I, CLAUDIA

I, CLAUDIA

DAVID POTTER

First published in Great Britain in 2026 by
The Book Guild Ltd
Unit E2 Airfield Business Park,
Harrison Road, Market Harborough,
Leicestershire. LE16 7UL
Tel: 0116 2792299
www.bookguild.co.uk
Email: info@bookguild.co.uk

The manufacturer's authorised representative in the EU
for product safety is Authorised Rep Compliance Ltd,
71 Lower Baggot Street, Dublin D02 P593 Ireland (www.arccompliance.com)

This work is entirely fictitious and bears no resemblance to any persons living or dead.

Typeset in 10.5pt Adobe Garamond Pro

Printed and bound in Great Britain by 4edge Limited

ISBN 978 1835743 843

British Library Cataloguing in Publication Data.
A catalogue record for this book is available from the British Library.

*To all my writing friends - but especially to
Lynda for all her patience and support.*

ONE

Do you know any decent hitmen? Seriously. I'm asking.

It's not as if I can look on the Checkatrade website for killers for hire or search the internet for assassins with a five-star Trustpilot rating. I mean, where do you find these guys? Assuming hitmen are men, of course. Not that I've got anything against female killers: I'd happily employ a fellow middle-aged crazy woman if she could get the job done. I'm not fussy. Just insanely angry. Well, that's what my psychiatrist reckons, and he should know. Although it didn't stop him making a pass at me when I told him my husband had left me for his female business partner. His *young* business partner, I might add. The one with the fake tan, tits and eyelashes. Obviously.

When I say he left me, Gary hasn't actually left the house yet or even admitted to the affair. And I can tell that Dr Rosencrantz is dubious about my suspicions.

He said to me: "Now then, Claudia, you are taking your clozapine, aren't you?"

I said: "Of course." *Wink wink.*

It's all right for him, but he's not the one putting on weight and suffering from a dry mouth and constipation. If I'd wanted to shit bricks and drink endless cups of tea all day I'd have

1

become a builder, not a pharmacist. Besides, my subscription to the Craft Gin Club counts as medication, doesn't it?

Dr Rosencrantz thinks I'm imagining the affair. But a woman knows, doesn't she? It's those telltale clues. Quite apart from the stray blonde hair on his jacket, the lipstick smear on the waistband of his boxers and the scent of Miss Dior permeating everything, it's the chest waxing, nipple piercing, teeth whitening, fat reducing, body shaping, eyebrow threading, fake tanning and ultrapeeling beauty treatments, not to mention the gym-going, the clothes buying, the late working, the defensiveness and the furtive WhatsApping. And the happy smile. Especially the happy smile. What's Gary got to be happy about? He's an accountant married to a psychotic middle-aged woman with frizzy hair and paranoid delusions – according to the doctor.

By the way, if you're in the market for a dodgy accountancy firm, the business is called Alcock and Bull. He's Alcock – or behaves like he is – while she's full of bull. Did I tell you her name's Alexa? Fancy being called Alexa. That's a potential disaster in this age of the 'internet of all things'. You mark my words, it's just a matter of time before one smutty demand too many sets off the leaf blower in the shed.

So, do you know any decent hitmen?

When I say decent I mean *reliable*: someone who takes a bit of pride in their work. Someone who plans meticulously and covers their tracks – and mine. And cleans up afterwards; I do hate mess. I did find someone promising on the Dark Web: promising in the sense he was full of promises, providing I paid him in bitcoins first. But how does that work? It's not as if I can stroll into my NatWest branch and withdraw a handful of non-fungible tokens along with the housekeeping. Why bitcoins? It's taking all the vicarious pleasure out of planning an assassination. What's wrong with stuffing a Tesco carrier bag full of used tenners and leaving it behind Professor Moriarty's tomb in Highgate Cemetery? Sometimes the old ways are the best ways.

As for the would-be hitman, he called himself TheManOnTheGreasyKnoll. I'm not sure if he realised it was actually the *Grassy* Knoll, or if he was just trying to be satirical, but he didn't seem to have much of a clue or a sense of humour. You've got to retain a sense of the absurd when it comes to killing people, haven't you? I mean, look at Jean-Paul Marat – if only he'd asked his plumber to install a shower, the French Revolution would have turned out differently. Arguably. Anyway, I asked the Greasy Knob Man if he did special offers.

What do you mean? he messaged me back.

Well, I said, *my main target is that cheating husband of mine, but I wouldn't mind if Alexa gets hers as well. Do you do Buy One Get One Free deals, like Aldi?* He got the arse after that and didn't get back to me. Very unprofessional.

I'd do it myself but, as I said, I hate mess. In fact, I can't stand the sight of blood, which I think you'll agree is a major setback for anyone planning a career as an assassin. It's called hematophobia, so any death involving the shedding of blood is an absolute no-no as far as I'm concerned. That rules out stabbing, or shooting due to my hoplophobia. I've thought about strangling him with a rope, but that's out because of my linonophobia. And I can't drown him, as I'm aquaphobic.

As you can see, my polyphobia is a bit of an issue, so it's a good job I'm OK with poisons. Although having said that, it's more difficult for me to gain access to them these days as I can't get a job as a pharmacist, not since the unfortunate death of my first husband (another cheating bastard). And my second husband (yet another cheating bastard). Not that the authorities ever managed to pin their deaths on me, which is a relief considering my aichmophobia.

You don't think I'm imagining all this, do you? Only I've read that unreliable narrators are a thing with some of you more writerly types. And what's more unreliable than a schizophrenic with paranoid delusions? Or more deadly, come to that. I guess you'd have to ask Dr Rosencrantz about that, although you'd better be quick because he's on my list, too.

Anyway, look at the time! And you didn't drink that cup of tea I made for you. Or touch those angel cakes. Never mind. But if you want to know what *really* happened to my previous husbands, it'll have to wait until our next little chat. I might even show you my diaries.

Do you know any decent hitmen? Seriously. I'm asking.

TWO

"Have you missed me?" asked Alexa.

"More than mere words can express," said Gary, clasping her to him so tightly that Alexa could feel every button on his shirt. And more. It may only have been a two-week trip to see her family in Greece, but it had felt like a fortnight in purgatory for Gary. His pleasure at seeing her again was palpable. It even warranted a small groan for good measure.

Holding onto her with all the desperate fervour of a drowning man clinging to a lifebelt, he tried to manoeuvre her around a small occasional table and towards a two-seater couch in the corner of his office. He was in the momentary grip of what the French might call a *grande passion*, Alexa not so much, at least not at 9am on a Monday morning, when she'd just eaten a full English and spent over an hour doing her hair and applying her make-up. And definitely not when Gary's office door remained unlocked. There's passion and there's recklessness – in Alexa's opinion. And Alexa's opinion held sway as she swayed out of Gary's grasp, wagging an admonishing finger as she did so.

"Buckle up, sweetie, before someone comes in," she said.

5

Gary sighed and adjusted himself, before sitting down on the black leather couch: a satisfyingly expensive piece of furniture and practical too: so easy to wipe clean. He patted the seat next to him.

She said: "Only if you promise to behave yourself."

He said: "Only if you insist."

Alexa sat down with a practised elegance and crossed her legs. She'd made a special effort with her outfit this morning. Her V-neck white blouse and short navy skirt had been carefully chosen to reveal just enough of her newly acquired tan to entice, while remaining plausibly businesslike. It had certainly enticed Gary.

"Perhaps we can meet at lunchtime for a quick conflab?" he suggested.

"Hmm. I've got such a ton of work to catch up on," said Alexa. She pulled a face and the small flame of hope that Gary had been kindling inside flickered and died.

"Oh," he said, shoulders slumping.

Alexa leant towards him and whispered: "But you could always come round to my flat tomorrow evening. That's if you can come up with a good excuse to tell the wifey." As a provocative reminder of previous encounters, she licked his ear, her tongue uncoiling deftly like a hungry hummingbird's.

"I'll think of something," he said, "but why not tonight?"

"Because I'm seeing the girls tonight. But talking of the wifey, how are things at home?"

Gary groaned yet again. But not in a good way. "She's gone bonkers," he said, resisting the temptation to run a hand through his perfectly coiffured hair.

"I know it's difficult for you, sweetie, but you must try not to exaggerate. Claudia's a bit eccentric, but I wouldn't call her bonkers."

"Eccentric? You don't know the half of it. I'm convinced

she's stopped taking her medication and now she's started drinking and talking to herself."

Alexa raised an expensively shaped eyebrow. "You mean, as opposed to her talking to you, but you not listening to her?"

"Not exactly. She's bought one of those silicone dolls, you know, the ones with the realistic skin, hair and everything. It's so lifelike it's creepy. And she talks to it as if it's, well, a real person."

Alexa's eyebrow kept rising until it touched her hairline. "Oh my God! I saw a late-night programme on Channel Four about those dolls. I thought they were for lonely men who couldn't get a girlfriend. What's Claudia want one of them for?"

"What?" said Gary, frowning. "No, no it's not a sex doll, if that's what you're thinking. It's baby-sized, like a traditional doll. And the worst thing is, she takes it to bed with her, and it lies on a pillow between us, gazing up at the ceiling. One night, when I was half asleep, I accidentally touched it, and it blinked at me and started breathing. Jeez! I nearly crapped myself!" Gary shifted uneasily on the couch.

"Breathing?" said Alexa. "Are you sure you didn't imagine it, if you were half asleep?"

"Don't you start; that's what Claudia said. But look, I found this leaflet with the packaging she'd thrown in the recycling." Gary stood up and walked over to retrieve a sheet of paper from his Armani jacket, which was on a padded hanger behind his antique mahogany desk. He sat down again and handed it to Alexa, who read:

This Collector's Edition of the Totally Real® doll is handcrafted to recreate every detail of the original sculpting. Baby Ophelia's vinyl skin is as velvety soft as a real baby's, and her cloth body is weighted so she feels just like a real baby in your arms. You're sure to be totally captivated by her exquisitely hand-painted features, her baby-soft hand-rooted hair, long eyelashes and tiny manicured

fingernails and toenails. Best of all, she responds to your touch by
cooing softly and 'breathing' – you'll feel her tiny chest rise and fall
– an especially amazing feeling when you hold her close!

Alexa let the leaflet fall into her lap. "Oh my God! This does sound a bit weird. Maybe she's broody? What does she talk to it about?"

"Anything and everything, and for ages at a time. She claims she doesn't, but I overheard her chattering to it the other day. It was like she was telling it her life story. I'm thinking of buying a listening device to record some of this stuff."

"Why?"

"For evidence. Just in case she's plotting something. I always thought the rumours of what happened to her previous husbands were just old wives' tales, but now I'm not so sure." He grimaced and dabbed his top lip with a handkerchief to remove a prickle of perspiration that had made a disagreeable appearance.

"Collecting evidence won't help you if you're already dead, will it?" said Alexa bluntly.

Gary's high-pitched squeak would have made any rodent proud. And it was accompanied by a secondary outbreak of sweating under his arms that not even his Sure Men Nonstop Protection Anti-Perspirant was able to contain. Disagreeableness was now off the scale. And if the trickle reached the waistband of his trousers, he was going to sue the company. He really was.

"Just leave her," said Alexa. "You've been promising me you'll do so for weeks."

"I've told you I can't just divorce her without serious financial repercussions."

"The prenup? I thought you were getting advice about that."

"I was. I am. The solicitors are going over it with a fine-tooth comb. But in the meantime, we need to remain discreet. Careful."

Alexa let out a sigh of exasperation. "Define 'careful'."

"Well, when we meet up during the day, it's best we continue to leave the office five minutes apart. We don't want the staff tittle-tattling."

"You forgot to mention that silly phone you insist on using."

"My burner phone? It's essential in case Claudia checks my usual phone. And, of course, I always use breath freshener. Afterwards."

"So thoughtful," said Alexa with a hint of sarcasm. "You think that's enough to fool her?"

Gary shrugged, surreptitiously checking his armpits at the same time. "Who knows? She lives in her own little world most of the time. She's bonkers."

"So you said."

"Honestly, the things she says and does sometimes. I could kill her."

"Then why don't you?"

THREE

Do you like lists, Ophelia? I do. I think I'm a listophile at heart. They help me keep my thoughts in order. Or, as a friend's young son might say, they help me keep my shit together. Which is a great piece of advice as far as shit is concerned, don't you think? It's better if it's all kept in one neat pile rather than spread about the place in random dumps.

As for lists, I'm lost if I go shopping without one, but then so are half the people I see in Sainsbury's. They shuffle around in a daze, blocking the aisles with their trolleys while they try to remember if they came in for cheese straws or drinking straws. Get a grip, people! And familiarise yourselves with the store layout while you're at it. You're not going to find the Anusol in the same chiller cabinet as the salmon fillets now, are you? Make a list, cloth heads, or next time you're going to find yourself on a different kind of list: one of mine.

Am I making sense?

Talking of salmon fillets, I ought to tell you I'm also very fond of animals. I'm a bit of a dogophile, although not so much of a catophile. You can't really trust cats, can you? It's the way they look at you and slink around like they're up to no good. They're not loyal, like dogs. They'll go with anyone for a saucerful of Whiskas. Gary's a kind of cat, you know. He's a cheetah, a lying cheetah. A woman knows these things, doesn't she?

Apart from cats and dogs, I also have a soft spot for hedgehogs and bees. I bought some bee feeder liquid drops off the internet so I can try and save any distressed bees I find in the garden. You've got to do your bit for the planet, haven't you? Bees are among the good guys; bees pollinate flowers and make honey. Whereas what do cheetahs do, other than run around shagging anything in a fur coat? And tearing the heart out of their victims.

Excuse me a moment while I pour myself another drink. I know it's quite early, but I need something to wash down all these evening primrose oil capsules.

Right. I've probably mentioned hitmen before, but how about the guy who did for Jeffrey Epstein? I'd hire him in a flash. Money no object. I mean, Epstein *was* assassinated, wasn't he? I realise he was in a prison cell at the time, but weirder things have happened. Look at all the UFO researchers who have died suspicious deaths in the past fifty years. I read a book about it once, called *Close Encounters of the Fatal Kind*. If something is out there, then I want to hire it. Perhaps Scully or Mulder from *The X-Files* can help. I might give their agent a call later.

In the meantime, I've been making a list of the ways in which I could deal with Gary myself. If I have to. And allowing for my various phobias, which rule out things like cutting the brake pipes on his car. Unfortunately. By the way, have you seen his car? It's very big and flashy, and you know what they say about middle-aged men who drive such cars. According to an article I read on the MailOnline website, there was a survey carried out of the partners of men who drive flashy cars, and nearly half said their husbands were lacking in the trouser department. Ha! They didn't need to carry out a survey; they could have just rung me. Let's just say Gary's more of a Nissan Micra than a Hummer Monster Truck.

Anyway, here's the list I've made so far on my iPhone:

1. Falling down the manhole outside our house. Or being pushed. Whatever. That's if we're even allowed to call it a manhole these days. So maybe it's safer to say it's a hole of indeterminate gender for the time being. On the plus side, even if the fall didn't kill him, he'd die of starvation. Eventually. On the minus side, there's a chance that our elderly next-door neighbour Mr Robinson, who's blind, might fall down it by accident. However, every cloud has a silver lining because all that tip-tapping on the pavement with his white stick really gets on my nerves. As does the lack of eye contact when we're having a chat. Sorry if that sounds a bit heartless and crazy. In any event, I'm not sure there's enough room down there for Gary and Mr Robinson.

2. Persuading him to take up an extreme sport like scuba diving, sky diving or mountaineering and then sabotaging his equipment. On the plus side, plummeting ten thousand feet with a duff parachute is going to be terminal. It's definitely a bucket and spade job. On the minus side, it's going to be messy, and I don't like mess. I'm very mess averse. And I don't think he's got the time or the inclination for extreme sports.

3. Poisoning. On the plus side, household poisons are easy to obtain. And what's more appropriate for a love rat than warfarin? But on the minus side, they're far too easy to diagnose and trace. And as I said the other day, I don't have access to all the wonderful drugs and

poisons I used to. And whose fault is that? Maybe I ought to add the chair of the General Pharmaceutical Council to my list.

4. Arson. On the plus side it would be easy enough to get a couple of canisters of petrol, a pack of Zip firelighters and a box of matches. And he absolutely deserves to burn in the fires of Hell for all eternity. On the minus side, I'm not sure what to set fire to. The house is out, because it's in my name and I've no desire to make myself homeless. His office is also a non-starter, because I put up the money to buy the business, so technically it's mine. Spin on that, Alexa Bull! So that just leaves Alexa's flat. Yay! What's not to like about that? There's my BOGOF deal right there.

5. Poisoning. OK, so I've just mentioned this one, but it's worth reconsidering if it's coupled with the right burial site. How about *underneath* a garden pond? Ingenious, don't you think? As you know, this is a big house and garden, and I've often fancied creating an environmentally sustainable pond, even if I couldn't go too near it myself because of my aquaphobia. But otherwise it would be a win-win if I put Gary's body in a big hole underneath it. There'll be no rising from the grave on Hallowe'en if he's down there, unless he miraculously grows gills. And best of luck to the police if they bring in cadaver dogs to try and sniff him out under thirty thousand gallons of pond water, weed and assorted fish, newts and frogspawn. In any event, isn't it illegal to disturb a newt's habitat these days? Newts rule, OK.

So, what do you reckon? Do you think I still need a hitman?

FOUR

While Gary and Alexa were busily reacquainting themselves a few yards away, their office manager, Mrs Pinchess, was onboarding a new receptionist. Not that Mrs Pinchess referred to it as such. Calling it an onboarding may have been the modern term for the process, but she considered it to be an HR-inspired affectation, like referring to holidays as 'leave' or a training course as a 'career enhancement programme'. When she started work forty years before, an onboarding was simply referred to as 'showing the new girl round'. So that was what she was doing: introducing Timea Novak to the rest of the staff and showing her round the company's offices.

These were located in the town's former Victorian lending library, just off the main shopping street. The ground floor had been converted into a reception area, an office each for the two partners and a couple of meeting rooms. The first floor was now a large open-plan office that accommodated a group of socially awkward young accountants, who did most of the run-of-the-mill auditing work. Gary had once referred to them as a team but dropped the term after half of them failed to show up for an office Christmas party. Even the promise of festive nibbles, mince pies and all the eggnog they could handle had been an insufficient inducement to attend. It was therefore little surprise that eye contact was kept to a bare minimum when Timea was introduced to them.

"They seemed a little aloof," said Timea as she and Mrs Pinchess made their way back downstairs.

"They're accountants," said Mrs Pinchess in a tone that suggested that was all the explanation Timea needed.

The onboarding continued back in the reception area, where Mrs Pinchess was based. She also had a desk upstairs, but she preferred to be downstairs in reception. This was someone who liked to keep an eye on all the comings and goings.

"How long have you been in this country?" she asked Timea as the pair sat down together at the front desk. She was trying to work out from the strength of Timea's accent if the new recruit had an acceptable grasp of the English language. Mrs Pinchess believed it was part of her job to uphold standards, both in respect of Alcock & Bull and the country as a whole. One of the reasons she'd voted for Brexit and more latterly the Reform Party was to keep the riff-raff out, not to hand them decent jobs on a plate. And as far as she was concerned, a job at a respected accountancy practice like Alcock & Bull was a prestigious local employment opportunity for any eighteen-year-old. Employing Timea had not been her decision; it had been Gary's choice. And what Mrs Pinchess had noticed immediately about her, apart from the foreign accent, was that she physically resembled a younger version of Alexa. Interesting.

Timea forced a smile. "Although I was born in Slovakia, we came to Britain when I was only five, so I very much consider myself to be British," she said.

"Do you?" said Mrs Pinchess. The side of her mouth twitched. "Really? My, my. And what does your father do?"

"He runs an import and export business in Birmingham."

Mrs Pinchess's sour expression betrayed the picture she had created in her mind's eye: a dodgy back-street operation similar to Del Boy's in TV's *Only Fools and Horses*.

Timea recognised the look. She said: "It's a multimillion-pound business, actually. It was recently commended by the Government's business secretary as the kind of enterprise that's important to the future of Global Britain. My father wanted me to go and work for him, but I said it was more important for me to get a thorough grounding in business practices first. At somewhere like Alcock & Bull." Timea smiled. Again. Although – actually – the business secretary had said no such thing and nor did her father run a multimillion-pound company. But Timea had decided satire was the best way to respond.

Not that Mrs Pinchess was aware that Timea was making fun at her expense. Suitably impressed by the apparent governmental seal of approval, she smiled and patted the back of Timea's hand. "That's marvellous. Your family is a real example to all other incomers," she said, oozing smarminess like a *Love Island* contestant on a promise. "You may call me Penny."

Satisfied that Timea had passed scrutiny, Mrs Pinchess began to explain the meet-and-greet protocol and other routine office procedures. At the end of the explanation, she handed Timea a swipe card. "This is for the door over there," she said, pointing. "As you've just seen, the corridor beyond it leads to the partners' offices. We had to have the security lock installed to stop people waltzing straight in to see Gary or Alexa unannounced."

Timea frowned. "How rude. Did it happen very often?"

Mrs Pinchess looked around before leaning forwards conspiratorially. "We do have a bit of an ongoing issue with one person in particular."

"Who's that?" asked Timea, sneaking a furtive look around too, even though she had no idea who she was looking for.

Could it be Stinky Stan, who was often seen wandering around town in a dirty old overcoat and tennis shoes, muttering to himself, and smelling like a sweaty Limburger cheese in a heatwave? Not quite.

"It's Mrs Alcock, Gary's wife," whispered Mrs Pinchess. She opened a drawer and took out a photo of Claudia. Timea studied it. The picture was not very flattering. It looked like the kind that the paparazzi might take after sneaking up on a bleary-eyed, wire-haired celebrity as they put the bins out first thing in the morning. In an old housecoat. And wellington boots.

"It's not a very good picture, is it," said Timea.

"It'll have to do. Gary took it when our previous receptionist started." Mrs Pinchess shrugged and added: "But you'll soon get to recognise her because she has a habit of 'popping in'. Frequently."

"Really?"

"I'm afraid so. She only works across the road, if you can call it work. She helps out as a volunteer at the Newvale Animal Aid charity shop on Monday and Friday afternoons. And then on Tuesday and Thursday mornings she does the same thing at the Newvale Children's Action Fund shop two doors away." Mrs Pinchess paused and looked around again before continuing: "I think it's admirable that she supports these charities, but I don't understand why she doesn't simply donate money to them and leave it at that. It's not as if she and Gary are short of a bob or two. I mentioned this to her once and she said it was a more meaningful gesture if she donated her time as well as her money. Odd woman. Still, the rich don't think like the rest of us, do they?"

"You make her sound rather eccentric."

"Trust me, that's putting it mildly. If you ask me," said Mrs Pinchess, looking round a final time, "the only reason she does it is so she can spy on her husband. But be that as it may, when she comes in, don't 'swipe' her through the security door, no matter how urgent she says it is. Even if you know Gary's not in a face-to-face meeting with a client, always tell her he's on an important Zoom call. Then ring his extension to take further instruction. If he doesn't answer, then tell her he could be in a forward strategy meeting with the rest of the team and ring Alexa's office. That's where he'll be. Without fail. But let it ring a few times. And whatever you do, don't tell Mrs Alcock he's in with Alexa."

"Why?"

Mrs Pinchess flushed. "Just don't. And one last thing: if Gary ever suggests diarising a one-to-one with you, politely remind him that I'm your line manager. And let me know."

FIVE

Gary and Alexa lay naked and sheened in sweat on top of her double bed. The duvet, their clothes and even Gary's Emporio Armani socks lay discarded in a heap on the floor. And although the volume had been turned down on the wall-mounted TV, the weatherman on the early evening news could still be heard telling viewers that the heatwave was set to continue. Yet that wasn't the only reason why the couple were feeling distinctly hot and bothered.

Alexa was staring at a stationary ladybird on the blush-pink ceiling. "It's not the first time it's happened recently, is it?" she said. "I thought after two weeks without me you'd be firing on all cylinders. I thought you wanted me."

"I did. I do," he said, watching the same bug. He was waiting for it to come within swatting range. "I'm sorry."

"You do know you can buy something from Boots these days, don't you? That would be problem solved."

"I don't have a problem."

"Based on the last half-hour, sweetie, I beg to differ."

Gary gave up on the ladybird and glanced down the bed at something else that remained stubbornly motionless, supine. "It must be stress," he said.

19

Alexa's eyes followed Gary's. "Are you sure you haven't been expending your energies elsewhere?"

"I can assure you I haven't given Claudia a second thought."

"How about anyone else?"

"Like who?"

Alexa turned her head to scrutinise Gary's face. "No one in particular. Just checking."

"Claudia really has gone bonkers, you know," said Gary, changing the subject. "She's had a child's seat fitted in her car so she can transport that doll creature round with her." He finally turned his head to look at Alexa, a pained expression on his face. "She's also asked me when I'm going to get around to fertilising her eggs."

"What the fuck!" said Alexa, jerking upright with all the vigour Gary had previously been unable to muster. "I thought you said she was menopausal."

"She is."

"Then what's the point? And anyway, I thought you said that side of your marriage was over?"

"It is. She's fifty-five and well past her sell-by date as far as I'm concerned," he said, sitting up and reaching for a glass of water on the bedside table. "She's not asked me to have sex with her for some while, thank God. The thing is, though, she had some of her eggs frozen after the death of her second husband, Martin, so she could still have kids at a later date. And she's decided now is the time."

"Oh Jeez! So what does that involve? Do you have to perform into a petri dish or something?"

"God knows. I've no idea. Hopefully it won't come to anything."

"Judging by this evening, that wouldn't be a surprise."

Gary drained his glass and chose to ignore the jibe. "She's also started wittering about building a pond in the back garden. Who wants a stagnant pond only yards from the patio? Just imagine the smell and all the mozzies and other wildlife it would attract. Ugh!" Gary shivered despite the summer heat. "The next thing you know there'll be fox shit all over the lawn."

Alexa thought for a moment before making a suggestion. "If she wants a water feature, why don't you suggest a heated outdoor swimming pool instead?"

"Hey, that's not a bad idea! But, unfortunately, she'll never agree to it because she's got a phobia about water. It'll serve her right if she gets too close to her bloody pond, has a panic attack and falls in and drowns."

"Wouldn't it just," said Alexa, as she swung her legs off the bed and padded through to the kitchen-diner of her reassuringly expensive modern apartment to refill their glasses. When she came back she suggested they shower and ring Domino's for a pizza.

"That's fine by me," said Gary, "unless you want to try again first?"

Alexa gave a rueful smile and shook her head. "Best let sleeping dogs lie, don't you think, sweetie? You need to get yourself sorted. You're letting this business with Claudia get to you far too much."

"I know, I can't help it. I'd divorce her tomorrow if it weren't for the fact it would be a financial disaster for me. Er, for us, I mean."

"Have you thought about hiring a hitman?"

Gary frowned. "Are you serious?"

"Why not?" said Alexa, as she tidied up their discarded clothes. "They merely provide their clients with a professional service, the same as us."

"What? Please tell me you're not equating hired thugs with people like us. I've had to work hard to earn the respect of the Newvale business community. How many hitmen do you know who are in the running to be golf club captain next year?"

"Oh stop being such an arse. You've just admitted you'd be ruined without Claudia's money. If the root cause of your problems is the little wifey at home, then you need to deal with it. Stop being so squeamish."

"Yeah, well, I trust you'll let me know if you acquire a potential hitman as a client any time soon."

Alexa put the neat pile of clothing down on her dressing table stool and turned to face Gary, who was still sitting propped up on the bed. "Funnily enough, there is someone who comes to mind," she said. "Let me give it a bit more thought."

"Please do," said Gary. "Alternatively, there was an article in the paper this morning that caught my eye. It was about a shopper who came across a deadly spider in a bunch of bananas they bought from their local supermarket. I think it was called a Brazilian wandering spider. The article said they do turn up from time to time in imported fruit like bananas. I thought one of those little beauties could get the job done if I hid it in her pyjamas or something."

"Very diabolical. But what are the chances of finding a venomous spider in a bunch of bananas in Newvale in the next week or so?"

"I thought about getting our new receptionist Timea to visit all the town centre supermarkets at lunchtimes to check out their bananas and report back."

"That is quite possibly the most ridiculous thing you've said all evening. Oh, and by the way, I've been meaning to ask you about the new girl. Why didn't you wait until I got back before hiring someone?"

Gary fidgeted from one buttock to the other. "We needed a new receptionist to start pretty quickly so she beds in before Mrs Pinchess goes on holiday."

"That's an interesting way of putting it. And what's also striking is that she looks just like the last couple of receptionists you hired. It's almost as if you have a type in mind, except they're getting younger. What happened to Jasmine, by the way? She left very abruptly."

"She said she needed to take a break to prioritise her mental well-being."

"Really? You weren't harassing her, were you?"

"Of course not," said Gary. He paused and added: "I might have said something she misinterpreted, but you know what the kids of today are like. Snowflakes. But just to be on the safe side I got her to sign a non-disclosure agreement in return for an ex-gratia payment."

"Again?" said Alexa with a sigh. "How much this time?"

"Two grand… ish."

"Ish?"

"More or less."

"We need to talk about this in the office tomorrow. In the meantime, if you can't find a hitman to do your dirty work for you, you need to come up with a more realistic plan than hiding venomous spiders in Claudia's underwear."

"Like what?"

"How about tampering with the brakes on her car?"

"That wouldn't work. She drives so slowly she'd never notice the brakes weren't working."

"In that case, how about staging a fatal car crash? I remember reading about a guy who killed his wife by giving her a lift and deliberately crashing the car into a tree at fifty miles an hour."

"You have to be kidding me! A crash at that speed could easily kill me as well."

"I suppose there is that," said Alexa, "which also raises an interesting point. In the event of both of you dying at the same time, what happens to your gorgeous Edwardian house? And the rest of your estate? Without any kids of your own, does it all get left to the local dogs' home? Because if so, is that really fair on me? Quite apart from anything else, I am your business partner. Perhaps you ought to think about altering your will in my favour. Just in case."

SIX

Sorry if there's a bit of a fug in the car this evening, Ophelia, but I can't seem to stop farting. I know the Ford Fiesta's only small, so I've opened all the windows for you. It shouldn't be too bad if we can generate a through-breeze. To be honest, I'm not sure what's causing my IBS. It could be the thought of them up there in her flat. I know they're there. Canoodling. According to the GPS tracking device, Gary's parked his car two streets away. As per usual. But he's not fooling anyone, least of all me. He told me he had a Lodge meeting tonight, but I know exactly what's being lodged – and where. I know all about their silly rituals. She'll have him blindfolded and begging for one of her funny handshakes.

I daresay all the Haribos I've been eating aren't helping. Or the evening primrose oil capsules. I've been taking quite a lot of them recently. They're supposed to be very good for all my menopause symptoms. And since taking them I've also noticed I've been miraculously clear of other problems, like osteoporosis, asthma, eczema, neuropathy, dry eye, high cholesterol and heart disease. Not to mention scaly skin. Because who wants to look like a lizard? Especially with David Icke around. Although to be fair, I never had any of these symptoms before I started taking the capsules. But then you can never be too careful with your health, can you?

The only thing the evening primrose oil didn't help me with was my tardive dyskinesia, which was a side effect of the anti-psychotics that Dr Rosencrantz prescribed. It was manageable when I was home alone but could be really embarrassing if I had a funny turn when I was out and about. If you don't believe me, *you* try wiggling your fingers, flapping your arms and thrusting your pelvis at the person who's standing next to you in the check-out queue and see what happens. You'll soon know why I stopped taking the drugs. There's madness and there's madness.

As for the Gruesome Twosome up there, I'd forgotten Alexa had been on holiday until I noticed more blonde hairs on Gary's jacket last night.

I asked him: "Was it Take Your Dog to Work Day, today?"

He said: "Of course not. What are you on about?"

So I said: "Hmm. That rules out a golden retriever, then."

He looked at me as if I was mad. Which I absolutely am. Some of the time. And then he went off to play with that silly burner phone he keeps in his sock drawer. Oh, and the whiff of Miss Dior was back, so I knew it couldn't have been a dog he'd been petting. Or could it? I suppose it depends on your definition. I'm so glad I made him sign that prenup agreement. I thought it was too good to be true when a man who was ten years younger than me took an interest.

Anyway, when I was at the children's charity shop this morning, I popped into their offices to check up on her. It really annoys them when I call in like that, but there's nothing like getting under your enemy's skin, is there? And sure enough, she was there: I heard her laughing. It's unmistakeable. She sounds like a hyena. By the way, did you know hyenas scent-mark their territory using their anal glands? And there was me thinking it was Miss Dior. Unfortunately, Wikipedia didn't make it clear if hyenas and cheetahs eat each other. But I wouldn't be surprised. Would you?

I also found out something else: they've got a new receptionist. She looks just like the one who left but younger. That was a bit triggering, I must say. It brought back memories I thought had been well and truly buried. Although I've got nothing against speaking ill of the dead, that little revelation will have to wait until I'm properly in the mood. Aren't I a tease?

In the meantime I'm trying to focus on Alexa's flat, which looks like it might be worth a bob or two. They call it 'casing the joint', I believe. And from what I can see there are a lot of CCTV cameras surrounding the block, which'll make firebombing it tricky without being identified. You can't be too careful with forensic evidence nowadays. I might be mad, but I'm not stupid.

I've started watching Sky Crime and the Crime and Investigation TV channels for advice and inspiration. They have some great true crime programmes: *Meet, Marry, Murder; Buried in the Backyard; Buried in the Woods; Killer in My Village;* and especially *Sex, Lies and Murder* and *Deadly Wives*. It does get a bit irritating, though, when the police keep banging on about all the 'red flags' that were raised during their investigations. What is this: a crime show or *Baywatch*? And then, to cap it all, it's guaranteed the village idiot will pop up and say: "Nothing like this ever happens in our town." It just has, numpty. That's why they're making a TV programme about it. It's enough to drive you to drink. Well, it is for me.

As I say, you can't be too careful these days and I don't want to draw any unnecessary attention to myself, especially after the visit from the police this afternoon. Oh, sorry. Didn't I tell you about that? Apparently, my neighbour complained I've been harassing him. Can you believe it?

The policeman said to me: "Is it true you called Mr Robinson a 'vile old man' and a 'dickhead'?"

I said: "What's wrong with that? The *Daily Mail* calls people 'vile' all the time. And have you seen the shape of his head? It speaks for itself."

He said: "Yes, but the *Daily Mail* doesn't threaten vulnerable blind people with physical harm. You shouldn't have told him you were going to 'shove his white stick where the sun don't shine'."

So I said to Plod: "That's fine. But did he also tell you that he hits his guide dog Honey with that bloody stick? The only reason he's come snivelling to you lot is because I threatened to report him to the RSPCA and the Guide Dogs for the Blind Association."

That stumped him. He went away mumbling that it might still be classed as a hate crime. A hate crime? Ha! If he wants to see me commit a hate crime he needs to stick around. Not that he was a proper policeman anyway. He was one of those 'pretenders' – a community support officer – all hi-vis jacket and superiority complex. Pompous arse. You don't think I'm making this up, do you?

As for Robinson, he's going to get his. Trust me. I happened to follow the officer out of the house and saw the old blindie standing at his front window and smirking at me. *Smirking!* How is that even possible when he can't see beyond the end of his nose? Allegedly. Later on, I deliberately dropped a pound coin at the end of his driveway as a test. And sure enough, when he came out of his house, tip-tapping away, he reached the coin and bent down to pick it up. So as well as hitting Honey, he's scamming the benefits system. I do hate cheaters.

SEVEN

Apologies for the other evening, Ophelia. You'll be pleased to know things seem to have settled down bowel-wise. Having said that, it might be an idea to keep the air freshener handy, just in case. I'm also feeling a bit calmer, so maybe the two things are linked. "Peace of mind is the basis of a healthy body," said the Dalai Lama. Wise words from a wise man but it's so much easier to achieve a state of Zen after a handful of Valium in my experience. Even so, I've had a bit of a chat with myself, and I now have a clear plan of action to focus on. That's good. I know I'm a schizophrenic, but it doesn't mean I like being in two minds.

Am I making sense?

Anyway, would you like to see some of my old diaries? I did promise you the other day. They usually live in a locked suitcase in my attic, a bit like Anne Frank, but I've brought down the one from 1988 to show you. I thought I would read out one or two entries as they might help to explain a few things. Here goes:

Monday, 7 March 1988
Well, today was the first day of my pharmacist's foundation training year at Harrisons the Chemist. What an eye-opener

– I could have done with sticking my whole head in a bath of Optrex after that. I couldn't believe the number of old people kicking and elbowing their way to the counter. Where were they all coming from? They were like a swarm of locusts descending on a field of green shoots. They even sounded like them, with their arthritic knees and hips clicking away.

"Is it pension day?" I asked Manisha the pharmacist.

"No, it's like this every day," she said.

I can't believe old people have so many complaints. I did little else but fill out prescriptions for dodgy kidneys, hearts, lungs, prostates and thyroids. And then there were those with arthritis, asthma, bronchitis, diabetes, high blood pressure, low blood pressure, high cholesterol and shingles. Not forgetting the ones with dementia, although I suspect some of them thought they'd come into the library for the warm. If the NHS wants to sort out its waiting lists and save a ton of money, it should stop all their meds and let nature thin out their ranks. What's wrong with the survival of the fittest? I'm with Darwin on that one.

And then, just as I was about to go for lunch, in sauntered this greasy, spotty schoolboy. I was just thinking what acne treatment to recommend when he asked for a packet of condoms. Urgh! I was so repulsed, it felt like something had shrivelled and died inside me. Thankfully it wasn't him.

I nearly said to him: "Who's the lucky girl? Would you like a free booklet on how to administer CPR?" But being the consummate professional, I put my personal feelings to one side and handed him one of the standard packets.

"Oh, no," he said, "I'll need a pack of twenty. Ribbed. Please." The cocky little sod then winked at me. Something for the weekend? I hope that packet of twenty lasts him a lifetime.

PS There was one bonus to filling out all those oldies'

prescriptions: I discovered it's quite easy to sneak a tablet here and there. Today's mood: happy daze!

I'm not sure I'll have the time or the energy to write anything tomorrow (or for the next day or so, fingers crossed!), so here's hoping the Big Day is a Big Success. Obviously, things haven't gone entirely smoothly in the run-up to the wedding, what with Sarah being taken to hospital with a bad case of food poisoning(!) and all. The doctors aren't sure what's caused it, but as she likes to stick her snout in the trough at every opportunity, who knows what she's eaten? Everyone else has sympathy for her, but Miss Piggy was lucky I chose her as one of my bridesmaids in the first place. I still haven't forgotten the despicable prank she played on me at uni.

And then, of course, there's been Simon insisting that his cousin Birgitte takes her place. Strange girl. I think she was supposed to be called Brigitte, after the actress Brigitte Bardot. But that's what happens when you ask a dyslexic father to register a birth. I'm glad I don't have to partner him at Scrabble. I can't say I'm very fond of Birgitte. She's eighteen but only looks about fourteen, so the dressmaker had a nightmare adjusting Miss Piggy's dress to fit her. I certainly wasn't going to pay for a totally new dress to be made. And I only gave way to Simon's badgering because he's been depressed. It's due to his diabetes. Or so he said. But it's surprising how quickly his mood improved once I slipped him a handful of Nobrium and agreed to Birgitte coming on board.

I'm glad Dad's been able to fight off his cancer long enough to give me away; that means a lot to me. Mind you, I'll bet it's the first time he's ever given anything away in his life! You don't get to become a successful businessman by giving things away. Interestingly, I wonder how much Simon would have paid for me if he'd had to? Hmm, best not go there.

Mother won't be there, of course, but least said about her the better. Today's mood: contemplative.

<u>*Sunday, 25 September 1988*</u>

Back from honeymoon in Barbados. Trust Simon to book a holiday to the sunny Caribbean during the rainy season. Summed up the honeymoon really: not the right kind of wet blanket. Only just dodged a hurricane into the bargain. Simon had his wallet nicked and I had my arse pinched – several times – by one of the dishy waiters. To be honest, he showed more interest than Simon. I was tempted!

Got home to find out Miss Piggy had died in intensive care. According to the doctors it was kidney failure, probably caused by eating poisonous mushrooms. Who am I to argue with them? Obviously didn't bother telling them she'd been for dinner at ours. Good riddance! Today's mood: grim satisfaction.

<u>*Tuesday, 6 December 1988*</u>

Dad died. Can't write at the moment. RIP, my hero.

EIGHT

Gary was in Alexa's office, scrutinising a sheaf of papers she had pushed across her desk for his attention.

"Interesting," he said, nodding in approval. "So, according to your detailed report, his financial shenanigans have put him in serious jeopardy on two fronts."

"Exactly. Not to put too fine a point on it, Bob Flint is deep in the ploppy stuff," said Alexa. "And I'm not sure which would be the worst outcome for him: the taxman, or his soon-to-be-ex-wife finding out he's been trying to hide a chunk of his money. And having met her at a sherry reception once, I can testify his wife's a seriously scary-looking woman. Mind you, that could have a lot to do with the number of failed facelifts she's obviously had. The skin's been stretched so tight you could play a drum solo on it. It's also left her with eyes like the slits on a jouster's helmet and a permanent grimace."

"Scary? If you think she's scary, you want to try living with Claudia for a few days."

"Don't worry," said Alexa, "with Flint's help, you won't have to live with her for much longer. Along with Mrs Flint,

33

she'll soon be an ex-wife. Or, to be more accurate, she'll be an ex-person."

"You think Flint'll do it?"

"I'm sure. He knows that unless we're prepared to cover his backside for him, his life isn't going to be worth living."

Gary rubbed the stubble on his chin. He had been so disconcerted by Claudia's recent behaviour that he'd even forgotten to shave that morning: a regrettable fall in personal grooming standards. He wanted to believe his problems could be solved by employing the tax-dodging demolition contractor to do his dirty work for him, but he still had doubts. "If we cover up Flint's unlawful activities, that's going to put us at serious risk as well."

Alexa had a glint in her eye. It could have been the way a beam of sunlight had evaded the window blinds, but Gary didn't think so. Not that he was the type who usually spent too long looking deep into a woman's eyes. Not when there were other options.

She said: "No one's going to find out, though, are they." It was a statement, not a question. "Only three people will know about our arrangement: you, me and Flint. And if Flint becomes a problem…"

Gary didn't linger on the 'if' solution. "How's he going to do it?" he asked.

"The less we know about that, the better. But he demolishes big buildings for a living so he must have access to all kinds of equipment. Including explosives."

Gary's eyes widened in alarm. "I don't want him blowing up the house," he said. "I quite like it. And I'd like it even more without Claudia in it."

"Yes, without Claudia. But very much with me in it instead," said Alexa. The glint was back.

"Of course," said Gary, smiling. Nervously.

"Just checking, sweetie. And don't worry. I'll make sure he leaves the house untouched. It would be such a shame otherwise as I've already decided on the window shutters I want to replace your awful net curtains."

Gary shrugged. The fate of his net curtains was the least of his worries. "How much do you think he'll want?" he asked.

"He won't be getting anything up front, other than a delay in his day of reckoning with the taxman and Mrs Angry. If it turns into Mission Accomplished, then I'm sure you – or rather we – will be in a financial position to consider a cash bonus."

"Very good. It sounds like you've covered most eventualities. Payment by result will definitely help my current financial position."

Alexa permitted herself a small smile of satisfaction. Men were so easy to manipulate. When you knew which buttons to press. However, there was one thing she was still hazy about. "Out of interest, how did your wife manage to become so rich? You've never really explained that to me."

Gary allowed himself a reciprocal smile. Women were so gullible. When you knew which levers to pull. However, he needed to decide exactly how much to tell her. "Her father was a successful businessman. When he died he left the house in The Avenue, and the rest of his estate, to Claudia as his wife had pre-deceased him. She eventually became a client of Templeforth Accountancy, which is how we met. With Claudia's help I bought out old man Templeforth when he wanted to retire. Later on you joined the business and the rest is history, as they say." It was the truth. But not necessarily the whole truth and nothing but the truth. That would be telling.

Alexa nodded. Gary wasn't telling her anything that she hadn't already discovered for herself. But it was reassuring that he was being honest with her, up to a point. She had the feeling there was more to the story than he was letting on. However, there was something else she was genuinely in the dark about. "So, has she always struggled with her mental health? Or is it a fairly recent development?"

Gary sighed. "I was once told that when she was at university studying pharmacology, one of her friends spiked her drink with a hallucinogenic drug of some kind at a party. It was supposed to have been a harmless prank, but it turned into a one-way trip to a hospital intensive care unit after she went into a coma. She was never the same after that, although she managed to keep her problems largely hidden. Things have got a lot worse recently though. She's far more easily triggered."

"Some friend, doing something like that. I trust she fell out with them."

"I wouldn't know," said Gary with a shrug. He didn't know and he didn't care. He should have done, but he didn't. He was more concerned with Claudia's latest scheme. "She's going ahead with that pond, you know. She's hired contractors to dig the biggest bloody hole you've ever seen."

NINE

My dad.

I bet you thought, *poor Claudia, growing up with daddy issues,* after reading last week's diary extracts. Well, for your information, I did *not* grow up with daddy issues, thank you very much. My dad was great. No complaints. What I grew up with were 'mummy issues'. Not wishing to beat around the bush, so to speak, she was a slut. There. Said it. Wash my mouth out with soap and water.

If bed-hopping was a sport, Mother would have held the British all comers' record. No doubt about it. If she had replaced her bedroom door with a turnstile, I wouldn't have been in the least surprised. I don't know if there was something wrong with her, mentally, I mean. I came home from school once and caught her in flagrante delicto in the kitchen with one of her men friends and a pot of Ski yogurt. *My* Ski yogurt, for Chrissakes! The one with the bits of cherry in it. The one that *used* to be my favourite. No wonder I've had a yogurt phobia ever since. No wonder I don't like mess.

I said to her: "Why do you behave like this?"

She said: "I don't know. I think I must be cock-eyed."

Never a truer word.

Poor Dad. He just turned a blind eye, though I know he was hurting. I hate cheats.

I mentioned Mother to Dr Rosencrantz once and he said hypersexuality can be a symptom of a borderline personality disorder, as well as a schizo-affective disorder. That worried me. All things considered.

Rosencrantz asked me what happened to her, and I just glossed over it. As you do. Well, as I do. I told him while Dad was away on a business trip, she just upped sticks and left. The only clue the police had to go on was a typewritten note explaining she'd eloped with one of her lovers and not to look for her. A detective called it a 'Dear John' letter, which was ridiculous considering Dad's name was Bill. How can the police hope to solve a case if they don't get the basic facts right? Anyway, a suitcase was missing, along with some clothes and a few pieces of jewellery. They never found her, so who knows where the yogurt-despoiler ended up? Dad was upset, but it was the best thing that could have happened to him, in my opinion. And my opinion matters, right? Eventually he accepted she'd disappeared without trace, and after seven years the court made a declaration of presumed death. So, all's well that ends well, don't you think?

OK, I need a drink after that. I know it's early, but I bought this Seville Marmalade Gin especially to drink at breakfast. Or instead of. Whatever. But it beats porridge every time.

Anyway, I suppose you'd like to know what happened to my first husband, cheating Simon. Well, after our less-than-inspiring honeymoon, the marriage continued on its ho-hum way for a couple of years until around the autumn of 1990. It was about then that I suspected something was up. And the thing that was 'up' was most definitely not being pointed in my direction, if you get my drift. But it was really bizarre the way Simon's dirty little secret was uncovered, as you'll see.

Saturday, 6 October 1990

*HOLY MOTHER OF CRAP WE'VE WON THE POOLS!
I don't really know how it works, but Simon says we've got
eight draws and that means we've won the jackpot! He's
phoning the claim line right now. Update later. Got to go and
change my knickers first cos I've literally wet myself! I haven't
had a soggy gusset since primary school – other than on my
one and only date with Danny Beckett when I was in the fifth
year. Shit, I'd forgotten about that. Should have kept him.
God, I need a couple of Valium. Today's mood: off the scale!*

Thursday, 11 October 1990

*OK, so the good news is Littlewoods have confirmed we've
won the jackpot. But the bad news is that we've got to share
it with another winner. Bummer! Even so, we've still won
£749,546. And 38p. I'm so glad I made Simon tick the 'no
publicity' box. I can't do with the thought of all those begging
letters. It's been bad enough telling the neighbours and his
grasping mum and dad to f*** off after Simon went and
blabbed to them. Idiot. Today's mood: middling.*

Monday, 15 October 1990

*UNBELIEVABLE!! Simon reckons the money belongs to
HIM and not to US! What a total and complete arsehole
that man is. He says he was the one who forecast the results,
and it was his name on the coupon. True. But when the
pools collector came round to pick up the coupon, it was me
who paid the stake money. Again. Anyway, the cheque's been
made out to him, although he says he'll transfer it to our joint
account IN DUE COURSE. He's already talking about the
things HE wants to buy with the winnings. He hasn't asked
me what I want. Today's mood: seething.*

Happy Valentine's Day. Not. Had a totally inappropriate card from Simon that I suspect he bought from the off-licence at the last minute. As far as I could tell it featured one teacup holding a biscuit and saying to the other teacup: "Please can I stick my Hobnob in?" Which I'm sure you'll agree is absolutely hilarious and a complete joke on so many levels. We're not going out tonight because he's got to attend an utterly pointless meeting of the council's Health and Leisure Committee. His boss is off sick with the flu (apparently) so he's the most senior environmental health officer still standing. Apart, that is, from Birgitte. Yes, you read that right. Cousin Birgitte, who still only looks fifteen. Can't they give the poor girl growth hormones or something? Or, at the very least, persuade her to wear a padded bra? I don't know how he did it, but Simon managed to wangle her a job working with him at the council. More on that imminently. Today's mood: very dark.

Friday, 22 February 1991

Brace yourself. Had a meeting with Gerry Coulson, the private detective that Dad's old accountant, Mr Templeforth, recommended. I went to get the results of his investigation into Simon's 'activities'. I have to admit I was moderately impressed by Gerry's office above the A1 Snacks Shop. It was reassuringly seedy, with peeling paint, shabby furniture and piles of papers everywhere, and smelt of Peperami sausage sticks and old farts. To be fair, the old farts could actually have been Gerry and his less-than-glamorous assistant, Mrs C, who both look well past retirement age. But credit where credit's due: they struck gold! I'm amazed at how calm I'm feeling at the moment, but that's probably down to the strip of lorazepam tablets I liberated from work. I don't know if the old duffer I short-changed will notice. And I don't care. I really don't. Which is rather to be expected, considering lorazepam is an anti-anxiety medication. More tomorrow when I've read the full report. Today's mood: ~~beyond chilled~~ ice cold.

<u>*Saturday, 23 February 1991*</u>

ARMAGEDDON! The End Times! Call it what you will. As I feared, Simon has been having an affair with Birgitte the midget. Although whether their squalid couplings deserve to be called an 'affair' is a moot point. She's his cousin, for Chrissakes! It's practically incest! Not to mention she's twenty, going on fifteen. Is there such a thing as Paedophilia by Proxy? Because if there isn't, there should be. No schoolgirl in Newvale is safe with him walking the streets. And what's more, it turns out he's been blowing OUR winnings as fast as she's been blowing him. It's disgusting. I need something to dull the pain. On Monday I'm going to try and swipe some liquid morphine. Simon is a dead man walking! Today's mood: sulphurous.

<u>*Sunday, 24 February 1991*</u>

What a turn up for the books. Simon went off to some football match or other with his mates and within minutes the front doorbell rang. It was Birgitte, or Lolita, as I prefer to think of her. She'd been hiding behind the rhododendrons and waiting for him to leave. Anyway, she must have got wind of something because she wanted to confess. Or, as she put it, bare her soul, which makes a change from everything else she's been baring recently! Trollop. I like that word, don't you? It sounds a bit like wallop, which is what I wanted to do to her. But although she doesn't realise it, she might just have saved her skin by throwing herself on my mercy. I can be compassionate when I want to be, you know. Besides, it appears Simon's ardour is cooling towards our helpless little fawn. It seems he's turned his attention to Birgitte's younger sister Lora (chalk up another one for the Dyslexic Dad). She is thirteen and a half. What can I say? Today's mood: murderous.

What did you make of all that then, Ophelia? Did any of my revelations surprise you? You probably guessed what Simon had been up to before I told you, but I bet you never saw the pools win coming, did you? I suppose you want to know what happened vis-à-vis Simon.

Oh, hang on a moment, though, I think that's someone at the kitchen door. It's probably one of the landscape gardeners who've been working on the new pond I've been telling you about. Won't be a minute.

Uh-oh! You're not going to believe this. As I suspected, it was one of the workmen.

I said to him: "Can I help you, or have you come to badger me for another cup of tea?"

He said: "Another cup would be nice, considering."

"Considering what?"

"Considering we've just found human remains in your garden."

TEN

Gary was drumming his manicured nails on the desk in Alexa's office. *Where was she?* It was 8.30am – a good half an hour before he usually arrived at the office – and there was no sign of his partner. It was so unfair that on the very day he had chosen to turn up early, she was late. *Where was she?* It was so utterly inconsiderate of her.

He stopped drumming long enough to glower at his watch once more, just as Alexa walked into the office. Her eyebrows lifted at the sight of Gary occupying her chair, his demeanour betraying a sense of entitlement reminiscent of a medieval monarch.

"Hello?" she said; it was half-greeting, half-query. "You're in very early. For you. To what do I owe this undoubted pleasure?"

Gary transferred his glower to Alexa. "Where have you been? I've been trying to get hold of you all over the bank holiday weekend." In Gary's mind he was being authoritative, yet to Alexa's ear it sounded more like a childish whine.

She said: "You know I went on a spa weekend with a couple of the girls. You're not still sore because I wouldn't let you come as well, are you?" Alexa turned away as she put down her attaché case and rolled her eyes.

"No," he said, even though he was. He'd looked at the treatments on the spa's website and had fancied the idea of having the men's hand maintenance treatment, the super boost facial for men and the hot stone massage. But most of all he'd warmed to the idea of spending three days in a fluffy white dressing gown, in the company of a country house full of similarly underdressed women. Not only underdressed but wealthy. He was sure the combination would have been a potent pick-me-up for his recent difficulties. Yet that lost opportunity wasn't the only reason for his annoyance. "Why have you been ignoring me? I've been calling and texting you all weekend."

"Ah," said Alexa. "Sorry about that. I dropped my phone as we were unloading the cases and Jess accidentally reversed over it. I need to sort out a replacement this morning, ASAP."

Gary squinted at her as if he couldn't make up his mind whether to believe her or not. "I see. So you haven't seen my messages?"

"Of course not. What's the big emergency?"

Gary took a deep breath. "The police have spent the whole weekend digging up our garden."

"Excuse me?" said Alexa, staring at him wide-eyed. "Digging up the garden? What are they doing? Looking for a body or something?"

"They're not just looking – they've found them!"

"Them?"

"Two. At the last count."

"You're kidding me!"

"Do I sound as if I'm joking?"

"No, of course not," said Alexa. She paused for a moment and added: "Do we know who they are? Or rather, were?"

Gary shook his head. "The police are being very tight-lipped about it. They've called in one of those forensic archaeologist types to try and identify the bones."

"Oh, so they're just skeletons then."

"Just skeletons? Isn't that bad enough? What else did you think they'd be?"

"I wasn't sure if you meant the bodies were reasonably recent. You know, fresh corpses. Ones a medical examiner could get stuck into and carry out a proper autopsy."

"That's grotesque. You've been watching too much of that crime drama *The Coroner*."

"You think? I've often fancied being a forensic pathologist."

Gary frowned. Alexa had that glint in her eye again. She was beginning to disturb him. Not as much as Claudia, that was for sure. But even so. A forensic pathologist? At what point did a normal person decide they wanted to cut up dead bodies for a living? It was the same with rectal surgeons. Did they start out at medical school wanting to become brain surgeons, but then have to lower their ambitions when they finished bottom of the class?

Alexa was quick to interrupt his wandering thoughts. She was eager to know more about the bodies. "Are they both adults?" she asked.

"They haven't told us anything officially," said Gary, "but I heard the archaeologist say one's an adult, although he wasn't absolutely sure about the age of the other."

"Oh my God! Not just a common or garden killer then, but a child murderer to boot."

"Hang on a minute. He didn't say it was definitely a child."

"Maybe not. But whoever's killed them has been using your back garden as a deposition site."

"Please don't," said Gary, holding up his hands. "There's already talk of the police extending the search for more bodies."

"Really?" said Alexa, trying to keep a growing excitement out of her voice. "One more and that means there's a serial killer on the loose."

"I don't even want to think about that possibility."

"Well you wouldn't, would you? Living under the same roof as Claudia, what with her questionable history. Has she been taken into custody yet?"

"No. But it might be only a matter of time. She's been behaving very strangely."

"I thought you'd already told me she was bonkers?"

"She is."

"And has she stopped taking her medication?"

"She has."

"And has she started drinking?"

"She has."

"And is she menopausal?"

"She is."

Alexa shook her head. "Well, there's your answer right there. It wouldn't take the discovery of bodies in the garden to tip her over the edge. Burning the toast would do it."

"Yes I know all of that, but this has been a very different kind of strangeness. It's almost as if she knows something about the bodies that no one else does."

ELEVEN

I'm feeling really evil today, Ophelia. It's a combination of factors. But what's new? The appointments didn't help. Fancy getting an invite for a smear test *and* a mammogram on the same day. What are the NHS playing at? It's almost as if they don't care about my mental health.

Gary said: "But these tests are a good thing, surely?"

I said: "I beg to differ. Ben & Jerry's ice cream is a good thing."

He said: "Well, you can always use it to cool things down afterwards."

Sarky bastard. He knows I don't like mess. And he'd be singing a different tune entirely if someone stuck a spatula up his John Thomas and then waggled it around. Just to make sure. And then, after all that, they squeezed it through a mangle. Mind you, who knows what he gets up to with Alexa. You read about stranger things than that in the *Daily Star*.

Getting old really is the gift that keeps giving, though. What's not to like about hot flushes, headaches, palpitations, mood changes, brain fog, digestive problems, bloating and sore boobs? Not to mention night sweats. What are you supposed to do about them? Duvet on, or duvet off? Legs in, or legs out? Gary's moved into the spare room. He says he doesn't want to be sleeping in a puddle of sweat, especially when it's not his. Which is fair enough, I suppose. But it also saves me having to smell Alexa's residue on him all night. So that's a small win.

And then there's the fluctuating libido. It's not as if I've ever been a raving sex maniac like my mother, but I wasn't averse to a modicum of jiggery-pokery. Up to a point: the point where it got a bit messy. But at the moment I don't know if I'm coming or going. There are days when the skeletal Deliveroo kid looks desirable, despite his wart. And then there are days when I wouldn't let even George Clooney have a lick of my Toblerone. Sod Mother Earth, I've got my own battle with climate change to worry about. One day I'm as dry as a rift valley riverbed and the next it's as if there's been a flash flood and it's in full spate again. Maybe HRT treatment would even things out? It might even prepare the ground for Gary's replacement. Possibly. I shall have to ask my GP about it.

In fact, I've decided I'm going to have to make more of an effort with my appearance too. I had a shock this morning when I inadvertently caught sight of myself in the full-length mirror on the inside of Gary's wardrobe door. I was naked at the time, as I always strip off before searching Gary's clothing for evidence of Alexa so I can decontaminate myself in the shower immediately afterwards. But when I caught a glimpse of my reflection, I thought one of Macbeth's witches had crept up behind me. I don't know what was sagging more: my tits or my spirits.

They were hardly given a lift as I sat drinking my breakfast gin and reading the TimesOnline on my tablet. I saw a headline that read: 'How sitting down for eight hours a day harms your mental health'. Well, I've got news for whoever wrote that because it doesn't do the size of your arse many favours either.

Quite frankly, I'm not surprised Rosencrantz wants to medicate me – someone like me shouldn't be walking the streets outside of a zombie film.

Talking of zombies, there's also the business with the bodies in the garden. I could tell that Gary thought I had something to do with them. And the police kept giving me funny looks as well. So I decided to play along. I can be such a mischievous devil when I want to be. But I knew the bodies had nothing to do with me. Obviously. Did they seriously think I'd get the gardeners to dig in the same spot where I'd buried someone? I'm mad but not that kind of mad.

It didn't surprise me when the archaeologist said they were probably medieval. I thought everyone knew there used to be a priory on this site. Besides, there is an upside to all this. Having dug there once, the police'll never look in the same place again. Will they? The downside, though, is that the County Archaeological Service now wants permission to dig test pits all over the garden to see if there are any more bodies or buildings. That would seriously delay my plans. And I really don't want them digging at the top end of the garden where the rhubarb is. That wouldn't be good. As it is, I'm surprised no one's asked what I've been using for fertiliser.

Anyway, I'm sure all this faff about the bodies has been a major distraction, when all you really wanted to know about was Simon. So here's a bit more from my diaries for you:

Sunday, 10 March 1991

ARE THEY MAD!!! Simon's football club has asked him to take over as the manager of their under-fourteen girls' team. I kid you not! He didn't so much as tell me about the appointment; he GLOATED about it. So have a guess who their star striker is. That's right: Dyslexic Dad's youngest progeny. No doubt Simon will be hoping to stick one in the back of her net before the end of the season. Besides Lora, it'll be like giving a fox the free run of the chicken coop. And some of those young chicks have barely grown any feathers yet. Disgusting! I can't allow that to happen. Can I? Today's mood: determined.

Wednesday, 20 March 1991

Phew, had a close call at the pharmacy today. Manisha almost caught me adding to my Valium stockpile. I have a suspicion that one of our 'regulars' has ratted on me, so she's keeping an eye out. And let me tell you that's not easy when you're as cross-eyed as Manisha. I've often wondered whether if I gave her a sharp slap it would knock them back into alignment. Who knows? I might try it one day. As for the snitch, I think it's Ted the Twitcher. To be honest, I'm not surprised he's on tranquillisers. You'd need sedating too if you acted like you'd got a ferret in your pants. Talking of which, I slipped a couple of strong laxatives into Manisha's coffee so I doubt she'll be in tomorrow morning. She'll be a brave woman if she risks it. It's not called the rush hour for nothing. I need time to alter the insulin records. Today's mood: focused.

Thursday, 28 March 1991

All set for tomorrow. We've booked a luxury cottage in Wales for the Easter weekend. Simon says he's looking forward to it – shame he won't be coming with me. In fact, if all goes according to plan, he won't be doing much at all, except preparing to meet his Maker, and I don't mean his mum and dad. They're in Cleethorpes. He's fast asleep at the moment, which is only to be expected after all the Valium I mixed in with his dinner this evening. I'm not entirely heartless, though; it was his favourite: coq au vin. But then 'he who lives by the sword' etc. A jab tonight and another before I set off in the morning should do it. Today's mood: expectant.

Wednesday, 3 April 1991

It's done. More tomorrow. I need to catch up on some sleep. Today's mood: relief.

Thursday, 4 April 1991

Update on the Wales weekend: it was really relaxing. I spent most of my time reading Stephen King's The Dark Half – *that guy is such an inspiration. I thought about going pony-trekking but decided against it. If I'd wanted a beast between my legs, I'd have stayed at home with Simon. Or maybe not.*

When I got back on Tuesday I dutifully phoned for an ambulance. I knew it was fairly pointless, but one has to go through the motions, doesn't one? The doctors tried to save him, bless 'em, but it was too late. They asked me why I hadn't rung 999 as soon as he went into a coma, but I said I'd been away all weekend. That was the truth, wasn't it? I told them he must have become confused by the tablets he was taking for his depression and then accidentally overdosed on his insulin. I cried. A lot. I felt they expected me to. Today's mood: serene.

Thursday, 2 May 1991

Bugger! I've been suspended while Harrisons carry out an internal investigation. It's that bloody cross-eyed fuckwit Manisha's doing! I don't like swearing, but really! She could have turned a blind eye to the missing Valium – it would have been easy enough. For her. I was all apologetic and remorseful, begging her not to tell. I even bought the fat little pig an iced doughnut from Greggs, but it made no difference.

Before leaving I made her a special cup of coffee to show no hard feelings. Ha! If she spends the next week shitting through the eye of a needle, it's her own fault. She'll need to examine her conscience as well as the toilet bowl.

Luckily they'll never know about the insulin. But even so, I'll probably lose my job. Today's mood: fuming.

TWELVE

Apart from its excellent menu, Rossellini's offered Gary and
Alexa – but especially Gary – a discreet place to meet after
work. The owner, Fredo, was a client of theirs and always made
sure that when the couple wanted a table, they were allocated a
cosy alcove at the rear of the first-floor dining area: away from
prying eyes. Fredo wasn't judgemental. Besides, Fredo knew
which side his ciabatta was buttered – if, that is, he wished to
keep the child maintenance payments he was making to one of
his waitresses a secret from his wife.

Rossellini's was located in the middle of a historic row
of Georgian buildings in Newvale, with a faux Georgian
shopfront, boasting antique glass windows and rich burgundy
paintwork. The exterior colour scheme was reflected in the
interior decor, which featured dark mahogany woodwork,
burgundy brocade curtains and burgundy carpets. Fredo was
proud of the ambience he had created for his diners.

"It's like a bloody Turkish brothel in here," muttered Gary
darkly. The subdued lighting matched his mood.

"You'd know about that, would you?" asked Alexa as she
picked her way through her caprese salad.

"No, of course not. It's just how I imagine such a place would be," said Gary, wincing slightly at the memory of an ill-judged, hedonistic weekend city break in Istanbul. *What did that little minx call herself again? Ah yes: Fatima. Thick-thighed, heavy-lidded, light-fingered Fatima, who had taken his wallet in exchange for an antibiotic-resistant infection.* His guilty thoughts were interrupted by the sudden appearance of Fredo, hovering over him like Banquo's ghost. Or possibly Basil Fawlty.

"Is everything to your satisfaction?" asked the restaurateur, wringing his liver-spotted hands together.

"Yes, good, thanks," said Gary. "I have to say the tagliatelle is up to your usual standards." He wanted to add "which isn't saying much" but resisted the temptation. Instead he settled for the equally unsettling: "How is little Maria?"

Fredo's face froze and he glanced around before lowering his voice in response: "She is fine. Thank you. She has just started school so growing up fast." He paused and added "Please enjoy the rest of your meal" before scurrying away.

Alexa raised her eyebrows. "That was a little unnecessary, wasn't it?"

"Well, I wish he wouldn't creep up unannounced like that. Gives me the willies. And anyway, I'm surprised a man of his age was capable of impregnating a waitress."

"Envious?"

"What?"

"You're a bit tetchy tonight. Wifey been playing up, has she? Been requesting your fertilisation services again?"

"No, thank God. She seems to have gone off the idea. And just to be on the safe side, I've moved into the main guest room."

"What then?"

Gary put down his fork, picked up his glass of chianti and drained it. "She's been keeping secret diaries, you know."

"Diaries? About what? The bodies in the garden?"

"No, not about that. She knew they were medieval all along. She just pretended she could have had something to do with them to wind me up. Although, there's definitely something going on with that garden. I saw the look on her face when the archaeologists said they wanted to dig test pits."

"Well, go on – what kind of secret diaries?"

"I found a diary of hers from 1991 behind a cushion on the sofa. When I told you I'd heard her chattering to that doll thing of hers about her life story, I think she must have been reading to it from the diary."

"So you picked up someone else's private diary and started reading it. Is that what you're telling me?"

"Of course I did. Don't be such a hypocrite. You'd have done exactly the same. And although I only had time to quickly scan it, let me tell you the bits I read made my blood run cold. If I didn't know it before, I know it now: that woman's a psychopath."

Alexa edged forwards in her seat, her salad abandoned. "Go on then. What did it say?" she urged. The glint was back.

Gary dropped his voice until it was no more than a strangled whisper. "She admitted murdering her first husband Simon."

Alexa suppressed a gasp. "She actually said she killed him?"

"More or less."

"More or less? What does that mean? Tell me slowly. I want *all* the details," said Alexa, leaning even further forwards until her breasts were almost nestling among the rocket leaves.

"What I mean is, she made it clear she was responsible for him going into a diabetic coma – although she stopped just short of saying she had injected him with a fatal insulin overdose."

"Maybe you should tell the police."

"I've thought about that, but the police investigation at the time didn't come to anything and Simon was cremated, so I doubt the diary by itself would be enough new evidence. And who's going to believe the confessions of a madwoman? Besides, the only way I'm going to get my hands on her money is if she's dead. Sending her to prison won't help."

Alexa turned her attention back to her salad, picking up her fork and idly playing with her food as she mulled over what Gary had said. A hint of a smile appeared as she speared a cherry tomato with a quick jab and looked up. "Blackmail," she said.

"Pardon?"

"You need to find out where she's hidden her diaries and appropriate them. If they're as incriminating as you say, you can blackmail her into signing over control of her money to you. It's either that, or you go to the police with them. Simples."

"Brilliant!" exclaimed Gary, sitting back. "Why didn't I think of that?"

"Because I'm the brains of this outfit."

Gary scowled. "I hardly think so. I couldn't see the wood for the trees. That's all."

"Whatever you say," said Alexa, with an imperceptible shake of her head.

"I'm pretty sure she keeps them in a locked trunk in the attic. When she's out do-gooding, I'll have a go at opening it."

"Hmm. You'd better hope they are incriminating, though. Because otherwise…"

"Otherwise what?"

"Otherwise she's not going to be happy when she finds out what you've been up to," said Alexa, skewering another tomato. "If she did kill at least one of her previous husbands, and she's as mad as you say, you'll be living on borrowed time."

Gary's stomach flipped. He wondered if Banquo's ghost had put something indigestible in his dinner. Or was it fear? "Perhaps you'd better give Bob Flint a call and hurry things along. Just in case."

THIRTEEN

I've given up on Gary fertilising my eggs. He's not even offered
to make a token effort for old times' sake. All that's required is
a quick 'splash and dash'. That's not asking for too much, is it?
It's all he was ever good for anyway, but even that seems to be
beyond his powers nowadays. Maybe all those steroids he buys at
the gym have shrivelled his interest? Something has. I was in town
at lunchtime and saw Alexa going into Boots, so I followed her;
I'm sorry, I just couldn't help myself. It was the way she clickety-
clicked in there on those ridiculously high heels. I kept thinking,
*with a bit of luck she'll fall over, legs akimbo like a drunken stilt-
walker. Then I can pretend to administer CPR while choking her and
whispering, "Die, bitch, die."* That would have been a proper Tena
Lady moment. Right in the middle of Boots.

But no such luck. Alexa teetered straight up to the girl on
the prescriptions counter and pointed at the Viagra Connect
display on the shelf behind her. I couldn't hear what was being
said because I was hiding behind the facial cleansers at the
time. But she went away empty-handed except for a packet of
Strepsils and a bottle of Oral-B mouthwash. Eh? Your guess is
as good as mine.

To be honest I'm not even sure Gary's sperm would be up to the job anymore. I doubt those weary little tadpoles could swim a width these days, let alone manage a length. I read a report in *The Times* the other day that said male fertility drops off a cliff after the age of fifty. Ha! Droops off a cliff, more like. Gary may have four or five years to go to that milestone birthday, but if it wasn't for Just for Men, his hair would already have more white patches than a badger's arse.

I think it's time I looked around for a younger donor, don't you? I'm not too old to be a mother, am I?

I don't know what Alexa sees in him. Well, I do: she thinks he's going to get his hands on my money. As if. The pair of them were at Rossellini's the other night, you know. Fredo's wife, Francesca, called me to say they were having a cosy tête à tête in one of the upstairs booths. So much for Gary's tale about a business strategy meeting with a producer of quality screws. I didn't realise extramarital affairs required a strategy these days. Perhaps they do? If so, Francesca's seen through Fredo's strategy as easily as I've seen through Gary's.

I often compare notes with Francesca about our cheating husbands when we're volunteering at the children's charity shop. I've told her she would be better off without him – and that serving girl of his. Strangling them both with shoelace spaghetti, or drowning them in a vat of pesto, would be poetic justice, don't you think?

I imagine Gary was telling Alexa about the diary I left behind the cushion for him. I'll bet that spooked him. I daresay he'll be nosing around the loft for the rest of them. What a pity I moved the diaries somewhere else. I won't tell you where for the moment in case walls have ears, but it took me a while: all those stairs. I was up and down more times than Lizzie Borden's axe. I'd love to see his face when he realises the trunk is empty. I might even buy one of those miniature spy cameras off the same surveillance website where I bought the GPS tracker.

I didn't give him a lot of time to look at the diary, so I don't know if he read what happened in the aftermath of Simon's death. But I can see you're interested, so let me have a quick drink and then I'll tell you.

Friday, 10 May 1991

Poor old Manisha. Not! I bumped into one of the girls from Harrisons this morning and she told me the backstabber has spent the last couple of days in hospital. She nearly crapped herself to death. As fast as they were pumping liquids into her at one end, her sphincter was pumping them out at the other. I'm not sorry, but I'm glad I wasn't there to see it. I don't like mess. Today's mood: vengeful.

Wednesday, 7 August 1991

Three cheers for PC Plod! I'm in the clear. They've not found enough evidence to charge me over Simon's death. I knew they wouldn't. He deserved to burn in hell for what he did. Or at least in Newvale Crematorium's oven, which was the closest thing I could find this side of Hades. Celebrated at the Butcher's Arms with a flame-grilled steak. Today's mood: exhilarated.

Tuesday, 17 September 1991

I KNEW IT! That sanctimonious bitch Manisha set me up! With the help of Ted the Twitcher and another of our regulars, Granny Green Teeth, she monitored my tranx dispensing. Thanks to her 'evidence', I've lost my job at Harrisons and had my licence revoked by a Fitness to Practise Review. I wish I'd also collected evidence on the number of times Manisha swiped tubes of Canesten cream. That woman's been visited by thrush more times than my bird table. I'm not sure what to do now. I suppose I could always apply for a job at the new Argos warehouse. Thankfully, I don't need the money. Today's mood: depressed.

I'm sorry, Ophelia, but I can't read any more for the moment: I've just heard Honey squealing. I was going to make Robinson an offer: if he treated his dog better, I wouldn't report him. But any goodwill gesture is on hold now. I can't see me burying the hatchet, unless it's in the middle of his sternum. I need to check if that hole's ready yet.

FOURTEEN

Mrs Pinchess was already seated at her desk in reception, her coat hung up and her computer switched on, when Timea arrived for work. Mrs Pinchess looked up, looked at Timea and then looked at her watch with pursed lips. It was 9.01am. "Good morning," she said, but the greeting lacked an accompanying smile.

"Oh, good morning," said Timea, her eyebrows lifting in surprise. "I thought you weren't due back until Monday."

"There was a change of plan."

Timea waited for an explanation, but as none appeared to be forthcoming, she ventured: "Everything's OK, is it?"

"Yes."

"How was Wales?"

Mrs Pinchess fixed Timea with a stare. "It rained. For the whole time we were there."

"Ah. I see."

"Do you, Timea? Do you really? Have you ever spent ten days in Wales in the pouring rain? In a caravan?" She could have added "with only Mr Pinchess, a dog-eared copy of JG Ballard's *The Drowned World* and a chess set that was missing two pawns and a knight for company", but she refrained. She wasn't sure the younger woman, whose last holiday had comprised seven days of unremitting sunshine and hedonism in Ibiza, surrounded by a bevy of buffed young bodies, would understand.

"I'm sorry," said Timea, who was doing her best to empathise.

"So am I. So was Mr Pinchess, believe me. It was *his* idea to book a fortnight's stay at a campsite at the base of a mountain called Cader bloody Idris. I was promised the views were going to be spectacular, but as we couldn't see anything through the blanket of rain and low cloud, I couldn't possibly comment. We cut the holiday short when I saw a frog hopping around the bedroom."

Timea pulled a face and sat down next to Mrs Pinchess, turning on a radio on the reception desk shelf as she did so.

Mrs Pinchess had no idea what genre of pop music was emanating from the speaker, but what *was* clear was that Timea had changed stations during her absence. She reached over and changed it back to Radio Newvale. "It's intended to be an informative service for the benefit of our business clients while they're waiting for their appointments to begin," she said, admonishing Timea. "This isn't Glastonbury."

"Sorry," said Timea.

"Just so long as you bear that in mind. Now, have there been any problems while I've been away?"

"No, it's been quite quiet."

"There haven't been any issues with the partners, have there?"

"No. I've not seen much of them at all, although Gary did call me into his office to make a strange request."

Mrs Pinchess felt the hair on the back of her neck prickle as her mind went back to the non-disclosure agreement signed by the previous receptionist Jasmine. "What exactly did he want?" she asked cautiously.

"He asked me if I had a thing about spiders. When I said 'no' he asked me to go round the supermarkets a couple of times a week and look to see if there are any spiders hiding in the bananas. And to report back if I see any. He told me he was an amateur entomologist."

Mrs Pinchess frowned. "What on earth's one of those?"

"I looked it up. It's someone who's keen on studying insects."

"What? It's the first I've heard about such an interest. I think he must be playing some kind of joke on you."

"He didn't seem to be joking."

"Hmm. I need to get to the bottom of this. Alexa's in with him at the moment, but when she comes out I'll go in and have a word with him. Bug collector, indeed."

Inside Gary's office, the couple were sitting on the two-seater couch as Gary tried to persuade Alexa to invite him to her flat that evening.

"There doesn't seem to be much point, does there?" said Alexa. "The last couple of times have been a bit of a flop."

"I wish you wouldn't exaggerate. You're making a mountain out of a molehill."

"If only. Which reminds me, I popped into Boots last week to ask the pharmacist about buying Viagra for you."

Gary's face puckered as if he'd just been slapped by a wet kipper. "What? You talked about me to that little bottle-blonde? I'll never be able to show my face in there again!"

"Erectile dysfunction is nothing to be ashamed about. And if it's any consolation, I didn't mention you by name, so feel free to chat her up, if that's what you had in mind. But just remember it would be a pointless exercise without some of those little blue pills to give you a helping hand, as it were. And another thing, you have to buy them yourself, because you have to complete a questionnaire first."

"No way! That's not going to happen! I have no intention of allowing myself to be questioned by that girl. What would she know about it?"

Alexa rolled her eyes. "Well, you need to do something. You could always ask Fredo if he would give you one of his to try."

Gary recoiled as if he'd received a couple more slaps from Mr Kipper. "Fredo? You've talked to Fredo about this? Oh my God, it'll be all round Rossellini's! I'll be a laughing stock!"

"Calm down. Fredo's the soul of discretion. Besides, he wouldn't dare mention my chat to anyone else. He knows what the consequences would be."

Gary didn't respond. He sat in silence, eyes closed, practising his deep breathing and nursing his bruised ego.

Alexa allowed Gary a few minutes to regain a measure of control before switching to an equally contentious topic. "What about Claudia's diaries? You haven't mentioned them since last week. Did you find them?"

Gary's eyes blinked open. "Sort of," he said and explained that the trunk was still in the attic, where he'd last seen it, and still padlocked.

"And?" queried Alexa.

"While Claudia was out do-gooding yesterday morning, I got Jimmy B, the locksmith guy, to have a look at it. He opened it without any problems."

"And?"

"And it was empty. Except for a note that read 'Curiosity killed the cat!' "

"Yuk! Not good," said Alexa. "Any ideas where she's moved them to?"

"Not yet, no. But I'd be a lot less stressed if you simply gave Mr Flint the hurry-up."

"Don't worry – he's on the case."

Gary was about to make a comment when there were two sharp raps on the door. He glanced at Alexa before calling out: "Come in."

Mrs Pinchess poked her head round the door. "I'm sorry to interrupt but there's just been a newsflash on the radio. They're saying there's been a huge explosion in The Avenue."

FIFTEEN

Detective Sergeant Kevin Kenneth sighed deeply, knocked and entered the office of his superior, Chief Inspector Julian Catesby. As far as DS Kenneth could recall, it was the first time he had been summoned to a one-to-one briefing with his boss since the younger man had been appointed six months previously. He wasn't even sure that Catesby knew who he was.

"Take a seat, Ken," said Ch Insp Catesby, confirming his suspicions.

"Thank you, sir. But it's DS Kenneth. Or Kevin – should you bump into me at the Golden Lion and wish to buy me a pint and divvy up a packet of pork scratchings."

Ch Insp Catesby frowned and pulled a face, suggesting this was unlikely to happen. Ever. He looked down at his notes, offering DS Kenneth a view of his poorly disguised, mid-life bald spot as he did so. "Kevin? Yes, of course it is," he said with more than a hint of irritation, while continuing to study his pad for a few moments longer.

DS Kenneth took the opportunity to covertly inspect the office, noting the beige colour scheme, utilitarian furnishings, the neat stack of papers to one side of the chief inspector's desk and the obligatory computer terminal. The sole concession to embellishment was the equally obligatory family photo depicting Catesby's strawberry-blonde wife and their two slightly ginger pre-teen children (one boy, one girl) petting a golden cocker spaniel (gender unknown). At least DS Kenneth assumed they were his family, assiduously collated and curated by Catesby to form part of his career-enhancing CV. It was an open secret throughout the station – a fine example of outdated 1960s brutalist architecture – that in addition to his police service, this included details of his membership of the Newvale Masonic Lodge and the Newvale Golf and Country Club. Ch Insp Catesby liked to think that the modern, inclusive police force was especially keen to include masons and golfers.

But if DS Kenneth was impressed, his face didn't show it; it rarely showed much at all. If anything, his expression tended towards the hangdog after a lifetime filled with disappointments. Tall and pale, with cadaverous cheeks and thinning grey hair, he was divorced and lived alone with only a mute budgie called Elvis, and his thoughts, for company. These included vague notions of what he was going to do with his time when he retired the following year on his sixtieth birthday; being a policeman was all he knew and the only aspect of his life that had been relatively successful. Even so, this was down to doggedness and persistence rather than intellectual brilliance.

Nor had anyone ever invited DS Kenneth to join the masons – not that he would have been able to manage the secret handshake as most of his right forefinger was missing and had been since he was a teenager. And the loss of the top two joints had been subsequently followed by phantom limb syndrome that remained unresolved. The episode had begun innocuously enough when his finger was bitten by his pet rat, Robin, named after the toothsome former Bee Gee. But by the time he was taken to A&E by his mum, the finger was so badly infected, most of it had to be amputated. As Gibb himself sang, it was a 'Tragedy' as the amputation cut short – quite literally – a promising career as a young pianist.

It had been the first of life's blows to land and was followed by romantic misfortune when the love of his life left him for his best mate. That was bad enough, but midway through the wedding reception? They hadn't even had time to cut the cake before she severed relations. As the years went by there were other disasters. On one occasion his house burnt down. The cause of the fire was traced to a faulty VCR that had been programmed and left unattended to record *Towering Inferno*. The VCR was an obsolete Betamax device. Naturally. And then there had been various accidents involving kitchen cutlery, household tools and sundry electrical gadgets that had required more hospital attention.

But DS Kenneth didn't like to dwell on past misadventures. He gave a discreet cough and Catesby finally looked up, now wearing his 'grim news' face. "There's been an explosion in The Avenue," the chief inspector said. "A couple of our units have just arrived on the scene and we're waiting for a situation report from them, but I understand there could be fatalities."

"That's bad luck," said DS Kenneth, attempting to scratch his nose with his imaginary finger. It was not an unexpected reaction from someone who viewed life through the prism of misfortune, but it unsettled Ch Insp Catesby.

"Is that an appropriate response to an incident involving the loss of life, Kenny?" he said.

DS Kenneth tried again. "It goes without saying my thoughts are with the victims and their families at this difficult time," he said, parroting the phraseology used on the recent media training course he'd attended, "but at the same time I was also thinking: *The Avenue? Again?*"

"Quite. That's why I asked you to pop in and see me. You're one of my best detectives," said Ch Insp Catesby, although it was more accurate to say he was the *only* detective left standing following an outbreak of norovirus that was sweeping through the station. Strangely, DS Kenneth's guts had so far escaped its clutches, although he accepted it was only a matter of time. Shit happens.

"So," continued Ch Insp Catesby, "I want you to go along to The Avenue and have a good old poke around. See if the explosion's linked to the recent hate incident and the dead bodies that were found."

DS Kenneth balked. *Have a good old poke around?* He glanced down at his missing finger and wondered if Catesby was taking the piss. If so, two could play at that game. "With respect, sir, those bodies were seven hundred-year-old skeletons. And seeing as there was no evidence to suggest they were the subject of a modern-day black magic ritual, I think we can assume that no one had been attempting to raise the dead – other than the forensic archaeologists, of course."

Ch Insp Catesby's eyes narrowed. "Was that supposed to be a joke, Kelvin, because this is a serious matter. There could be ramifications."

"Ramifications?"

"Indeed. The accountant who does the books for my wife's beauty salon lives in The Avenue. I need to know if he's involved in any of this. It's not a good look for me if he is. Or for the golf club. Or the Lodge."

"I doubt the people killed in the explosion are over the moon, either, sir."

"There is that, too," conceded the chief inspector. Although he couldn't help wondering how far they might have travelled if the explosion had been as big as reports suggested.

SIXTEEN

The last few bars of Lulu's Eurovision Song Contest winning entry from 1969 were fading out as Gary and Alexa followed Mrs Pinchess into the reception area to catch Radio Newvale's latest news bulletin.

"Please tell me they weren't just playing 'Boom Bang-a-Bang'," said Mrs Pinchess, her lips pinching in disapproval. "Such poor taste in the circumstances. And that woman's accent is so grating at the best of times," she added.

"Completely inappropriate," agreed Gary, with a look he hoped conveyed the appropriate degree of sincerity.

"I think someone in the studio must have pressed the wrong button," said Timea. "The DJ said it was going to be 'Congratulations' by Cliff Richard."

"Ah. That would have been so much more appropriate," said Gary, allowing his facial muscles to relax into the hint of a smile.

"Would it?" said a surprised Mrs Pinchess.

Alexa intervened, covertly spearing Gary's foot with the stiletto heel of one of her Jimmy Choos.

"No! Probably not." He gasped and took out a monogrammed silk hankie to wipe away the tears.

"You poor thing," said Alexa, patting his hand. "The swirl of emotions at a time like this can wrong-foot even the strongest amongst us." Then, turning to Timea, she asked if there'd been any more news on the explosion.

Timea said the police had cordoned off The Avenue while they dealt with what they said was a major incident. "They haven't said if anyone's been hurt, but there's been a lot of damage to houses in the street and people are being evacuated."

"Good God!" said Gary, still dabbing at his tears. "If the explosion was that big, someone *must* have died, surely. When's the next bulletin due?"

"Anytime soon," said Timea, just as Don 'Cheesy' Straw's award-winning Mid-Morning Show was interrupted by a news update:

It is believed that at least two people died in an explosion in the Old Hill district of Newvale that occurred just before 9am this morning. The police say it is too early to determine what caused the explosion at a house in The Avenue, which has also resulted in widespread damage to property in the area. A fleet of ambulances has been standing by to take casualties to Newvale Royal Infirmary. The Avenue has been cordoned off by the police and residents have been evacuated while the cause of the explosion is investigated. Initial reports suggesting a faulty gas appliance may have been to blame have not been discounted, although police say they are keeping an open mind at this stage. We will bring you further updates as more details emerge.

"Oh dear," said Mrs Pinchess, shaking her head.

"I hope Mrs Alcock's OK," added Timea.

Gary's hands were shaking, and his mouth was all of a quiver. It might have looked to Mrs Pinchess and Timea as if he was overcome by fearful anxiety, but in reality he was struggling to suppress an impulse to shout "yes!" and high-five Alexa. He was surprised to hear there had been two deaths but assumed the 'bonus ball' was Flint himself. That would take care of any loose ends and save them a quid or two into the bargain. So what was not to like? He momentarily considered if he should grab his jacket and head home to give the impression he cared about Claudia's well-being. But he was so caught up in the excitement of the moment that the thought was just as quickly forgotten.

"From the sound of it there must have been enough explosive to bring down a tower block," he said, as Don 'Cheesy' Straw resumed his show with the Rolling Stones' 'Jumping Jack Flash'.

Mrs Pinchess pursed her lips again and turned down the volume. She quite liked the Stones, but there was a time and a place, and this wasn't it.

Timea frowned. Unlike Mrs Pinchess, she didn't care for the Rolling Stones at any time. And she was also puzzled by Gary's remark. "Explosives?" she queried. "I thought the announcer said it could have been a faulty gas appliance?"

Alexa found herself intervening once more. "I'm sure you're right," she said, in a voice as smooth as liquid velvet, "but we'll have to make allowances for poor Gary. I think he's confused by the shock."

"Am I?" asked Gary.

"Most definitely," said Alexa, turning away from the others to give him a full-on glare. "Why don't you go and have a sit-down in your office for a few minutes? When you're feeling a bit calmer I'll drive you home."

"Why?" said Gary.

"So we can make sure Claudia's OK."

"It's pointless," said Gary with a shrug. "We both know she's going to be dead."

Timea began to sob. "I can't believe it," she said.

"Nor can I," said Alexa as she continued to glare at Gary.

"Right," said Mrs Pinchess, picking up her mug and Timea's, "why don't I make us all a cup of tea while we wait for the next update?"

A few minutes later she returned from the kitchenette carrying a tray with four mugs of tea and a plate of Club biscuits.

"Ooh, orange ones, my favourite," said Gary, his eyes lighting up as he helped himself to one of the bars. He had barely removed the wrapper before Don 'Cheesy' Straw's show was interrupted once more. Mrs Pinchess turned up the volume as the announcer said:

More now on the explosion that killed two people in a quiet residential street in Newvale this morning. Police have confirmed that a man and a woman died in the explosion that also caused widespread damage to property in The Avenue. Three other people, who were walking a dog nearby, were taken to Newvale Royal Infirmary for treatment, but their injuries are not believed to be life-threatening. The dog was unhurt. An investigation is underway into the cause of the explosion, but it is not believed to have been due to a faulty gas appliance, as initial reports suggested. An eyewitness has told Radio Newvale that he saw a car explode, and a police forensics team can be seen examining pieces of metal that have been strewn across the road. Police are not releasing the names of the two people who died until their next of kin have been informed.

"I'm sorry! You'll have to excuse me," said Gary, biting his bottom lip and hurrying to his office. The door slammed shut behind him and from inside could be heard loud wailing. Or so it seemed to Mrs Pinchess and Timea. But Alexa knew better. She'd witnessed how watching reruns of *Fawlty Towers* reduced him to hysterical laughter. Especially the episode with the talking moose head.

"I think I'd better go and make sure he's OK," she said, while wondering if a talking moose head would show more self-control than her co-conspirator. It was a concern. He was becoming a liability. "I'll talk to him and then take him home," she added, before following him to his office.

"Poor Gary," sobbed Timea, refusing Mrs Pinchess's offer of a Club biscuit.

Mrs Pinchess shrugged and took a bite out of it. "I don't think I've ever seen him quite so distressed," she said between mouthfuls, catching herself before she added: *Apart from when Jasmine initially refused to sign her NDA.*

By the time of the next bulletin at 11am, Alexa and Gary had already left the office en route to The Avenue and what they hoped would be a satisfyingly large hole in the driveway where Claudia's car had been parked. During the short journey, Gary daydreamed about what he'd do with the money, and that future didn't necessarily include his current mistress and business partner. At the same time, Alexa prayed that Gary didn't behave like an idiot in front of the police investigators, or she might have to decapitate the talking moose head sooner rather than later.

Meanwhile in the office, Mrs Pinchess and Timea listened with growing alarm as the station cut from the studio to their radio car for a breathless up-to-the-minute update from their on-the-spot reporter Kylie McCrystal:

An explosion that killed two people in Newvale this morning could have been caused by a car bomb, police sources suggest.
Eyewitnesses have told me they saw a Ford Fiesta explode on the driveway of a home in The Avenue shortly before 9am,

showering the area in metal and glass fragments. A police forensics team is now examining the debris as well as the remains of the vehicle. It is believed the two people who died were in the car when it blew up.

Three other people, who were walking a dog nearby, were taken to Newvale Royal Infirmary with minor injuries and have since been released.

The police have not ruled out a link to terrorism and won't be allowing residents back to their homes until they are satisfied there is no risk of further explosions.

The Mayor of Newvale, Councillor Sharon Wilde, told Radio Newvale a short while ago that she was concerned to hear about the incident and deeply saddened by the deaths. She said her thoughts are with the families of the deceased and she will be opening a Book of Condolence at the district council offices for people to sign.

The MP for Newvale, Jonny Truslove, who is on an extended fact-finding visit to Patong Beach in Thailand, sent a message via his secretary to say his thoughts are also with the victims' families.

Finally, reports that a dog may have been caught up in the incident have caused widespread concern. Worried listeners have been contacting us throughout the morning for reassurance that Spot, who is a chug, is all right. I'm happy to confirm he is unhurt and has been inundated with goodwill offers to cheer him up. The Castle Street butcher's shop On the Bone has offered Spot a year's supply of free bones and selected offal, while Jack Leadsom, a Newvale dog trainer who specialises in treating canine trauma, has offered a free course of therapy and bespoke mindfulness.

And for those who may be wondering, a chug is a cross between a chihuahua and a pug, rather than a charity street collector.

And now back to Don 'Cheesy' Straw in the studio.

"Oh dear," said Mrs Pinchess. "I'm fairly certain Mrs Alcock drives a Ford Fiesta."

Timea burst into tears once more as the sound of Elvis singing 'Hound Dog' filled the airwaves.

SEVENTEEN

Well, that didn't do an awful lot for my mental health, Ophelia. It was a good job I was out in the back garden when the Robinsons' car blew up, or I might have been forced to raid my secret gin reserves. I'm sorry we had to make such a quick exit, but the long arm of the law wanted to pull us out of the house ASAP for safety reasons. Or so they said. I thought for one horrible moment they wanted me out of the way so they could excavate the rest of the garden for more bodies. But then I realised they'd got their hands full with the Robinsons. Or what was left of them. Did I say hands? I meant buckets. Obviously.

It was such a rush I only had time to pick you up, along with a spare pair of knickers and a lipstick. You might wonder why I bothered with either of those other items, seeing as we're only staying here for a day or two. But this is a hotel, and you never know who you might bump into and want to lure up to your room. And when it comes to luring, there's nothing better than a generous application of Lancôme's L'Absolu Rouge Drama Matte and a pair of peekaboo pants. They're leftovers from my last honeymoon. Unfortunately, I didn't have a lot of use for them, so no surprises there. But I kept them just on the off-chance they might come in handy again. You never know. I live in hope.

Mind you, any illicit encounter would have to go some to beat this morning's Big Bang. It was stunning. My ears went pop, and it almost blew my wellies off. Gary's never come close to achieving that. The only one who has, was my schoolgirl crush Danny Beckett, when he dragged me into an empty bus shelter for an extended snogging session. It was hot. Trust me. But even then, the earth only moved because a double decker rumbled past. It was not at all like yesterday morning when all the windows were blown out and there were shards of glass everywhere. Now that's what I call a climactic event.

I'm sorry if I'm rambling a bit. I should have brought my meds with me – the ones that come in bottles labelled Gordon's and Gilbey's.

Anyway, Gary's pulled a few strings to get us to the front of the glazier's queue, so he does have his uses. I actually felt a bit sorry for him when he turned up at the police cordon yesterday. He looked like he was going to burst into tears when he saw me standing there. I thought, *that's touching. Maybe there's hope for him yet.* But then I saw *her* standing next to him. Why was *she* there? If he needed an emotional support animal, what was wrong with cuddling a guinea pig? Or me, even? On reflection, leopards don't change their spots, and nor do cheaters.

It must have been a bit confusing for him, though, after Radio Newvale said it was a Ford Fiesta that exploded, what with me driving the same make of car as the Robinsons. Maybe I ought to get my car checked out by the garage, just in case the explosion was caused by a common fault? Fred Henderson, who lives the other side of the Robinsons, wondered if it could have been a car bomb. He used to be in the army, so he knows a thing or two about blowing people up. But if it was a bomb, who would do such a thing, other than old man Hendo? Or me? And it definitely wasn't me – unless I've been sleepwalking again. I must check with Dr Rosencrantz if somnambulism and bomb-planting is a 'thing' with people taking anti-psychotics. I once woke up while peeing in a wardrobe, so nothing would surprise me. Although waking up and finding myself having sex with Gary would be well off the scale of probability.

Hendo also said he'd seen Mrs Robinson just before the explosion. She'd told him that the dog-beating benefits cheat she lived with had food poisoning and she was going to take him to the doctors. You don't think that could have been down to the mushroom risotto I made for him as a peace offering, do you? And when I say 'peace offering' don't take me too literally. I had to do something to stop him, didn't I? Especially when one of the other Children's Fund volunteers told me what he and that desiccated stick he was married to got up to when they lived in Africa. So I'm not sorry what's happened to them. They deserved everything they got.

Actually, the explosion did me a favour. Talk about covering your tracks, the pair of them covered the whole street. It was very messy. And as you know, I don't like mess. I'm hoping the fire service will hose down the front of the house before we move back in. As it is, I had to point out to the police forensics girl that there were a couple of bits of bone embedded in our front door frame. I daresay that'll need fixing with Polyfilla.

My main concern after the Robinsons went up in smoke – or atomised mist, more like – was what to do about Honey. Thankfully, Newvale Animal Aid are looking after her in the short term. But if the Guide Dogs lot don't want her back, I said I'd take her. I can give her the love and attention she was sadly lacking next door. And in return, she would be a godsend if I go shopping after having one gin too many. Who needs driverless car technology when you've got an ex-guide dog to take you home?

What I can't understand is why the media have ignored Honey's plight. Even the bearded busybody with the French bulldog who runs the neighbourhood Facebook group failed to mention her. Is it because she's a working girl? Instead, they've been all over that chug Spot, just because he's cute looking. Even the *Daily Mail* used his photo this morning rather than one of the Robinsons. Mind you, they were so pig-ugly it was hardly a surprise. A picture of them would have been enough to put anyone off their Corn Flakes.

Excuse me for a minute because the room phone's ringing.

Uh-oh, that was the front desk. The police are on their way up. They want to ask me a few questions about the explosion. And the previous hate incident. From the tone of the detective sergeant's voice, it sounds a bit ominous.

EIGHTEEN

Alexa was naked and curled up like a big cat on the sofa in her apartment – a big cat that's just got the cream. In her hand was a glass of Prosecco and on her face was a self-satisfied smile. It was smug, even.

"What did I tell you?" she said, snuggling herself deeper into the red velour upholstery. "A little hurried, granted. But nevertheless, it was a promising start worth celebrating."

Gary wasn't so much curled up as sprawled, manspreading-style, next to her. He, too, was naked except for his Armani socks and his handmade suede loafers, which he'd neglected to remove in his haste to disrobe, a little more than ten minutes previously. His grin of triumph, though, was turning into a frown.

"How long do you reckon before I get a 'second wind'?" he said.

"Stop stressing about it, sweetie," said Alexa as she passed him a glass. "Just relax, have a drink and let the chemistry work its magic. Fredo said the effect lasts for around four hours, so we've got the rest of the evening to reap the benefits."

"What if it doesn't and I need a booster. How many tablets did he give you?"

"Only the one, just to see if it worked. Besides, Fredo said he'd only got a packet of four and he needed the other three for the rest of the weekend."

"Selfish old goat," said Gary, glancing down apprehensively.

"Oh, do stop it!" said Alexa. "This evening was only meant to be a proof of concept. Now that we know they work, you can get your own supply and stop relying on me to do your dirty work for you."

The thought of approaching the young bottle-blonde on the Boots pharmacy counter unexpectedly perked up Gary's interest. It didn't go unnoticed.

"Hold that thought a moment – whatever it was," said Alexa. "First, we need to talk about that other bit of dirty work."

Gary forced himself to focus on the aftermath of Wednesday morning's debacle; thoughts of the little snake charmer in Boots might come in handy a bit later. "Mrs Pinchess told me the police are looking for a person of interest," he said. "She heard on Radio Newvale that the police want to trace someone who was seen on CCTV leaving the scene on an e-bike just before the explosion."

Alexa had just picked up the half-empty bottle of Prosecco from the coffee table but put it back down. "Uh-oh. Have the police issued a description?" she asked.

"Black, they think."

"Black?" queried Alexa.

"With orange forks, although it wasn't a high-quality recording. Apparently."

Alexa shook her head. "Not the bike, you idiot, the so-called person of interest."

"I was just getting round to that," said Gary, his voice whining in protest. "According to Mrs Pinchess, all they've said is that the suspect was wearing a grey hoodie."

"Thank God that's all they've got to go on, then," said Alexa as she picked up the bottle again and poured herself another glass. "Bottoms up, eh?"

"Really?" said Gary, raising an eyebrow expectantly.

Alexa's face puckered. "That's not what I meant! Try concentrating your dirty mind instead on the fact that Bob Flint has been in touch, demanding payment."

Gary sat up. "You're joking," he said. "If the police catch him and look at his mobile phone data, we'll be toast."

"Don't worry, we arranged beforehand that we'd only communicate by Telegram."

"Do people still send telegrams?" said Gary, scratching his groin in a clear demonstration that his mind was wandering elsewhere.

"Honestly, Gary, pay attention," said Alexa. "I'm talking about the encrypted communications app. I'm not that stupid, you know."

Gary drained his glass, taking the time to mull over Alexa's words. How to gauge her level of stupidity? Clearly she was good with numbers and anything to do with money, but hiring someone as incompetent as Bob Flint had been a big mistake. The dynamite-happy nutcase had almost demolished the whole street, killed the wrong people and was now demanding money with menaces. Alexa was in danger of becoming a liability. He might have to act sooner, rather than later, even though it was going to take him a while yet to groom Timea. And that still left Flint to deal with.

"So what does he want?" he asked.

"Five grand," said Alexa.

"Five grand!" spluttered Gary. "He's having a laugh!"

"Plus an extra grand in the form of a health and safety surcharge."

"A what?"

"He says this is to compensate him for being hit by debris in the aftermath of the explosion," said Alexa. Her face puckered again as she added: "Human debris."

Gary pulled a face that mirrored Alexa's. "Serves him right. And why should we reward failure?"

"That's exactly what I said. I told him he's not getting a single penny because he botched the job. It was the wrong house, the wrong car and the wrong person."

"What did he say to that?"

"He wasn't happy. He blamed it on 'duff intel'. He said he was told to target the grey Ford Fiesta and that's what he did."

"Didn't he look at the house numbers?"

Alexa paused for a moment and let out a deep sigh. "He claims he's dyslexic."

"A demolition contractor with dyslexia? If he can't read the instructions on the box it probably explains why he used enough explosive to blow up a Chieftain Tank, let alone a Ford Fiesta. Remind me never to accept an invite to a fireworks party round at his house. The guy's not safe to be walking the streets. Even if he was last seen on a bike."

"From our perspective he's become a bit of a loose cannon," said Alexa, smiling momentarily at her own joke. "But seriously, can't you find out from your masonic police buddy what's going on? Surely you can catch him with his trousers rolled up and ask him if the police know who the suspect is? Better still, find out their plan of action."

Gary grimaced as he stood up and flexed his leg. "Bloody leg's gone stiff now," he said, ignoring the question. "Do you think it's a side effect? Not much good if it spreads, is it?"

Alexa rolled her eyes. "I think it's already affected the organ between your ears. Did you hear what I said? What about your detective friend, Inspector Gadget of the Lodge?"

"I heard," said Gary, "but I wouldn't bargain on too much help coming from that quarter. I doubt Catesby could detect a snowflake in a blizzard, let alone Newvale's answer to Guy Fawkes." He stopped flexing his leg and began poking it with his finger, just as his stomach gave a loud rumble. "I'm starving. Haven't you got anything to nibble?"

"No," said Alexa. "It may surprise you to know this, but I've been too busy with other things to go shopping this week."

Gary stopped poking and turned around to face her. "Are you sure there's nothing?"

"Hmm," said Alexa, studying him, "you've just reminded me – I think there might be some Cheesy Wotsits in the cupboard." She didn't need to study him at length, though, to see that the business with Claudia was taking its toll. He was starting to let himself go. In her view, his paleness and slight flabbiness was in stark contrast to her own golden tan, sculpted figure and all-round gorgeousness. In his present condition, she even queried if he deserved her. She needed to encourage him to start going to the gym again, without wounding his fragile ego in the process.

"I think I'll skip the Wotsits if you don't mind," said Gary, who had forgotten about the needs of his stomach. "We can always ring up for a pizza afterwards."

"After what?"

"Round Two?" suggested Gary, proudly waggling his hips back and forth, like a stage magician waving his magic wand. It was a wonder he didn't shout "abracadabra!" for good measure.

Alexa smiled as she thought, *the things you have to do to secure the lifestyle you so richly deserve,* while telling him: "Only if you take your shoes off this time. Are they Hush Puppies? Because last time the squealing sound was putting me off."

"Hush Puppies?" said Gary. "Do I look like a prole? That wasn't the shoes – it was me."

"Well take them off anyway. And the socks. You look ridiculous, and I don't want tread marks all over my Egyptian cotton sheets."

Gary grinned as Alexa led the way to the bedroom. Once inside her boudoir, he kicked off his shoes, flicked his socks across the room and cried: "Geronimo!" as he bounced onto the bed. On balance, Alexa would have preferred 'abracadabra'. Or even 'alakazam'. Although definitely not 'open sesame'.

Later, after Gary had consumed Alexa and most of the pizza, she asked him if he intended to stay the night in the flat, seeing as the house was still off-limits. She wasn't too keen on the idea herself, but she thought she ought to make the offer to keep him sweet. But Gary said Claudia would be very suspicious if he didn't go back to the hotel.

Alexa frowned. "I thought you said the hotel had put you in separate rooms?"

"They have," said Gary, "after I had a quiet word with the manager. I couldn't bear the thought of sharing such a confined space with her and that doll thing. But she'll be on the prowl anyway, waiting for me to return. And I don't want to fuel her paranoia – especially after Wednesday's disaster."

"That's a good point. And who knows? Her vigilance could pay off for her if the tablet's still working. I hope you've left something in the tank."

The colour drained from Gary's already-pale face. "Don't joke about that kind of thing. It brings back uncomfortable memories. Talking of which, what are we going to do about Flint?"

"I've told him if he wants paying he needs to come up with another plan," said Alexa.

"What did he say to that?"

She picked up a neglected slice of pepperoni and popped it into her mouth. "Well," she said, in between chews, "I don't want to worry you unnecessarily, but he said he might just target us instead."

NINETEEN

Home sweet home. Although, it would be a lot sweeter if it was just the two of us, Ophelia. Did he wake you up when he got back to the hotel on Friday night? Or should I say Saturday morning? He told me there'd been a heated meeting of the golf club's rules subcommittee that had gone on longer than expected – some rubbish about incurring a penalty stroke if players handle their balls inappropriately. He'd know about that kind of thing, of course.

And judging by the smell of Miss Dior, he wasn't the only one taking a hands-on interest in the outcome. Would it be appropriate if I drugged him and pegged him out naked on the eighteenth green, smeared his precious balls with jam and let the fire ants get to work? It would be symbolic if nothing else. Remind me to check what kind of jam ants like the best. Otherwise, I've still got a batch of prune and orange marmalade the woman across the road made a few years ago. That might do the trick. I'm certainly not eating it. I tried it once and didn't leave the toilet for a week. Mind you, that might just be the state of my bowels. It doesn't take much.

Talking of which, the unexpected visit by the police didn't do me any favours either. Did you see that Detective Sergeant Kenneth? Odd man. Half a finger's missing, but his brain seems to be all there. He asked me some interesting questions. But apart from looking like he'd just spent a wet weekend in Bognor Regis, his expression didn't give much away. So not just odd but dangerous. He thinks I did it. I could tell. I've watched every episode of *Columbo*, several times, so I knew what he was up to. He even tried to trick me with his opening question.

He looked at me, straight-faced, and said: "When was the last time you saw the Robinsons?"

So I said: "Do you mean before they pebble-dashed the front of my house?" Because I can be just as disingenuous when I want to be.

It was obvious he'd been running background checks on me. He brought up the so-called hate incident the other week – as if threatening to give Robinson a damn good rodding with his white stick could be compared to sending his Fiesta on a manned mission into deep space. He knew he was on shaky ground with that one. Though not as shaky as the ground the Robinsons had been on at the point of lift-off.

Having warmed me up with that one, he moved on to Simon and Martin. How had I felt about having two husbands die in unusual circumstances? Well, truth be told, I was deliriously happy. But I wasn't going to tell *him* that, was I? I may be mad, but I'm not *that* kind of mad. So I simply said: "Some people's marriages do end in unfortunate ways, don't they?" That made his face twitch, which was interesting.

He also brought up my used-to-be-best-friend Sarah's death and Manisha's hospitalisation. He asked me if I had an opinion on what substances had made them so ill, seeing as I was a trainee pharmacist at the time. Sarky bastard. I gave him one of my puppy-dog-lost looks I've practised over the years. And as we know, practice makes perfect.

I said: "I can't help you with that, I'm afraid. I'm not an expert on self-harm."

He said: "Self-harm? Are you sure about that?"

So I said: "Yes, I'm sure that's what it was." Which wasn't really a lie. The way I look at it, by harming me in the first place, they both committed acts of self-harm.

Am I making sense?

He then tried to hit me with a sucker punch by asking about my mother. What did I think had happened to her? And did she have a fondness for mushrooms, like Sarah? That was a bit sneaky.

I said: "You're quite good at digging, aren't you? Would you like to help me with the pond in the back garden?"

He said: "I thought it was a grave site."

I said: "It was, but it could always be resurrected." I laughed. I don't know why; I think I had a touch of the devil about me. Or it could be because he tried to scratch his nose with his missing finger. It was a wonder I didn't wet myself.

I told him I wasn't sure where fungi sat on Mother's list of likes and dislikes, although she had a fondness for yogurt, if that helped. Along with various types of vegetables. And men. But I wouldn't like to hazard a guess which she preferred the most. It was probably all three at the same time. She had an eat-as-much-as-you-want approach to life's buffet of pleasures. That made him blush, so I'm guessing he's a TV-dinner-for-one type. I told him I had no idea what happened to her after she left with her fancy man as I've always imagined she died of exhaustion a few months later. There's only so much even a sex maniac like my mother can take – or so often. If there's such a thing as orgasmatitis, then she died from it. Ha! That made him blush even more. I actually did wet myself at that point. Well, just a dribble.

That's when he left. He'll have to try a bit harder than that if he wants to finger me for anything. I could tell I'm one of his 'persons of interest', though, just by the way he looked at me when I crossed my legs – despite the fact I was wearing tracksuit bottoms. I told you he was odd. Maybe he goes for the athleisure look? Or more likely the 'look-what-the-cat's-just-dragged-in' look. As you know, I wasn't looking my best. If I ever do. Perhaps he's not the only one who needs to try harder.

Anyway, work on the pond has been put on hold because of all the police activity. And DS Kenneth's interest. I'm not sure I want him nosing around my curtilage uninvited. Do you like that word? I came across it in the deeds to this place. I tried it out on the archaeologist who's still wittering on about digging test pits in the back garden.

I said to him: "I'd rather you didn't make a mess of my curtilage, thank you very much."

He pursed his lips and said: "I can assure you the area of land next to the house will be fully restored when we've finished."

Liar. Does that mean they'll put back whatever they find and cover it up again? I think not. And I wasn't keen on the lip-pursing, either. So I told him he ought to be satisfied with evaluating the big hole in next door's driveway for the time being. Not to mention the spoil heap. There ought to be enough human remains to sift through to keep his team going until Christmas. And it's got to be more fun than finding endless bits of old pottery.

Mind you, the crater in the Robinsons' driveway has given me ideas: it might make an even better deposition site than the pond. Who's going to want to dig it up again after it's been filled in? Other than an archaeologist. And if he doesn't watch his step, he could easily join Gary and Alexa, so a bit of forward-thinking would solve that problem. In any event, I daresay it will take a while before the Robinsons' house undergoes structural repairs and is sold. If they can find a buyer after what's happened. Then again, who would want to buy *this* place if they knew what had gone on here?

By the way, I've moved my diaries back into the trunk in the loft. It's the safest place for them now that Gary's already looked there. I've told him that unless I'm around to supervise, I don't want any workmen checking whether the garage has been damaged by the bomb. The expression on his face told me everything, so I fully expect him to spend the next few weeks fruitlessly searching through all the junk in there looking for them. You have to be cruel to be kind. Or is it the other way round? In any event, the next time we chat, I'll fetch down the 1999 diary and tell you all about Martin.

TWENTY

Holy mother of crap! Between the two of them, my GP and Dr Rosencrantz have changed my meds. I don't know what they've given me – well, actually I do, but I'm not telling you in case you snaffle some for yourself – but now I'm feeling positively turbo-charged. I asked them if they could even out my moods a bit, especially my up-and-down libido. But wow! I've been evened out all right, but with the dial turned up to the max. OK, so the dial probably needs turning down a notch or two, but they're not to know, not yet anyway. I don't know if the new treatment plan's altered my hormones, my state of mind or both. But this rocket is now fuelled to go to the moon and back.

I can't remember if it was Bill Shakespeare or Cosmopolitan's sex therapist who once said: "There is a tide in the affairs of men which, taken in the flood, leads on to fortune." Well, let me tell you I'm riding on the crest of a tsunami. I've had to put my Rampant Rabbit in the fridge this morning to cool it down. And I almost climbed in there with it. It's costing me a small fortune in batteries. At this rate I'm either going to invest in a rechargeable model or buy shares in Duracell.

I ordered a takeaway three nights on the trot with the intention of ambushing the Deliveroo kid, but a leery middle-aged bloke with BO and a smoking old Honda Accord kept turning up instead. Creep. I wouldn't even let him enter the front porch, let alone my inner sanctum. Not even I'm that desperate. Yet. And then this afternoon, I saw this gorgeous man walk past the Animal Aid charity shop and I almost ran out and hit him over the head with the Babyliss curling iron I was pricing up just so I could give him the kiss of life afterwards. That's not normal, is it? Not even for me.

I'm thinking about changing tack with Dr Rosencrantz. I know he's interested. As well as rich. And he comes with access to a treasure trove of pharmacological delights. So what's not to like, as the youngsters say. It's not as if I'd want to keep him forever, is it? Unless I have him embalmed and put in a glass case in the hallway. A bit like they did with Lenin. And it beats having an elephant's foot umbrella stand as a talking point.

On the downside, it would mean having to put DS Kenneth on the back burner for a while. But hopefully I can keep him simmering until I decide what to do with him.

Boy, I could do with a drink.

I've got so many ideas whizzing around my head at the moment my ears are like the flippers on a pinball machine. I've been thinking I need to do more to help the animal kingdom. Animals need all the help they can get in this world, don't you think? I'd like to open a donkey sanctuary, or a hedgehog hospital, or even fund a scheme to introduce beavers to the River Vale, which runs alongside the golf course. Or maybe all three. Of course, when I mentioned it to Gary, he was horrified.

He said: "It would be a colossal waste of our money."

To which I pointed out it was *my* money.

He then said: "But the golf course will be overrun. Half my time as captain will be spent chasing after beavers."

So I said: "I thought you liked that sort of thing."

He glared at me and said: "What are you suggesting?"

But I just shrugged and left it at that. The non-disclosure agreements speak for themselves.

Talking of useless husbands, I promised I'd tell you more about Martin. At the time we met in 1999 I was working as a receptionist at High Cross Vets and in an on-off relationship with one of the vets, Gerald. To be fair, it was mostly off than on, but that was because I couldn't stand him most of the time. I was drawn to him because he was a vet. But then there are vets and there are vets. Just as there are serial killers and serial killers.

I'm not sure he'd ever heard of the milk of human kindness. Or any kind of kindness, come to that. Still, I'll let my diary speak for itself.

Tuesday, 9 February 1999

I'm finally done with Gerald! I can't stand his so-called 'tough love' approach anymore. He was such a prick again today, making Miss Grant's cat cry when he gave Cherie her annual inoculations. He's so rough. It's about time someone loaded up a hypodermic and gave him a taste of his own medicine. Preferably a syringeful of ketamine. Trouble is, the drugs cabinet is closely monitored. Never mind, where there's a will there's a way. Today's mood: angry watchfulness.

Wednesday, 10 February 1999

Told Gerald last night it was over between us. Do you know what he said? "Easy come, easy go." Heartless bastard! Not to mention ugly. His new sideburns look ridiculous – like two dead guinea pigs stapled to his cheeks. Maybe they are. I was going to put a couple of worming tablets in his coffee this morning and watch him squirm before I handed in my resignation. But then I thought, I can do better than that. And almost immediately this cute new client called Martin Williams walked in. He's got dark eyes, sensuous lips and delicate hands: I noticed them as he stood in front of the counter stroking his hamster. Ha! Now there's a thought!! He even winked at me on his way out. Claire told me he sings in a band that plays at the Queen's Head every Thursday night. Guess where I'm going tomorrow! Today's mood: eager anticipation.

Friday, 26 February 1999

Went to see Martin's band again last night – that's twice – and on both occasions he's virtually ignored me. Bummer! Yesterday was a bit humiliating, to be honest. I wore my spangly crop top and sexy miniskirt (even though my legs have seen better days) and stood right at the front so he couldn't miss me. Short of hanging a sign around my neck saying 'fancy a shag' I couldn't have been more obvious. Maybe I was too obvious. Or maybe it's the age gap. He must be four or five years younger than me. In fact, the whole crowd looked younger. I even heard a fat girl behind me say: "Who's that frizzy-haired old groupie?" To top it all, the drunken young lad who was standing next to her tried his luck and put his hand up my skirt. Uninvited. As they do. I allowed him five seconds of misguided hope before kneeing him. He squealed and I'm sure the little pervert's eyes crossed over. Even better, he threw up all over the fat girl's shoes. That saved me from having to deal with her later. As for Martin, I'll give it one more go and then find someone else to fixate on. Today's mood: disenchantment.

Sunday, 7 March 1999

THE EAGLE HAS LANDED!! Martin has finally

succumbed to my charms! Well, sort of. I hung around at the end of Thursday's gig, thinking I might have to kidnap him on his way to the car park, when bingo! As the band was packing up, I heard them saying they'd got nowhere to practise for the next month because their usual rehearsal room at the Queen's Head is being refurbished. So quick as a flash I offered them my garage. To begin with they were dubious – not helped by the negative attitude of that fat girl who got puked on the other week. She was there too. It turns out she's the drummer's girlfriend, so I'm guessing he must be partially sighted as well as deaf in one ear. Her name's Candy, probably because she's always stuffing her face with it. Suffice to say she's now on borrowed time.

Anyway, I easily dissed her by telling them it's a double garage – and a big one at that – with its own power supply and plumbing. That got their interest. So on Friday after work, I picked up Martin from the flat where he lives and took him back to mine to show him the garage (he doesn't have a car or a proper job, so I don't know what he does for money). His eyes lit up when he saw it and said it would be perfect for the band. They're called Marmite Sandwich, BTW. I haven't liked to ask why. Maybe because they're an acquired taste.

Martin said to me: "How come you own such a big house?"

And I told him: "It's a long story. Would you like to have a look around?"

So I gave him a guided tour. Good job I cleaned the toilet the other day, although I don't think he would have noticed, judging by the doss-hole where he lives. I could tell he was impressed. Afterwards I heated up a lasagne and we sealed the deal with a bottle of Chianti from Dad's wine cellar. I then put Dire Straits on the stereo, and we adjourned to *the sofa for a 'getting to know you' snogging session. I don't know if* Brothers in Arms *was putting him off or what, but he needs to practise his kissing a bit. Mind you, it was still preferable to Gerald: being kissed by him was like being orally molested by a wet sink plunger.*

Yesterday we went to the cinema to see the romantic comedy There's Something About Mary. *That was my idea. I thought it might give him a few useful tips. But when we got there he ended up dragging me to see* Velvet Goldmine *instead. As best as I could tell, it was a homoerotic offering about a glam rock singer in the 1970s. Not really my cup of tea and not very instructional on the seduction front. Still, I understood why he was interested in it, being as he's a musician. And fair's fair, he was more enthusiastic in the car afterwards. Today's mood: unrequited horniness.*

So that was how I met Martin. As we got talking, he told me he came from a broken home and had been abused as a child; that had me weeping buckets. Genuinely it did. I think you know me well enough by now to know I can't stand cruelty to children and animals. It does my head in. Well, what's left of it after my mother and Sarah had finished with it. When he asked me about my past – I think he was still intrigued by the house ownership thing – I told him the truth. Well, I told him *my* truth. Which didn't bear an awful lot of resemblance to the facts, but that was all right because I've always been more comfortable with *my* truth. And that's what it's all about, isn't it? Besides, he didn't need to know all the gory details.

Anyway, he told me that because of his unhappy childhood he had a deep-seated feeling of insecurity and a need to be cared for and loved. Understandably. And muggins fell for it. Understandably. Within a very short space of time, he moved in with me. On a practical level, as well as an emotional one, it made sense because he didn't have a job and was struggling to pay the rent on his flat. So while I went to work, he spent most of the day rehearsing in the garage. Not that all the practice seemed to improve his singing voice much. He called it distinctive, but trust me, it was very peculiar. If I'm being kind, I'd describe his singing as a weird mash-up between Rod Stewart and Bjork. But if I'm being brutally honest, he sounded more like a strangled badger. But then he explained the lack of improvement by saying most of the time was taken up with his band mate Marcel teaching him to play the keyboard. Or so he said.

And then, after moving in, it wasn't all that long before we decided to get married. And that's when things started to get very puzzling.

TWENTY-ONE

Detective Sergeant Kevin Kenneth sighed deeply, knocked and entered the office of his superior, Chief Inspector Julian Catesby, who was standing at his window gazing out over the car park.

Without bothering to turn around he said: "Do you know what I'm looking for, Kent?"

"Your car, sir?"

The chief inspector finally turned, giving a snort of exasperation as he did so. "I'm looking for your enquiries to advance my ambition for the Newvale Policing Unit. I want us to embrace the seamless sharing of large volumes of data between individuals, teams and partners, while at the same time preventing human cognitive overload and simultaneously revealing actionable insights."

DS Kenneth's face remained inscrutable, but behind the mask he was thinking. He was impressed by his superior's ability to communicate such a convoluted ambition in a single sentence and without pausing to draw breath. But what the man was on about remained something of a mystery to him. He took a stab at it.

"I see," said DS Kenneth. "So in other words, you want me to update you on what I've found out so far. Is that it?"

"In a manner of speaking, yes. As a consequence of you sharing any new information with me, I can then facilitate its cascade, promulgating necessary actions where appropriate."

"Of course."

Catesby sat down at his desk, closing what appeared to be a lavishly produced document from the force's chief constable. Even upside down, DS Kenneth could read the title: 'Policing in Newvale: My Vision for the Future'. *Ah,* thought Kenneth, *that would explain the sudden outpouring of gobbledegook from Chief Inspector Toady.*

"Well?" said Catesby. "What have you found out? Are we ready to make an arrest yet?"

DS Kenneth opened a slim manilla folder he had brought with him and looked down at the top sheet. It might have seemed to Catesby as if he was refreshing his memory, but DS Kenneth was perfectly well acquainted with the information contained in the printout. The gesture merely helped him to gather his thoughts. He told the chief inspector that background checks had been carried out on the Robinsons and it had been discovered they had a dark past. While working as missionaries in Africa, Mr Robinson was alleged to have been involved in a child abuse scandal, and his wife had covered up for him. Ultimately, no charges were brought because those involved were reluctant to testify, but the consensus at the time was that they had been lucky to avoid prosecution.

"Hanging's too good for people like that," growled Ch Insp Catesby, glancing at the photo of his children.

"Quite clearly someone felt the same as you, sir," said DS Kenneth. "Hence the decision to wipe them completely off the face of the earth. Except for the residue, of course."

Catesby pulled a face. "Thank you for your observation,

Calvin," he said sourly. The delight he had experienced earlier in the day at being asked to attend the media launch of the Chief Constable's Vision was now fading fast. And it wasn't just DS Kenneth's flippant comment that was to blame: the prawn vol-au-vents he had eaten at the accompanying lunch were beginning to move around ominously. He wasn't sure if prawns were bottom feeders, but he had a feeling that's where they were headed. A very strong feeling. He clenched internally, trying to buy time against the inevitable, in the hope the detective sergeant's update was a short one.

DS Kenneth noticed the strained look on Catesby's face and the prickle of sweat on his forehead. "Are you OK, sir?" he asked. "We can continue this later if you wish."

"Get on with it, man!" grunted Catesby. "Just tell me if you think revenge was the motive."

DS Kenneth shrugged. "We've had the CCTV footage of the escaping suspect forensically enhanced and his hoodie has a distinctive logo on the back. It's a circular design with a round-shaped bomb in the middle and the words 'Flint Demolitions' arranged around the outside."

Catesby was still clenching as DS Kenneth continued: "I've interviewed Bob Flint, the owner of the business, who said he has two dozen employees, all of whom have the same hoodies. So we're now in the process of checking all their alibis. There's no obvious link between Flint himself and the Robinsons, and he has provided me with an alibi of sorts, so—"

Ch Insp Catesby stood up abruptly, interrupting the other man. "I'm sorry, Kenworthy, but I have to attend to something else as a matter of some urgency," he said as he hurried to the door. "I'll be back shortly."

As the door closed behind the chief inspector, DS Kenneth sighed once more. "Another one bites the dust," he muttered to himself, still surprised that he had so far escaped the virus, if that's what it was. He decided he would give the chief inspector ten minutes, max, and then return to his office. It was a shame because he had just been getting to the interesting bit of the briefing.

The minutes passed slowly, and DS Kenneth was on the point of leaving when Ch Insp Catesby returned. That was another surprise. But the pasty-faced Catesby waved away Kenneth's concerns and sat down with a grimace. "I think you were about to tell me about Flint's alibi," he said.

"Ah, yes," said DS Kenneth. "He says he has someone who can vouch for him – a lady friend – but he doesn't want his wife to know. He says he's been seeing a cosmologist but was reluctant to tell me who it is unless it becomes imperative. I did wonder what a rough and ready type like him was doing with a scientist, but then I realised I'd misheard and what he actually said was 'cosmetologist'. And they're not the same thing. Did you know that?" Kenneth's face remained impassive, but inside he was smiling.

"Of course I know the difference, dunderhead," said Ch Insp Catesby irritably. "I'm married to one. A cosmetologist, that is."

"Really?" said DS Kenneth. "What a coincidence. And here was me thinking she was just a hairdresser." He moved quickly on before his boss could respond. "And here's another interesting coincidence: according to Flint's wife Holly, Flint Demolitions use the same accountants as your wife. You did say that Alcock & Bull are her accountants, didn't you? And that Gary Alcock lives next door to the Robinsons?"

"What are you suggesting?"

"Only that it's a small world," said DS Kenneth, who resisted the temptation to add, "and getting smaller with every day of this investigation." Instead he said: "As an aside, I also went to see Mrs Alcock. She's a strange woman. Rather unpredictable – like the weather. Overall she was quite wary but given to sudden outbursts of excitability. She reminded me a bit of the 'mad professor' type, although quite disarming in her own way."

"And? Is she a suspect?"

"I don't think so, but I'll come onto her in a minute, if I may. In the meantime I wanted to add that I went back to reinterview Flint and – surprise, surprise – he wasn't there. His wife said he's gone away for a couple of weeks 'on a big contract'. I get the impression she would like to speak to him as much as I would. And I daresay the cosmetologist's husband would like to do the same. Don't you agree?"

"Oh shit!" groaned Ch Insp Catesby as he leapt to his feet and ran for the door.

DS Kenneth shrugged once more. No doubt Catesby was on his way to facilitate a further cascade. He couldn't blame the chief inspector, all things considered, but he had been hoping to tell him an awful lot more about Claudia Alcock's background.

TWENTY-TWO

The summer-long heatwave had finally broken, replaced by an autumnal chill. The drop in temperature had been enough to persuade Alexa to turn on the heating in the flat, but even so there was a noticeable coolness in the air. She stared at Gary, who was sitting on the other side of the circular, white kitchen table, seemingly oblivious to her presence. While Alexa had already finished her Chinese takeaway meal, Gary had lost interest in the food. He was absent-mindedly spearing his chicken balls while scrolling through Alexa's laptop.

"Coo-ee. I'm over here," she said, waving her hand. "Just in case you've forgotten."

"What?" said Gary, looking up momentarily.

"What?" parodied Alexa. "How about paying me some attention? You've been looking at that computer for the last hour."

Gary looked up again. "Attention? I've already told you that you'll have to wait until my website order finally gets here."

"Charming! And for your information, I wasn't referring to *that* kind of attention. A show of interest and a bit of conversation wouldn't go amiss. And now you've mentioned it, I don't know why you had to buy Viagra off the internet when you could have walked into Boots and got some there and then."

Gary's imagination conjured up an image of the young bottle-blonde on the pharmacy counter, handing him a box of tablets while shaking her head sadly. "You wouldn't understand," he said.

"I think I do. It's called fragile male ego. And to make matters worse, you don't know what you're buying. You hear such horror stories of people buying duff medication from foreign websites."

"It'll be fine," said Gary. "The company's site carried some decent reviews from their customers."

"I'm sure it did," said Alexa, rolling her eyes. She paused for a few moments and added: "And talking of websites, what are you looking at? It's not those webcam girls again, is it?"

Gary put down his fork and turned the laptop around so Alexa could see a web page populated by images of stab and bulletproof vests for sale.

"What the fuck!" said Alexa. "Flint has really got you spooked with his threat, hasn't he."

"It's not just him. It's her. I've had to get Jimmy B the locksmith guy to put a lock on my bedroom door."

"That's a bit extreme, isn't it? Are you sure you're not overreacting to another one of her mood swings?"

"Mood swings?" said Gary, pushing aside the laptop. "That's putting it mildly. She's taken her madness to new levels. She's gone bonkers plus."

"Really?"

"Yes, really. You wouldn't recognise her. She's been to the hairdressers and had that frizzy grey bird's nest on the top of her head straightened and dyed silver with a lavender quiff at the front. And she's had her eyebrows shaped, or whatever it is you women have done to them these days."

Alexa frowned. "It sounds to me like she's making a bit of an effort with herself."

"Well, I wish she wouldn't; it's very disturbing. She's even bought a gym membership – thank God it's not the one I go to – and made an appointment with a personal trainer."

Gary picked up his fork and started stabbing at his chicken balls again. Alexa watched him and wondered if there was a Freudian explanation for this behaviour, not that she had any intention of mentioning the possibility to him. She tried to push the thought out of her mind and consider instead what Claudia might be up to. Had there been an especially powerful full moon that might explain an uptick in her all-round craziness? Or was it part of a cunning plan to win back Gary? Either was a concern. Alexa's plans for her future prosperity relied on Claudia's demise, preferably sooner rather than later. Claudia bumping off Gary or, at the other extreme, winning him back, was unthinkable. If anyone was going to be responsible for Gary's demise it would be her, once Claudia was out of the way and Mr Chicken Balls had changed his will.

But if what Gary had told her so far was concerning, there was more to come. "She's gone on a crash diet and lost some weight already," he said, "and she says she's going to replace her entire wardrobe when she reaches her target weight."

"When did she tell you all this?" asked Alexa.

"Yesterday evening when I got home from work. I walked into the kitchen to get a beer out of the fridge, and she was standing there with a strange look in her eye. It was as if she'd been waiting for me. I went to squeeze past her, but she backed me up against the Aga."

"And?"

"I panicked and told her to keep away from me. But she started cackling and said she just wanted to get to the cooker to boil a couple of eggs for a salad she was preparing. For a moment, though, I thought she was going to kill me."

"With a hard-boiled egg and a stick of celery?" said Alexa, who was beginning to wonder if Gary was overreacting.

"Don't even joke about it," he said.

"I'm trying not to. But given the efforts she is making with her appearance, hasn't it occurred to you that she had a different kind of intimate encounter in mind?"

"Oh God, no. Death would be preferable."

"Are you sure about that?" said Alexa. "Because it could be worse. You've heard of the black widow spider and the praying mantis, haven't you?"

"What are you suggesting?" said Gary.

"C'mon, you're supposed to be the entomologist. Whatever you do, don't give in to temptation in case she's planning to bite your head off afterwards."

"Don't worry, I don't think seduction is what she has in mind. She thinks more of stray dogs, lame donkeys and three-legged weasels than she does of me," said Gary, pouting. "She's still mad at me for the way I reacted to her animal rescue plans. She told me I was only interested in her because of her money."

"Well, it's true. And she's said it before, hasn't she?" said Alexa.

"Yes, but this time she said it would serve me right if she left it all to her favourite charities."

"She's bluffing. She only said it because she's annoyed."

"I wouldn't bank on it in her current state of mind. She said she's arranged to see her solicitor next week to discuss her options."

There was a sharp intake of breath from Alexa. Would Claudia really cut Gary out of her will? This was serious. "Her options?" she said. "She can't cut you out of her will completely – you're her husband. You'll have grounds to contest it."

"I know that, but what worries me is what she'll do when she finds that out. We need to get hold of Flint and do whatever it takes to get him back on our side. He needs to draw up a new plan to deal with her. It's the only way."

TWENTY-THREE

Sorry, Ophelia, but I've been so busy lately we haven't had the chance for a proper chat. So anyway, what do you think of my makeover? It was about time I did something. I caught sight of myself in a shop window the other day wearing a headscarf: I looked like one of those old Greek women guiding a donkey down a lane with a stick. Not that Gary's keen on the change; he said I look like a drag act that's failed the audition, but he's just jealous of all the admiring looks I've been getting. I even caught the Deliveroo kid licking his lips when I opened the door last night. At least I hope it was the new-look me he was lusting after and he hadn't been licking the cheese topping off my pizza again. Being as it was another of Gary's Lodge nights (what a surprise!) I did toy with the idea of inviting him in for a more substantial nibble, but he looks like he needs all his energy just to ride his bike. Let alone anything else.

As for Gary, I don't know why he's suddenly become so picky, not when Alexa boasts more filler than a rusty old Ford Cortina. Not that he was ever really interested in me; I realise that now. It's just my money he wants, and the same goes for that tarted-up banger of his. Well, I've warned him they're not getting any of it. He thinks it's because I'm cutting him out of my will, but as you know, it's because he won't be here for much longer. He'll be joining the Robinsons in a jiffy. A large Jiffy bag, if I get my way. And I usually do.

I've found out that the person responsible for planting the car bomb was a man called Bob Flint, who runs Flint Demolitions. Francesca told me this when we were talking at the shop the other day. She said that Chief Inspector Catesby had been to the restaurant with his wife to celebrate some special occasion or other. Some celebration, by the sound of it. According to Fredo, he overheard them arguing: Catesby was telling her she shouldn't be 'associating' with Flint as he's their main suspect in the car bombing. 'Associating'? Fancy that. And Flint obviously does, although I'm not sure why. She's so stick-thin, with that mop of strawberry-blonde hair, she reminds me of one of those caramelised toffee apples you get at the fair. Maybe Bomber Bob's got a sweet tooth and swapped her for a prize goldfish? Whatever, it's a pity I didn't know all this when Jennifer Catesby did my hair the other week, or I would have asked her for his contact details. I still might, because he sounds like he could be the solution to my Gary and Alexa problem.

In fact, I think I'll ring up her salon, The Beauty Spot, tomorrow and make an appointment to have my plume recoloured. Do you like it? I like being different. The last time I was there it was full of women my own age, all having their hair dyed exactly the same colour as each other. I've never seen so many blondes in one place since watching *The Midwich Cuckoos*. I'm not one to swim with the tide, or for swimming in general come to that. If I wanted to splash my face with other people's urine I'd join a fetish club.

The thing is, I've given myself permission to explore the new me; as if I was ever going to say no. I've been doing some soul-searching, such as it exists, and realised I've spent the last few years retreating from the world. Well, no more! It's time to throw away my inhibitions – although maybe not the ultra-thin Always Discreet for the time being – and embrace the future!

I was talking to Dr Rosencrantz about this last week when he asked me how I was getting on with the new regime.

I said: "Oh, has there been an uprising by the proletariat while I wasn't looking?"

"No, no," he said, "I mean your new medication."

So I said to him: "I feel like a butterfly that's emerging from its dowdy old chrysalis into the sunlight of a new dawn." Which was quite poetic for me. Usually, I'm more at the Pam Ayres end of the poetry spectrum than William Wordsworth. But who knows where this journey is taking me?

Rosencrantz said that one of my problems is that I've gone through life as a victim. Well, up to a point. But as I assured him, anyone who's victimised me has usually ended up as one themselves. Fair's fair, after all. He then suggested I should show a little more kindness to people in general and not just to animals and children.

"A little kindness goes a long way," he said. "You might be surprised by what you get back."

I wasn't entirely convinced by that. It's called gaslighting, isn't it? So I said: "Kind? Why should I be kind? Just because I'm a woman. Where has kindness ever got me?"

He knows all about my past relationships, so he didn't argue. Although when I say *all* I don't mean I've told him *everything*. I know he's my psychiatrist, but that would be crazy. Wouldn't it?

In any event, I asked him what kindness has done for women down the centuries. I mentioned Catherine the Great. Look at all the things she did for Russia. Quite apart from all her other achievements she played a key role in the Russian

Enlightenment and founded the first educational establishment for women in Russia, as well as the Hermitage Museum. That's kindness for people on an epic scale. But guess what: all most people know about her is that she was a nymphomaniac who died having sex with a horse; only she didn't. Not even my mother attempted that. At least I don't think she did. It was just a story invented by inadequate men to belittle her. Which is odd when you consider the men behind the lie probably wish *they* were built like horses themselves. Probably to go with their donkey brains.

Anyway, talking of men built like stallions – not! – I've brought my diary down from the loft so I can tell you what happened once me and Martin decided to get married.

Friday, 27 August 1999

Well, that wasn't exactly a case of 'light the blue touchpaper and stand well back'. Talk about a damp squib. I don't know why I bothered spending all that money on a honeymoon in Rome when we could have gone to Margate and had an equally disappointing time. There's no getting around the fact it was an expensive flop, in more ways than one. He blamed it on the stress of the wedding. STRESS!! He did bugger all except turn up on the day and say "I do." I was the one who did all the arranging and cheque-writing! The least he could have done was show willing every once in a while. I might just as well have left my sexy new lingerie in the suitcase. Or run it up the hotel flagpole and left it at half mast.

To make matters worse it was too bloody hot to go traipsing round all the sights. And in any event, me being me, I refused to go to the Coliseum. Martin tried to drag me there. He said it would be the cultural highlight of our trip. CULTURAL HIGHLIGHT?!! Since when has slaughtering thousands of innocent animals for fun been a high point of Western bloody culture? I would have strangled him there and then and thrown him in the Trevi Fountain if there hadn't been so many witnesses hanging around. Bloody tourists!

So we ended up in our room a lot. Yay! Except Martin spent more time on his new mobile phone, talking to Marcel, than trying to seduce me. It was very FRUSTRATING! I was in the bar on my own one evening(!!) when I got chatted up by this guy who was an Australian tour guide. I say chatted up, but his eyes never left my boobs. It was a first for me – I can't say I've ever been groped by a pair of eyeballs before. He asked me if I fancied popping upstairs and letting him explore the bush country. But seeing as he must have been at least fifty and smelt of rancid sausages – unless it was dead kangaroo – I punched him instead and reported him to the hotel management. That cooled his ardour and got rid of a lot of my own pent-up emotion into the bargain, I'm relieved to say. Today's mood: rancorous.

<u>Tuesday, 7 December 1999</u>

Christmas is coming and I don't know what to get him. The ideal gift would be NOTHING! He doesn't deserve anything, not even a packet of stale Twiglets. I went a bit OTT in the summer when I offered to pay for him and his precious band to record an album as a wedding present. Yes, I know, generous to a fault as usual. And what have I got in return? You guessed it – NOTHING! He's got the attention span of a gnat, at least when it comes to showing ME some attention.

He blamed 'stress' for his performance issues in Rome, so what's his excuse now? He says the intensive rehearsals before they go into the recording studio have left him 'exhausted'.

And there was me thinking musicians have legendary sexual appetites. I was going to replace the fruit in our bedroom with a family pack of Mars bars as a reminder of how rock stars used to behave, but I'd have probably ended up eating them myself, which is just too weird to contemplate, even for me. And anyway, I don't like mess. Besides, he'd better not be seeing someone on the side. If it turns out to be Candy, death will be too good for her! What's she got that I haven't? Apart from three stones of excess blubber. Maybe I ought to harpoon her? I could always get rid of her corpse by selling it to the Japanese for 'scientific research'. But if it's not Candy, I hope it's not history repeating itself. In which case, I may have to create a fifty-metre pre-teen exclusion zone around the garage.

As for the band, they don't seem to be getting any better despite all that practice. Claire at work asked me how I would categorise them. So I told her they were definitely more shitpop than Britpop. She thought I was joking! But she isn't the one spending a fortune on earplugs and paracetamol.

Claire also told me that Gerald is being investigated after one of our clients lodged a malpractice complaint against him. She won't tell me who it is, but I wouldn't be surprised if it turns out to be Mrs Brown. Her chihuahua, Charlie, died from an allergic reaction after Gerald gave him an injection. Today's mood: brooding.

Saturday, 1 January 2000

Well, he's still here. I woke up this morning hoping the Y2K Bug might have wiped him out – or at the very least reprogrammed his brain – but no such luck. So I'm stuck with him. For the time being. Marrying him wasn't one of my most clear-sighted decisions, but I ought to know better than trust my judgement when my blood's running hot.

Talking of which, we went to a New Year's Eve fancy dress party last night at The Angel. I threw caution to the wind and went as Lucrezia Borgia (aren't I a devil?!), although nobody managed to guess correctly. Mind you, the low-cut bodice was a bit misleading. One bloke, who was dressed as a pirate, came up to me and said: "Who are you supposed to be? Nell Gwynn?" So I said: "Excuse me, Capt Bird's Eye, but are you blind? Do these look like oranges to you?" It turns out he was the pub landlord and wears an eyepatch because he's partially sighted. He was a bit upset, so I let him have a quick squeeze as a goodwill gesture. I'm all heart. Sometimes.

Martin got hold of a ratty old leopard-skin leotard from somewhere (I didn't like to ask) and raided my underwear drawer for a pair of white tights (I shouldn't complain because it's the first time he's shown any interest in what's in there), then superglued a couple of balloons to each end of a stick and went as a circus strongman. It was pathetic! Strongman? He couldn't fill out a shopping list, let alone a he-man costume – he's nine stones dripping wet! He looked more like one of those starving cats the RSPCA use for their annual TV appeal. It's a wonder he didn't get people offering him £1 a week to get well soon.

Some of his band mates turned up as well. Marcel was dressed as an American footballer. He said he'd gone as a legendary tight end called Mike Ditka, which the others thought was hilarious, but it meant nothing to me. Then again, I'm not remotely interested in sport: too much mud for my liking. Candy was there as well, and fair's fair, she really looked the part as the Incredible Hulk. I asked her where she got the make-up from, and it turns out she's got jaundice. Ooops! But, as I said to her, "It suits you."

On a positive note, I discovered the delights of gin and tonic, gin fizz and negroni. In fact, pretty much anything that's got gin in it. Not sure it mixes too well with my meds, though, which might explain the Capt Bird's Eye incident. And I felt very strange this morning. Well, stranger than usual. Today's mood: otherworldly.

Tuesday, 25 January 2000

I AM FUMING!! I don't like to swear, but FUCKING HELL!! Gerald has got away with it. He told the investigators that he had no idea Charlie was allergic when he injected the poor thing. But I know for a fact it had been listed on Charlie's records. Yet when I double-checked today, there's no reference to it. Gerald must have altered the records to save his own skin. Well, you'd better believe me when I tell you he hasn't. Murderer! Today's mood: sulphurous.

TWENTY-FOUR

Detective Sergeant Kevin Kenneth sighed deeply, knocked and entered the office of his superior, Chief Inspector Julian Catesby, who was leaning back in his executive office chair and staring up at the ceiling tiles. Without altering his gaze, the chief inspector motioned with his hand to the sergeant to sit down.

"Do you think flies experience loneliness, Kenilworth?" Catesby asked. "Only I've had my eye on a fly up there for most of the day and it seems to be without a friend in the world – or a mate."

"I can't say I've ever thought about it," said DS Kenneth, abandoning an attempt to rub his chin with his non-existent forefinger. "Although there were enough of them in that old lady's flat I went to last week. Mind you, she had been dead for the best part of a fortnight so that wasn't surprising. Having a right old feast, they were."

Catesby abandoned his study of the fly and fixed Kenneth with a sour look. "Thank you for enlightening me, Sergeant."

"You're welcome, sir," said DS Kenneth, "and, if I might say, it's good to have you back. Are you feeling better now?"

It had been a month since their last meeting, which should have been ample time in which to recover from the sickness bug. But then the word around the station was that most of the chief inspector's absence was for compassionate reasons so he could deal with a 'domestic issue'.

"I'm as well as can be expected in the circumstances, thank you," said Ch Insp Catesby, enigmatically, "but getting back to business, I believe you have a progress report for me."

DS Kenneth nodded and opened his manilla folder, which was now a lot bulkier than it had been the month before. "Before I begin, all of Flint's employees have alibis that check out, except for Flint himself, so he remains the main focus of our investigation. However, I thought you might like to know I've also carried out some background checks on your, er, acquaintance, Gary Alcock."

Catesby leant forwards at the mention of the name as DS Kenneth explained that Gary began his career at a firm called Templeforth Accountancy, which was used by Claudia Alcock's wealthy father, Bill Nicholls. It was through this connection that Gary first met his wife-to-be. Later on, when Mr Templeforth retired, Claudia provided the funds for Gary to buy the business, having inherited a substantial sum of money when her father died. Sometime later, Alexa Bull joined the business, and it was renamed Alcock & Bull.

"But from what we can tell," added DS Kenneth, "Mrs Alcock retains the majority stake."

"Really?" said Ch Insp Catesby. "He's always given me the impression he's the man in charge. But what about criminality? Any whiff of impropriety?"

DS Kenneth said there had been an occasion, five years previously, when Gary had been under investigation for allegedly helping to cover up fraudulent activity by a client, Newvale Insulations. But insufficient evidence had been found, and no further action was taken. Was this sufficient to flicker the needle on Catesby's whiff-ometer?

"Hmm," said the chief inspector, who wondered if the information could be useful in the run-up to the Lodge's election of next year's junior warden. Gary Alcock was the current senior deacon and would normally expect to progress automatically to Junior Warden. But what if he should stumble? Assisted by a slight nudge? That would leave the way open for Catesby as Junior Deacon to accelerate his own progression. Providing, of course, his domestic difficulties didn't become an obstacle. Still, it was food for thought. In the meantime, there was also the other active business partner to consider.

"As for Ms Bull," said DS Kenneth, "her father is British but her mother's Greek. I was told that the maternal side of her family is strongly suspected of tax evasion in Greece, but seeing as that's almost viewed as a national sport over there, I'm not sure how relevant it is. And in any event, I've no way of telling if she's involved in any way."

"Good God, Kennedy. How many more cheats is your investigation going to uncover?"

"That's an intriguing question," said DS Kenneth, casting a sideways glance at the empty spot on the chief inspector's desk where the photo of his wife and children had previously stood. "A very intriguing question indeed."

"Is there anyone else?" asked Ch Insp Catesby.

"At this stage, there's only Claudia Alcock. As I said at our last meeting, she's an interesting character."

"Yes, but being an interesting character doesn't necessarily mean she's a person of interest."

"True, although her personal history, coupled with the fact her family is riddled with lunacy, suicide and internecine division, might prove otherwise."

"Is that so?" said Catesby, signalling to DS Kenneth to

continue. He didn't say it out loud, but it would be comforting to hear how other people's lives had been blighted by the mad, selfish behaviour of ungrateful family members. God rot their souls!

For his part, DS Kenneth couldn't help noticing a muscle in Catesby's cheek had started to twitch; no doubt something he said had struck a nerve. He looked down and shuffled through the sheaf of papers in his folder until he found the one he was looking for and began to read, explaining that Claudia first came to the police's attention in 1981 when she was fifteen years old and her mother Geraldine went missing. He said he had only just joined the force at the time and wasn't involved in the investigation, but he had since spoken to the retired officer who had been in charge and who remembered the case very well. The officer told DS Kenneth that Claudia was born only six months after Geraldine married Bill Nicholls, who was a few years older than her.

"I'm not one to cast aspersions," said DS Kenneth, "but it was suggested to me that she was attracted to him solely because of his wealth and had trapped him into marrying her. In any event, Geraldine wasn't a very good role model for Claudia. She had multiple lovers, of both sexes, during the marriage and at one point she was rumoured to have enjoyed a three-way relationship with her sister and her brother-in-law."

Ch Insp Catesby shook his head, twitched and shook his head again. "Disgusting behaviour," he said, while trying to suppress disturbing thoughts of his wife with Bob Flint. Not to mention naked images of his own sister-in-law, which he'd been unable to expunge from his memory, having called at her house unannounced during the summer and caught her sunbathing au naturel in the back garden. He had fled before she knew he was there and had assured himself he had done nothing wrong, morally or legally. But even so, he had been unable to forget what he saw: especially the way Kate's lithe, suntanned body had glistened seductively in the dappled sunlight. Dear God. The stirring it provoked! And taken together with the revelation of Jennifer's behaviour, was it any wonder his mind was in turmoil? Hopefully Dr Rosencrantz would sort him out. And sooner, rather than later.

However, the turmoil wasn't helped by DS Kenneth's continued revelations, including the information that Geraldine had tried to 'pimp out' Claudia to various of her lovers as her daughter was growing up.

It prompted another bout of head shaking from Catesby. "Do we know what happened to this awful woman?" he asked.

"No," said DS Kenneth. "A typewritten note was found, in which she said she'd had enough of her mundane, bourgeois existence and was eloping with one of her lovers. And, indeed, some of her clothes and personal possessions were missing, but there was no trace of where she might have gone. And the identity of the lover in question was never established. There was a suspicious blood-coloured mark on the note, but analysis showed it was a harmless fruit stain: cherry, I believe. With a hint of yogurt."

"So, do we think she was murdered?"

"Quite possibly, but although there was a lengthy list of jilted lovers to investigate – not to mention suspects like the husband and daughter – there was insufficient evidence to charge anyone."

"It sounds to me as if Mrs Alcock had a damaged upbringing."

"Very damaged," agreed DS Kenneth, "and it got worse. While she was at university her best friend, Sarah Goddard, spiked her drink with a hallucinogenic drug. It was only meant as a student prank, but Claudia had a fit and ended up in intensive care in a coma. At one point it was feared she might be brain damaged, or even die, but in a remarkable act of friendship, Claudia forgave her. Ms Goddard was subsequently poised to become Chief Bridesmaid at Claudia's wedding, only to die tragically on the eve of the ceremony."

"That's unbelievable."

"Yes, it is rather, isn't it?" said DS Kenneth, who added that tragedy had continued to dog Claudia with the deaths of her two previous husbands, both in unusual circumstances, and with serious misfortune affecting several other people closely connected to her.

"The woman's jinxed," said Catesby.

"That's one interpretation."

"But what about the lunacy and suicide you mentioned?"

"Ah. I was just coming to that. I think you'll be interested in the next bit," said DS Kenneth, who told Catesby that, just after the war, Claudia's maternal grandfather, Albert, committed suicide while playing a round of golf at the Newvale club. Although he was a manic depressive, his playing partners only realised something was wrong when he failed to emerge from the woods after hooking his ball badly off the third tee.

The chief inspector nodded sagely, which made a pleasant change from his previous twitching and head shaking. "That hole's an absolute bugger," he declared. "It's a par five with a vicious dog-leg. I've come to grief there a few times myself."

DS Kenneth arched an eyebrow. "I rather think that depends on how you measure grief, sir," he said. "The fact is, Albert's wife, Joan, had just left him. She was a singer and dancer, and during the war, while he was away, she apparently led a very energetic private life with a number of US servicemen who were posted over here."

Catesby's twitch returned. "How low can you get?"

"Not too low. She did have standards – it seems she never chose anyone below the rank of lieutenant," said DS Kenneth. He completed his briefing by saying that Joan left Albert for a former Italian POW, Major Gianni Rossellini, and together they opened the town restaurant with the same name. However, Joan was later admitted to a psychiatric hospital as she was suffering from delusions after coming to believe she was the 1940s burlesque star Phyllis Dixey.

"So although it might seem a bit of a tortuous link," he said, "Joan's second marriage to Rossellini means that Claudia is a distant cousin of Francesca, the wife of Fredo, who now runs the restaurant. Yet more wheels within wheels."

Ch Insp Catesby leant back in his chair and his eyes strayed back up to the ceiling. It might have looked as if he was lost in a moment of quiet contemplation but for the telltale twitch. "I don't mind telling you, Kennally, that all these people getting away with abhorrent, and possibly illegal, behaviour leaves a nasty taste in my mouth. I know the police are tasked with upholding the law, but the rules are such that it makes me wonder if vigilantes are such a bad thing."

TWENTY-FIVE

Alexa was sitting on the couch in Gary's office, looking smart and elegant in a pinstripe trouser suit and white blouse, as she scrolled through the updates on her phone. Gary was mooching around the room, hands in his trouser pockets and with a grumpy look on his face, like a truculent schoolboy who's just been told to stop pulling the wings off a dead fly.

Alexa looked up. "You'd think for the price you paid, they would have made those shoes of yours squeak-free," she said. "You don't suppose those poor alligators are still alive, do you?"

"What?"

"Come and sit down, you're making the place look ugly."

Gary pouted. "Is it time for elevenses? I could do with a cup of coffee."

"It's not even ten o'clock yet, and I think you've already had enough caffeine for one morning."

"Bugger," said Gary as he sat down next to Alexa. "Any word from Flint?"

"No, still no word. I can only assume he's decided to lie low for a while. I rang his office first thing on the pretext of needing to check something for the annual audit, but his secretary says he's working away on a big contract."

"Do you believe that?"

"Quite frankly, no. I wouldn't be surprised if he's gone on the run."

"Oh great," said Gary. "So there's a mad bomber on the loose who could be coming for us next."

"Relax. I doubt he'll be in any hurry to risk showing his face in Newvale for a bit. Unless…"

"Unless what?" asked Gary.

Alexa gave a sly smile and told Gary she'd popped into Rossellini's to see Fredo over the weekend and he couldn't wait to pass on the hot gossip about Flint and Julian Catesby's wife Jennifer.

Gary's snigger signalled an abrupt mood change. "Excellent! That'll be one in the eye for that sanctimonious prig Catesby," he said.

"I thought he was your friend."

"Friend? I wouldn't trust him further than I could throw him. I'm sure he's been trying to undermine my position at the Lodge. Maybe I can use this to even things up a bit."

He paused for a few moments while he let his mind conjure up a couple of scenarios that might lead to his rival's humiliation: a quiet word here, or an insinuation there, ought to do the trick. And as for Flint, he wondered if they could hire an investigator to keep an eye on Catesby's wife to see if she might lead them to him. But when he made the suggestion to Alexa, she was quick to point out that Catesby could be doing exactly the same thing, and he had a whole team of detectives at his disposal.

"Is she worth the bother?" she said.

Gary, who was busily recalling Jennifer Catesby in a less-than-flattering evening dress at the annual masonic dinner, misinterpreted Alexa's question. "It's debatable," he said. "I can't say I fancy her myself."

Alexa rolled her eyes. "Charming. That would make a change then. Have you gone off older women? Is that your problem?"

"What's that supposed to mean?" said Gary, who didn't like the way Alexa was now looking at him inquisitively. Or was it accusingly? And what was equally concerning was that the same thought had been niggling away at the back of his mind for a little while.

Nor was Alexa about to let him off the hook. "I just wondered if your tastes have changed. We never did have that conversation about Jasmine and her NDA, did we?"

"Ridiculous!" he said, even as the image of scrawny old Jennifer Catesby was replaced in his mind's eye by that of tender young Jasmine Shuttleworth. It was a shame she'd blown hot and then so cold. Still, plenty more fish in the sea. Or, to put it more accurately, school leavers looking for a job. But until Timea showed signs of living up to his expectations, he would have to settle for another well-worn cliche, such as beggars couldn't be choosers. Fixing Alexa with what he hoped was his most disarming smile he said: "So, I take it you didn't go to see Fredo just for some idle chit-chat?"

"I wondered how long it would take you to ask. I had hoped he might be able to spare another one or two of his little blue pills to keep you going until your delivery gets here. But no luck I'm afraid."

Gary's smile faded. "The greedy git!"

"He said it had been another busy weekend."

"Really? I hope it drops off. What the hell does that waitress see in him?"

"Forget about Fredo; it's you I'm concerned about. Would it help if I found one of those old St Trinian's School films for us to watch on Amazon Prime?"

"Ha, bloody ha. For your information my order's supposed to be arriving any day now."

"Let's hope it's worth the wait, then."

"Oh, it will be," said Gary, but his show of bravado was immediately undermined by a nagging thought: *what if the pills are duds?*

Alexa shook her head, as if she was a mind reader. "Anyway, let's move on," she said. "If we can't locate Flint we need to come up with an alternative plan."

"Like what?"

"I've had an idea," she said, as she leant over to one side and picked up her black leather attaché case, which was next to the couch. Resting it on her knees she flipped open the catches and retrieved an A4 notepad, before placing the case back on the floor. She flicked through the first few pages of the pad until she came to one that contained a mass of scribbled notes and doodles.

Gary peered at the page with a puzzled look on his face. "I take it you've not been busy compiling a list of ingredients for the perfect pipe bomb?"

Alexa ignored the comment and asked him if he remembered her telling him that Timea's father was thinking of transferring his accounts to them.

"Of course," said Gary, who had made it his business to take an interest in anything pertaining to their new receptionist. "Didn't she recommend us to him?" he asked.

Alexa nodded and said she'd had to contact his previous accountants to ask for clarification on a couple of points because they had only been prepared to issue a qualified set of accounts. As luck would have it, she had been on a course with the partner concerned and he had been a lot more forthcoming than Alexa had expected. In fact, he sounded relieved more than annoyed to hear that Mr Novak was moving his business.

"Why?" said Gary cautiously.

"He hinted at Mr Novak's business activities before he came to this country," said Alexa. "Without making any specific claims, he mentioned the names of one or two of Mr Novak's previous associates in Slovakia and suggested I might like to check them out before taking on his business."

"And?"

"And the people he mentioned ended up in jail. It was alleged in court that they were mafia-style gangsters. It seems Mr Novak and his family moved to this country around the same time the police over there started to leak lists of more mafia suspects to the media."

Gary started to lose the colour in his cheeks. "Mafia? Er, I'm not so sure about this, Alexa. Is it wise?"

"There's nothing to suggest his import-export business isn't a legitimate one," said Alexa with a dismissive wave of her hand. "It's just whether he's retained any additional less-than-legitimate interests. And if he has, well, maybe he could be persuaded to help us with our little problem."

But Gary remained unconvinced. He wasn't just concerned about the risk to their business reputation but the risk to them personally. Or, to be more accurate, to him. What if Timea had already complained to her dad about him? He'd become quite attached to his kneecaps and didn't fancy losing them anytime soon. Or any other part of his anatomy, come to that.

"It's too late to back out now," said Alexa. "As our American cousins might say, it's time to show some spunk!"

Gary winced. "That's what I was afraid of."

TWENTY-SIX

I've mentioned Dr Rosencrantz to you so much, Ophelia, that I thought you might like to see where we meet for our regular chats. I call them chats, although he prefers to call them sessions. He says it sounds more professional that way. Sod that. I'm paying for our chats, so it's only right we should call them what *I* feel comfortable with.

I suppose I could have gone to see someone on the NHS. But really? Why traipse across town to the hospital and sit with all those sick people in an overcrowded holding pen while waiting for an overdue appointment that starts two hours late? I've got better things to do with my time – like picking the fluff out of my navel – than spend it listening to some smelly old man with a strangulated hernia complaining about his pain. His pain? What about the pain he's inflicting on me! Sometimes you just want to take the old buggers outside and shoot them. Well, I do.

So no, slumming it with the *hoi polloi* is not for me. I much prefer coming here to see him in his private consulting room in this lovely old house. The ambience is so much more conducive to our intimate chats. Well, it was until this morning's episode.

The thing is, ever since I first came to see him, I've been keeping an eye on his body language. And it's been pretty clear he's been struggling to contain his interest in me. A woman knows these things, doesn't she? Especially when he's sat no more than two feet from the couch where I'm lying. Manspreading. Shamelessly. I'd have to be crazy not to notice something as obvious as that. So today was the day. Which you may have guessed from my outfit. Trust me, I was more than ready to help him unleash the monster that lurks within! Hence my new semi-transparent black blouse, sans bra: how daring! And this short black skirt. Not to mention my peekaboo pants, which enjoyed a long overdue airing. Because two can play at being shameless.

I know I've always said I don't like cheaters, but Gary's forfeited my faithfulness. Besides, I'm the one who writes the rules about what's acceptable and what's not; I'm very Gen Z like that. Although I did wonder – as I lay there, waiting for him to pounce on me like a ravenous tiger – if I'm turning into my mother. God forbid. Or even my nan, not that I was ever allowed to call her 'nan' or 'gran' when I was a kid. Nan said it made her feel she was past her best. Past her best what? She used to wear this long blonde wig and a feather boa and insist I called her Phyllis – right up until she went away 'for a rest'. I didn't see her again after that. My dad said she'd gone doolally. And it was only years later I found out it wasn't somewhere abroad, like Timbuktu or Wagga Wagga, and that my nan's real name was Joan.

But guess what: all the time me and Rosencrantz were chatting, I was waiting for something to happen. But it didn't. Can you believe it? He rejected me. And as you know, I don't take rejection very well. I was steaming, lying there like a turd that's been disowned by every dog walker within fifty yards.

I said to him: "What's wrong? Don't you like the new-look me?"

He said: "That's not the issue. There are boundaries that shouldn't be crossed."

So I said: "Boundaries my arse. Did Julius Caesar become ruler of the known world by staying on his side of the Rubicon? Did Michelangelo look at the ceiling of the Sistine Chapel and say to the Pope: 'Are you sure you don't want this Artexing?' Great men rise to the challenge."

He was halfway there – I could tell by the way he was sitting. Yet somehow he managed to resist my charms. How was this possible? He even suggested passing me over to a colleague because of my 'inappropriate behaviour' but then thought better of it when he saw the look on my face. Or, more likely, he remembered what's in my medical records.

As I left he said to me: "You're either the craziest sane person I've ever met or the sanest crazy person. And I still haven't made up my mind which it is."

Which you have to admit was praise indeed, because even I don't know.

Anyway, you don't mind if we sit here for a few minutes longer while I cool off, do you? I wish I'd brought my Thermos with me. It's an ideal way to keep my sloe gin fizz at just the right temperature. Especially in the winter. Not that I condone drinking and driving, of course. Why endanger someone else's life unless you mean to?

Talking of which, I went to Jennifer's Beauty Spot salon yesterday in the hope of getting her fancy man's contact details. I was going to tell her I wanted the old summer house demolishing. The rotting hulk used to be one of my mother's favourite haunts and it's about time it was pulled down. I haven't been inside for years, but I'll bet it still reeks of Brut aftershave and men's socks. And worse. However, Jennifer wasn't there. The girls said she's gone on holiday, although they couldn't tell me where. So unless she's embarrassed to admit she's gone to Butlin's, it all sounds a bit fishy. Quite apart from not getting my plume recoloured, I was annoyed that I won't be able to get hold of Flint for the time being. But you know what they say: 'as one door closes another one opens'.

So instead of the recolouring appointment I'd booked, they asked me if I fancied having a facial instead. I've not had one for years, but the girl was available, so I thought: *why not? It'll go with the new me.* Though when I say 'girl', Flossie must have been in her mid-twenties at least. Unusual name. I asked her if she doubled as an oral hygienist, but she gave me an odd look and said her expertise was more focused on manicures, pedicures, eyebrow tinting and spray tanning: you know, the usual beauticiany-type things. But she also said she was quite happy to give me an intimate waxing if that's what I'd like. To be honest, I thought she was being a bit forward, if not presumptuous, seeing as we'd only just been introduced. But I can be a bit that way myself, and as I'd seen her at the salon on my last couple of visits, I didn't take umbrage. Luckily for her.

In fact, you can blame my 'inner witch' for this, but I was drawn to her. She favours what I would describe as the 'skinny goth look'. She's thin, with long black hair, dark eyes, black eye make-up and dark red lipstick. And she always wears a black dress and black tights. I haven't told you this before, but when I married Gary, I wanted to wear a steampunk outfit at the wedding. Can you imagine? Well, I could, because wearing white and pretending to be a wide-eyed innocent hadn't worked with my previous two husbands, so why not go with the devil you know? Except, being a stick in the mud, Gary was horrified. So, no surprises there. And no steampunk wedding either. Pity. I wanted to wear a top hat like Noddy Holder's – you know, the one with the silver discs he wore on *Top of the Pops* – while the choir sang 'Mama Weer All Crazee Now'.

Flossie liked my new look. She said it was 'perfect' and asked me if I go to a gym. When I told her I'm a member of Get in Shape, she told me she's not happy at her current gym and is thinking of changing.

She said: "There's a guy there with rapey eyes who keeps staring at me."

So I said: "You need to have a serious word with him."

And she said: "I'd lure him to St Chad's graveyard at midnight and drive a stake through his heart if I thought I could get away with it. I really would. Do you ever have those kinds of urges?"

I tried not to, but I giggled. "If only you knew," I said.

I think I've found an interesting new friend to cultivate, don't you?

In the meantime, I think we should be heading back home now. I'll read you a few more extracts from my diary when we get there.

Hang on a minute, though. Isn't that Chief Inspector Catesby scuttling furtively up to Dr Rosencrantz's front door? I recognise him from a recent photo in the *Newvale Advertiser*, even though he's not in uniform. I wonder what he wants.

TWENTY-SEVEN

Gary walked over to his desk, opened the top drawer and took out a lavender-coloured stress ball. He gave it a couple of good squeezes before joining Alexa back on the couch.

"I'm not entirely happy with your new plan," he said.

"That much is obvious," said Alexa. She pointed at the ball and added: "How long have you had that?"

"A while. Claudia bought it for me. I think it was part of her campaign of psychological warfare against me."

"Which I would say is working. The colour suits you, by the way."

Gary shrugged. "She said lavender has a calming influence over brain waves and neurotransmitters. I'm not sure whether she got that from her pet shrink, Dr Rosencrantz, or the *Readers Digest*."

"I'm not entirely convinced it's having the desired effect, though. Are you?"

"It didn't stop her redecorating the bedroom the same colour. Or dyeing her ridiculous quiff to match. And God knows what else she's had dyed; I daren't ask."

Alexa frowned. "*The* bedroom?"

"*Her* bedroom," said Gary, who was now squeezing the ball continuously. "Just to clarify."

"Hmm. Perhaps you could stop playing with it for a minute or two – it's very annoying – and tell me what part of the plan you don't like."

"All of it. Basically. I don't think getting mixed up with the mafia is such a good idea."

Alexa sighed and consulted the notepad that was still resting on her lap, as if seeking confirmation and reassurance from the squiggles she had made on it. "There's no proof to say that Karol Novak was actually a member of the mafia, only that there may have been business dealings with mafia members."

"Hang on a minute," said Gary. "You said Carol. I thought we were discussing Timea's dad."

"We are. It's Karol with a K, not a C. He's a Slovakian, in case you've forgotten."

"I know that!" snapped Gary, squeezing the ball furiously. "I was just a bit confused for a moment, that's all. You need to make yourself clearer, woman."

Alexa's eyes narrowed. "What I said was perfectly clear," she snapped back, "but you're getting yourself so wound up you're not paying proper attention. And if you don't stop squeezing that fucking ball, I'll squeeze it for you! And then you'll be sorry."

Silence. During which Gary gave the ball a couple more defiant squeezes. He couldn't remember the last time Alexa had rounded on him like this, if she ever had. Maybe he *was* a bit stressed, but she was going to have to watch her step and remember who was the boss of this partnership. He turned his head momentarily as he put the ball down on the couch alongside him and didn't see Alexa mouthing the word 'twat' in his direction.

The uneasy silence was broken by a knock on the door. After a couple of seconds' delay it opened slowly and Timea's head appeared round the edge.

"Is it OK if I come in?" she asked.

"Of course," said Gary. "Why wouldn't it be?"

"I thought I heard raised voices. I didn't know if you were having an argument."

"We don't argue," said Alexa. "We sometimes have disagreements, but Gary eventually comes round to my way of thinking." She smiled, and although the lack of warmth didn't go unnoticed by Gary, he put aside his annoyance and focused on Timea instead.

"How can we help?" he said, beaming at their new recruit with a smile of such dazzling intensity it wouldn't have looked out of place in a toothpaste advert.

Timea nudged the door fully open with her shoulder. "I've brought you these," she said, as she walked into the office with a large bunch of bananas clasped to her chest. "Where would you like me to put them?"

Alexa looked at Gary and then back at Timea. "What are they for?" she asked.

"Gary asked me to keep an eye out for the right type of bananas for him. I got these from Aldi."

"Aldi?" said Gary. The thought that someone would shop at Aldi on his behalf appalled him. It appalled him so much he temporarily forgot why he had asked Timea to check out the banana supply in the first place. "Aldi? We only ever shop at Waitrose. Or Sainsbury's if we're desperate. Did anybody recognise you?"

"Oh," said Timea frowning. This was not the grateful reception she had been expecting.

"Ignore him," said Alexa, glaring at Gary. "He's in a bit of a funny mood today."

"It's OK, though," said Timea. "I didn't go in the shop itself. My brother works at Aldi's distribution centre, and he got them for me." She carried the bananas over to Gary's desk, and after putting them down, she turned and handed him an England's Glory matchbox. "You said you wanted one of these to add to your collection."

"A matchbox?"

"No, it's what's inside. It's a spider."

"Bloody hell," said Gary, putting the box down gingerly alongside the stress ball. "Is it a Brazilian wandering spider?"

Timea shrugged. "I've no idea. But my brother said it was wandering all over his bananas, which come from that part of the world, so I guess it must be. Will you be keeping it in a glass case when you get it home?"

For the first time in a long time, an image of Claudia's underwear popped into Gary's mind. "I think I know exactly where I'm going to put it," he said. "Thank you." He stood up, and before Timea could manoeuvre herself out of range, he gave her a hug. A big hug. As he did so, the mental picture of Claudia's underwear was immediately replaced by a vision of what Timea might be wearing beneath her white blouse and navy skirt. If Alexa hadn't been in the room, he might even have been tempted to give her bum a quick squeeze as well. Reluctantly, he allowed Timea to wriggle free, complimenting her as she did so on the perfume that was flooding his nostrils.

"It's called Black Opium," she said, taking a step backwards and out of arm's reach.

"Good name," said Gary. "I can see why it might become addictive. What do you think, Alexa?"

Out of the corner of his eye he could see Alexa shaking her head with a pitying expression on her face. "Sit down, Gary," she said. "I'm sure Timea doesn't have to fish for compliments from the older generation."

"I'm not that old," said Gary.

"You're old enough to be her father," retorted Alexa.

Gary was tempted to say there was no substitute for

experience, but with Alexa in such a funny mood, he decided that might be pushing his luck a bit too far. Instead, he asked Timea if she would thank her brother for him.

"Of course," she said. "Marián was only too pleased to help."

Gary burst out laughing. He couldn't help himself. It was an involuntary release of the stress that had been steadily building during the morning. But once he started there was no stopping him. "That's quite funny," he said between giggles. "You've got a brother called Marián, and your father's name is Karol. You wouldn't happen to have a sister at home called Roger, would you? I didn't realise you Slovakians were so far ahead of the game in these gender fluid times."

Timea's mouth dropped open. "Excuse me?" she said.

Alexa was quick to intervene, and not just because Gary had upset their young receptionist. She had recently read a magazine article warning employers that culturally insensitive remarks might be considered discriminatory by an employment tribunal. And that could mean another expensive payout. "Gary!" she said. "That's not funny at all. I think you should apologise to Timea."

Gary was not inclined to do any such thing: apologising wasn't in his DNA. Yet he reasoned it might be a worthwhile gambit if it improved his chances with the girl in the long run. "You're right," he said, trying his best to sound apologetic. "It was a thoughtless attempt at humour on my part, and I apologise."

Timea smiled hesitantly. "Apology accepted," she said, quickly adding, "and if there's nothing else, I really ought to be getting back to reception." She turned and left the room, closing the door behind her.

Gary shrugged. "Sensitive little soul, isn't she," he said to Alexa.

Alexa shook her head. "You've got no idea, have you?"

Gary was about to protest when his mobile phone pinged, alerting him to an incoming text. He walked over to the desk and picked it up. Looking at the screen, a smile lit up his face. "Yes!" he cried, punching the air. "My order's about to be delivered by DPD."

"That's good news, is it?" said Alexa.

"I thought you'd be pleased."

"So did I."

Gary ignored her less-than-enthusiastic response and smirked. "Come on, why don't I pop round this evening? Strike while the iron's hot, as it were?"

Alexa treated him to another one of her lukewarm smiles. "Sorry, but tonight doesn't work for me. I'm meeting up with a couple of the girls. And before you ask, no, they wouldn't be interested in joining us."

"Can't you put them off?"

"No. And to be honest, I'm not in the mood."

Gary pouted. "Really? Oh well. At least it'll give me a chance to try them out on my own and make sure they work. I guess you could call it a dry run," he said, smirking again.

"Oh, for Chrissakes!" said Alexa, turning away as she put the notepad back in her case.

But Gary was not to be deterred, deflated or delayed from his date with destiny. He took his Armani jacket off its padded coat hanger and put it on. "If you don't mind, I'm going to pop home. I need to be in when the delivery driver calls. I don't want Claudia intercepting the package."

"Perish the thought," said Alexa.

Gary picked up the stress ball and put it in his pocket. He then picked up the matchbox, frowned and held it up to his ear, giving it a shake as he did so. "I can't hear anything," he said.

"What were you expecting to hear? The Brazilian national anthem? Spiders aren't generally known for their singing voices."

"Very funny," he said. "But it had better not be dead. Because if all goes well, by tomorrow we won't need the mad bomber Bob Flint or Karol Novak. Clear your diary as we really will have something to celebrate."

TWENTY-EIGHT

Well, it's been an eventful day, don't you think? Mind you, every day's eventful where I'm concerned, Ophelia. You could say it's the nature of the beast, not that I'd tolerate anyone else saying that about me, mind. Especially not Rosencrantz after this morning's fiasco. I still haven't decided what to do about that, or him. But I mustn't let it distract me from my number-one objective: dealing with that preening popinjay I married. Do you like that word? I just found it in the dictionary while I was doing the not-so-quick crossword in the paper. It means 'a person given to vain, pretentious displays and empty chatter'. Which sums him up, don't you think? And I also discovered that back in the day, a popinjay was the name they gave to a figure of a parrot that was fixed on a pole and used for target practice. Who knew? I've no idea why anyone would want to shoot a parrot, or even a budgie come to that. I realise they can be a bit chatty sometimes and crap all over you if you let them out, but so can husbands. Which probably explains why there's nothing I'd like better than to see Gary impaled on the end of a long pointy stick and shot full of arrows. Sadly, it's a form of execution that's gone out of fashion these days. What's wrong with our ancient traditions?

He's up to something, you know. For starters, he came home at lunchtime, and he never does that, so it was a good job I'd changed out of my tart's boudoir outfit. There was no point giving him ideas as we've gone way beyond that kind of thing now. As it was, he was in a remarkably good mood and even attempted to kiss me on the cheek when we were in the kitchen. Thank God I had my non-stick spatula to hand. If that behaviour wasn't suspicious enough, he then hung around the hallway until that stunted little man from DPD turned up with a parcel for him. Why does DPD employ the guy when he can barely reach the pedals in that electric, so-called eco-friendly, van of his? Eco-friendly my arse: he drives it all over the grass verge, churning it up until it looks like one of Jennifer Catesby's organic face packs. That's how bad it is. It's just a shame Flint couldn't have taken out DPD man at the same time as the Robinsons. Still, maybe that's something I can bear in mind when I track him down.

Sorry, I got a bit distracted there. Again. I was going to say that Gary never buys anything online, so God knows what he's up to. Or what was in the package. Nose hair clippers, perhaps. God knows he needs them. He's started sprouting hair where I didn't know hair could grow. Whatever it was, he couldn't wait to take it upstairs to his bedroom. Even stranger, when he came down for lunch, he asked me if I'd got an empty jam jar he could have. Jam jars?

I said to him: "When was the last time I made you a jam sandwich?"

He said: "Never."

So I said: "Well, there's your answer."

I didn't tell him that jam was banned in this house after Mother disappeared. And lemon curd. Too many disturbingly messy memories. Even marmalade's a bit iffy, as far as I'm concerned. Anyway, when I asked him what he wanted it for, he ignored me, as per, and muttered something about needing more leg room. Bizarre. They look all right to me.

Even worse, while my back was turned, he found a jar of Hellmann's Vegan Mayo in the fridge and emptied it down the sink. Down the sink! Who does that? Except the kind of man who leaves the toilet seat up. And probably pees in the shower, too.

I told him: "When it blocks up, you can rod it out."

He said: "What with?"

So I said: "Work it out yourself, dickhead."

He looked a bit puzzled, but as he doesn't do cryptic crosswords, I'm guessing he didn't understand the clue.

Lunch was fun. I made him egg mayonnaise sandwiches but *without* the mayonnaise. Point made, I think. He only ate half of them – surprise, surprise – before taking his precious jar back upstairs with him. And then he went back to work. Bliss.

Obviously, the moment he left the house I went upstairs for a quick shufti in his bedroom. He doesn't know this, but when he had a lock put on the door, the locksmith gave me the spare key. Ha! Did he really think I was going to tolerate restrictions in my own home? Anyway, there was a small white cardboard box on top of his bedside cabinet. It was empty – I checked. I suppose it *could* have contained nose hair clippers. There was also a small matchbox that was empty too. He doesn't smoke so what's that all about? And no sign of my Hellmann's Vegan Mayo jar, so he's obviously hiding the evidence somewhere. I didn't have the time to look properly in case he came back unexpectedly again. But I'll have a good look tomorrow. Don't worry, I'll find whatever he's hiding; there's nothing I can't find – or hide – in this place.

And since dinner – when he was still insufferably joyful, despite my best efforts – he's been locked away in his room again. I dread to think what he's up to in there. But at least it means it's safe enough to read you the next diary extract without interruption.

Tuesday, 7 March 2000

Pancake Day. Yummy. One of my favourites. Made a stack of them before Martin told me – belatedly – that he doesn't like them. Why wait until I'm up to my tits in batter and lemon juice before saying something? Still, all the more for me – silver linings and all that. I had to have a lie-down on the sofa afterwards, though. Martin came in and said he'd been meaning to ask me if I was pregnant.

"No chance," I said.

"That's funny," he said, "you look as if you are."

"Ha! That's not an embryo you're looking at," I said, "but the after-effects of 110g of plain flour, two eggs, 295ml of milk, 56g of butter. And a pinch of salt."

Pregnant? As I pointed out to him, you have to have sex to become impregnated. He shrugged. I was fuming, but that's an issue for another day. He says tonight's gig might be his last with the band because of a problem with his voice. So how come he's only just noticed? But anyway, at least he'll be out of my hair for a few hours. It'll give me time to do what has to be done, providing I haven't overdone it with the pancakes. Today's mood: expectant.

Thursday, 9 March 2000

GERALD'S DEAD!! He committed suicide. Apparently. The police found him after Claire went to his house to check on him as he didn't turn up for work yesterday. When he didn't answer the door she called the police. Her brother's a policeman and he told her afterwards they found him lying naked on his bed next to an empty bottle of gin and a syringe.

She thinks he must have taken drugs from the surgery home with him to do the deed. He probably couldn't live with himself. Quite right, too.

The police turned up at work later to interview us, but we got the impression they'll rule out foul play: the house was secured and there was no sign of forced entry. Well, there wouldn't be, would there, if the intruder knew where he hid the spare key, as well as the code for the burglar alarm. Not that I mentioned this to the police. Obviously. Funnily enough, Claire had come to me in tears at the end of last week and admitted she'd covered up for his blunders several times in the past. How could she have done that? I still can't get over all the suffering he must have caused. Bastard! I hope he suffered too. Today's mood: vengeful.

Gerald's funeral at the crem today. I didn't go. Mark, one of the other vets, thought it showed a lack of respect on my part. As far as I'm concerned, Gerald can burn in the fires of hell for all eternity. So put that in your pipe and smoke it, Mark! Claire didn't go either; she's been off work for a few days with a stomach bug of some kind. Really? I think it's more likely her conscience getting to her. At least that's what I've told her. Today's mood: righteous.

All Fools Day. Never a truer word, or three. I can't believe how STUPID I've been. How did I miss something so obvious? When Martin suggested the other day that we should try 'poppers' to spice things up a bit, I just thought: already? We've only been married five minutes. Besides, how is amyl nitrite going to react with my medication?

Not to mention my favourite G&Ts? I like to be in control of my uncontrollability. And anyway, where did this 'poppers' idea come from? *Well, I only had to wait until this afternoon to find out. I came home early from work and heard groaning coming from our bedroom. Living with my mother all those years I instantly recognised the sound. I thought:* if he's in there with Candy, I'll make her groan all right. And when I've finished making her groan, I'll hang her by her tits from the guttering with a big sign round her neck, saying 'This Is What Happens to Fat Cheats'. *But guess what: when I flung the door open it wasn't Candy at all – it was Marcel he'd got with him! Fucking Marcel! Literally!! WHAT HAVE I DONE TO DESERVE THIS?? Today's mood: gobsmacked.*

<u>*Wednesday, 5 April 2000*</u>

OK, so I've calmed down a bit since Saturday. Good job because I don't think I can drink any more chamomile tea. Doreen, one of the receptionists at the vets, said it's great for anxiety. She told me she swears by it. Having tried it, so do I: IT'S FUCKING DISGUSTING, DOREEN! Even with a generous splash of gin to take away the nasty taste. Talking of which, Martin's behaviour since I caught him red-handed – quite literally, I might add – has been blatant. He's moved both himself and Marcel into the spare room and I can hear them going at it at all times of the day and night. It's not just me – the whole street can hear them. He doesn't care one little bit about my feelings. I mean, I realise he's gay, and I've got nothing against homosexuality, but does he have to shove it down my throat? Except, of course, when we shared the same bed and he didn't. Ironically, the reason he's quit the band is because he's developed this nervous condition called 'globus'.

He said: "It's like having a persistent frog in my throat."

I said: "Well, that's what happens when you employ a gay French organist."

Not that Marcel's really French. I belatedly went to the internet cafe in town and did some checking. It turns out he's not Marcel from Marseilles but Arnold from Barnsley. Until last year he was a care assistant in an old biddies' home – wiping people's bottoms for a living. I realise someone's got to do it, but it's not up everyone's alley, is it? Although I suppose it could depend on whose bottom we're talking about. By the way, I wonder if leading a double life is why Martin's started drinking heavily. Today's mood: simmering.

Tuesday, 11 April 2000

Martin was drunk last night. Again. He mentioned something about his past that's really set me wondering. I can't say anything more at the moment because I've got to get to the internet cafe before it closes. Today's mood: tense.

Oh my God! What the hell was that? Did you hear those thumps, Ophelia? It sounded like it was coming from upstairs. I think you'd better wait here while I go and find out what's happening.

TWENTY-NINE

Detective Sergeant Kevin Kenneth sighed deeply, knocked and entered the office of his superior, Chief Inspector Julian Catesby, who was sitting cross-legged on a mat at the side of his desk, with his eyes closed.

"Om," said the chief inspector.

"Sir?" asked DS Kenneth. "Is everything OK?"

"Everything's fine, thank you, Kenbold."

"I can come back later if you're having a nap?"

Ch Insp Catesby's left eye flew open. "Does it look as if I'm having a nap?"

"Erm," said DS Kenneth, his hesitation speaking volumes.

"I was meditating."

"Ah," said DS Kenneth, who could now see why Catesby's right eye was struggling to open as easily as the left: it was bloodshot, while the eyelid and skin around the socket was puffy and bruised. "I see you have a black eye, sir," he ventured.

"Very observant of you, Kencroft. Has anyone told you that you have a promising career as a detective behind you?"

DS Kenneth sighed. "Frequently," he said.

"I was doing some gardening at the weekend when I carelessly stood on a rake and the handle shot up, hitting me in the face."

"Ouch. Nasty." DS Kenneth's face remained impassive as he considered the chief inspector's explanation. He called on the skills he had honed during his long years as a detective to evaluate the truthfulness of what he was being told. And quite frankly, he found Catesby's story risible. He had often seen cartoons in which characters trod on rakes, resulting in the outcome described by Catesby, but he had never witnessed such a thing for himself. Nor had he heard of it happening to anyone else he knew. In addition to which, there had been a hard frost over the weekend, making gardening an unlikely task. So, on the balance of probability, he decided the story was highly improbable. Or, to give it the term often used by seasoned detectives, it was bullshit. In fact, it was so implausible that plausibility had jumped into a getaway car and was already halfway down the M1.

Conversely, his injury might lend plausibility to the rumour that Catesby's relationship with his wife had become increasingly fractious because of her relationship with Flint. DS Kenneth decided to test the office gossip. "I'm sure you must have been very grateful that Mrs Catesby was on hand to treat the injury," he said.

"What?" said Ch Insp Catesby, momentarily caught off balance. "Yes, well, I'm afraid Mrs Catesby's away at the moment."

"On holiday, is she, sir?"

Catesby finally stood up, brushing imaginary fluff off his trousers. "Not that it's any business of yours, but she's gone to look after her mother who's ill."

"Sorry to hear that. Does she live far away?"

"France," said Ch Insp Catesby, rather too quickly. "Yes, France. Somewhere in the Dordogne."

"That must be tricky for you, what with a demanding job as well as the two children to look after," said DS Kenneth, trying to sound sympathetic while looking around for the family photo. It was still missing. Though in its place, on the corner of the desk, he noticed two books: *How to Commit the Perfect Murder* and *Dealing With Emotional Conflict*. Intrigued, he attempted to scratch his nose in contemplation, only to fail for lack of the requisite finger.

"Thank you for your concern over my domestic arrangements," said Ch Insp Catesby, "but my sister-in-law is helping out."

DS Kenneth wasn't a family man, but it struck him as an odd arrangement. Why all the shuffling around? Wouldn't it have made more sense for Mrs Catesby's sister to have gone to France to look after their sick mother? And the grimace on the chief inspector's face suggested he wasn't too comfortable with the arrangement either. Unless it was his sister-in-law who was the issue. Although he hadn't come to Catesby's office to discuss the man's family, DS Kenneth's curiosity had taken over.

"It must be comforting, though, having your sister-in-law to stay," he said, still probing.

"Comforting?" said Ch Insp Catesby, grimacing again. "I wouldn't call it that."

"You wouldn't?"

"It's more of a trial. Not that you would understand," said Catesby as he took his seat behind his desk. "Now, can we please move on? Are you any closer to locating the whereabouts of that monster Flint yet?"

"I'm afraid not."

"Well, why not?" said the chief inspector, his damaged eye quivering with anger. "I want that man found, Kendal! Found! Do you hear me?"

"Yes, sir," said DS Kenneth. He didn't know how long Ch

Insp Catesby had been practising meditation, but he clearly needed to practise it a lot more, judging by his sudden mood swings. "The truth is we don't know where he is. We've spoken again to his wife Holly, and she believes he has been siphoning money from his business into a secret personal account for some time. Our enquiries suggest she may be correct, and we are now working on the assumption he may have created a new identity for himself."

"A new identity?" spluttered Ch Insp Catesby.

"Yes, sir. So he can start a new life. Somewhere else. With someone else. Sir."

"Are you suggesting he may have run off with... with another man's wife?" said Catesby, his voice rising.

"Yes, sir."

"And they're now cohabiting under an assumed name?"

"Yes, sir."

"Run off? Like the kind of degenerates who slope off to Brighton for a dirty weekend?" said Catesby, his voice now reaching a crescendo.

"I rather fancy they've gone a little further than Brighton," said DS Kenneth, who was trying to ignore the chief inspector's distinctly 1950s attitude towards extramarital relationships. And Brighton, come to that.

"Further?"

"Even further than France, I would suggest," said DS Kenneth mischievously. "I suspect he may be holed up in one of those countries that don't have an extradition treaty with the UK, such as Bahrain or the UAE in the Middle East. Or maybe somewhere in Africa or Central America."

"Hold on a moment. Africa? Isn't that where Robinson was accused of being a kiddy-fiddler?"

"It was," agreed DS Kenneth, "although Africa is a very large continent so it's too soon to say if there's a connection."

"Well get on with it, man!" said Ch Insp Catesby, his eye twitching furiously. "And when you find him, I want to interrogate him personally; do you understand? Who knows what we might also uncover when we find him!"

Such as the location of your wife, thought DS Kenneth, who refrained from giving voice to such a suggestion. Instead, he turned to Flint's finances.

"In view of the irregularities our financial investigators have uncovered with Flint's accounts, we are taking a closer interest in the role played by his accountants," he said.

"You mean that jumped-up snotbag Gary Alcock?"

DS Kenneth raised an eyebrow. Not for the first time, he hoped for his boss's sake the force's professional standards department was not secretly monitoring the office via hidden CCTV cameras. "Not so much Mr Alcock at the moment," he said. "More Ms Bull."

He explained that a more detailed examination of Alexa's background had revealed a poisonous family dispute when she was in her mid-twenties. Her wealthy Greek grandfather had fallen out with her mother, and it reached a stage where he declared his intention to disinherit Alexa's parents and their children. Although a 'clear the air' family meeting took place onboard his yacht, there were further arguments. Matters reached a head, at which point the grandfather did a Robert Maxwell: mysteriously disappearing overboard in the middle of the night. Suspicion fell on Alexa as she was the last person seen with her grandfather that evening, but nothing was ever proved. Ironically, far from his death securing their inheritance, Alexa's side of the family had since been mired in legal actions brought by other family members, together with a long-running tax investigation.

"It's rumoured the disputes have already swallowed up a large portion of the estate," said DS Kenneth, "and by the time they've been settled, the only thing Alexa will eventually inherit are big debts."

"Fascinating, I'm sure," said Ch Insp Catesby, who appeared to be more interested in securing a black eyepatch over his black eye, "but what's all this got to do with the Robinsons? Or Flint?"

"Probably nothing," said DS Kenneth, who wondered if the mention of piracy on the high seas had been the prompt for Catesby to adopt the persona of One-Eyed Willie from the *Goonies*. "Or it may be a piece of the jigsaw. Either way, I wouldn't want to be the person standing between Alexa Bull and a large sum of money."

THIRTY

Talk about killing two birds with one stone. Unfortunately, though, talk alone doesn't get the job done, Ophelia. Nor does wishful thinking. In my experience, action speaks louder than words and, as you know, I've never been shy about taking action – given half a chance. It's just a shame the chance never presented itself when I was at the hospital this morning. Still, I don't suppose killing one of those birds was *too* bad, even if the biggest turkey of all is still flapping about. It's a pity I don't know any Americans who could put Gary out of his misery in time for Thanksgiving.

It was quite a coincidence that he was admitted to St Chad's on the same day the NHS had rearranged my mammogram. I won't call it a lucky coincidence because there's nothing fortunate about going for one of those procedures. It's all flop, crush and squeal, followed by flop, crush and squeal for a second time, followed by a handful of paracetamol at regular intervals for the rest of the day. Not that I would turn down a shot of morphine if it was available. Or preferably two shots – one in each.

But that wasn't the worst of it this time. When I got there

and took my clothes off, I was a bit taken aback, and it takes a lot these days, when the nurse smiled at me and said: "I like your boobs."

So I plumped them up a bit for her, as you do – well as I do because there's not that much of them – and said: "Thanks. Glad you noticed them. I've been toning up at the gym."

But she gave me a really funny look and said: "I was referring to your boots."

I think she was more embarrassed by the misunderstanding than me. I don't do embarrassment; I was just angry. I almost said to her: "Whose fault was that then? Speak up, woman, and stop mumbling into your beard." Fortunately, I stopped myself. She looked the vindictive sort, and as she hadn't carried out the procedure yet, I didn't fancy coming home with my tits in a sling. But honestly, you'd think she'd do something about all that facial hair. She wasn't that old, and she works for the NHS for God's sake. Couldn't they give her some pills? Or a very large tube of depilatory cream? Failing that, get a razor, woman! Or at the very least a decent pair of tweezers. It's just a shame travelling circuses are a thing of the past, or she could have joined up and made a good living.

Anyway, after that I went back into the main building to check on Gary. I suppose I was hoping to find him with a sheet pulled over his head and a priest sprinkling him with holy water, but fat chance. Mind you, I did think my luck was in last night when I found him lying naked and half-dead on his bedroom floor. He was bright red, groaning and complaining of chest pains. I thought about checking for a pulse. But checking where? And what? Everything was pulsing. And I mean *everything*. How bizarre was that?

He said: "I'm dying. Help me."

So I said: "No worries, I'm happy to help. How does a pillow over the face sound?"

"Phone 999," he said. "Tell them I've been bitten by a Brazilian wandering spider."

That was a WTF moment if ever there was one. A Brazilian wandering spider?

I said: "What's one of those when it's at home?"

He gestured at a half-squashed spider on the carpet next to the empty Hellmann's jar and started moaning about its deadly venom. I thought he was hallucinating. For a moment I wondered if I'd overdone it with the Toilet Duck and he'd accidentally inhaled the fumes: you know how long he spends in there. Admittedly, though, the spider looked an ugly brute. So to be on the safe side I got a pair of tweezers, picked it up by one of its remaining legs and popped it back into the jar for later examination.

I was going to phone for an ambulance with his mobile, which was on the dressing table, but decided against it. What if the paramedics arrived too soon and saved his miserable life? You have to take these kinds of things into consideration. Besides, I didn't want to see him in his death throes if I could help it. They're never nice, and I don't like mess, as you know. So I told him to stop bleating and making a fuss and I would call from the landline downstairs. Naturally, I took my time and decided to google 'Brazilian wandering spiders' first. That was interesting because Wikipedia said they're one of the world's deadliest spiders. Who knew? It reported on some guy who'd been bitten by one of them. It didn't kill him, but the pain radiated to his chest and his heart began to race. He was dizzy, nauseated and then began to drool. But the amazing thing was the venom caused him to become priapic for several hours afterwards! Can you believe it? Because I struggled. I had to read that bit a couple of times to make sure I'd got it right. It would have helped if the article had also included a photo or two, purely for illustration purposes, but no such luck. Even so, it explained what I'd seen in his bedroom. And why. It turns out he wasn't that pleased to see me after all. Big surprise. Not.

Anyway, I made a mistake by not confiscating Gary's mobile when I was in the bedroom. I was just about to turn the telly on – Channel Four were showing a rerun of *Location, Location, Location* – when I heard him calling for an ambulance himself. He must have crawled all the way to the dressing table to reach his mobile phone. It was galling, but you have to give him ten out of ten for effort. I ran back upstairs to take the phone off him, but it was too late. He said the call handler had warned him there might be a delay before the ambulance got here. Which was cruel really, giving me hope like that.

I said to him: "You do realise that, even if you survive, you could be stuck with that monstrosity down there for several hours."

He said: "Isn't there anything you can do about it?"

I laughed. Ironically. "Why are you asking me?" I said. "What about if I call Alexa for you? I'm sure she'd be happy to give you a helping hand."

We didn't get any further with the discussion because the paramedics turned up. Spoilsports.

But as you may have guessed by the lack of bunting around the house, he survived. Not that he was ever in any real danger. It turns out he wasn't bitten by a Brazilian wandering spider after all but a common or garden cardinal spider. Basically, he overdosed on some dodgy impotence pills he bought off the internet. It would be funny if it wasn't so pathetic. Although, it didn't stop one of the nurses looking at me from time to time and sniggering. As if I'd got anything to do with his cockamamie problems.

They won't be letting him out until a bit later so I'm going to pour myself a drink – a stiff one, if you must know – and then I'll tell you what I discovered about Martin when I went back to the internet cafe.

Well, that was an eye-opener, and make no mistake. After Martin drunkenly mentioned he used to be in a band in Manchester, I went to the internet cafe to check it out. And it's true! He was the singer in a group called Foam Bandage. Ridiculous! I thought Marmite Sandwich was bad enough, but it seems he's cornered the market in stupid band names. And it doesn't sound as if his singing was any better back in the day either. According to a review I found for one of their gigs, '... the vocalist attacks the songs with all the screaming insensitivity of a WW2 Stuka dive bomber strafing a column of civilian refugees'. Harsh but fair, I'd say. And that's just the ballads.

The thing is, though, why didn't he tell me he used to be in this band? Or that he used to live in Manchester? Mark my words, there's something fishy going on. There were a couple of links to other stories that I didn't have a chance to check out as the cafe was closing, but I'll be back to do some more research. Hell hath no fury like a woman scorned, as they say. Well, as I say.

Talking of fish, or whales more accurately, Candy has gone missing. Shares in Cadbury's will plummet when the word gets out. Today's mood: inquisitive.

Bear with me, because I still can't quite believe this! It's taken me a few visits to the internet cafe to piece all the info together, but I'M LIVING WITH A MURDERER!! Holy mother of crap! Me! Of all people!!!!! It seems that when Martin was living in Manchester, he was in a relationship with a much older guy called Geoff Cattermole. The man died from a heart attack after going on a bender with Martin. And get this: they were sniffing 'poppers' and drinking heavily, just *the kind of session Martin tried to get me to take part in. Bastard! According to the reports I read, Martin took too long to call for an ambulance, and by the time it turned up it was too late. Interestingly, Martin had persuaded Cattermole to alter his will in his favour shortly before he died. Even more interestingly, Martin's been trying to persuade me to do the same thing.*

I told him last night I knew all about Manchester and Cattermole, and he laughed. He'd been drinking – again – and said Cattermole had outlived his usefulness. His only regret was that the money didn't last very long. I thought about dealing with him there and then, but these things take a bit of preparation, like making first-rate pancakes! Especially ones with warmed banana slices, drizzled in a classic banoffee sauce and piled high with ice cream and cream. Mmm. And apart from which, Arnold from Barnsley was hanging around like a bad smell: scotch eggs if I'm not mistaken. In the meantime, it goes without saying I shan't be altering my will.

Still no sign of Candy, BTW. I heard someone say she might have gone to Scotland. Loch Ness wouldn't surprise me: somewhere deep and cold would be ideal. Failing that, they could always check out the River Vale. Today's mood: calculating.

I'll have to leave it there for the moment because I've just remembered something I meant to do today. When I was picking up Gary's clothes last night, I couldn't help noticing his shirt had a different smell to it. And I'm not talking about man-sweat or Lenor with its promise of citrus zing, buttercup brilliance and ocean sparkle, because I'm telling you, there is no way Lenor can out-scent Miss Dior. But this was different. It was definitely not Lenor nor Miss Dior. I need to go into the office and take a good sniff of that new girl.

THIRTY-ONE

It was Monday morning and time to embrace the start of a brand-new working week with vim and vigour. But Gary was looking distinctly less than bright-eyed and bushy-tailed as he tried to slip unobtrusively into the office. It was very unlike him. Usually he liked to sweep rather than slip. Making a visible entrance was more his style, his wool and cashmere overcoat casually hooked over one shoulder by a manicured pinky. Wearing sunglasses and keeping his head bowed was not his normal demeanour.

He had hoped the cause of his dramatic trip to hospital in the middle of the night could be kept from the staff. Failing that, he hadn't been averse to them being told that he had been left hovering between life and death by the bite of a deadly Central American insect. That sounded dangerously exotic. Yet within hours of returning home the previous Wednesday, Alexa had WhatsApped to warn him that the story of how he'd overdosed on some dodgy Viagra knock-off pills he'd bought off the net was all around the office. Alexa swore she hadn't been the source of his discomfort, but Gary was suspicious as well as disappointed – it wasn't quite the Deep Throat experience he'd been expecting from her as he'd lain on top of his hospital bed.

He mumbled a greeting to Timea and Mrs Pinchess as he hurried through reception to his office. He'd hardly had time to hang up his jacket and sit down, when Alexa walked in, unannounced. As usual.

"Morning," she said as she sat on the couch and put down her obligatory A4 notepad beside her. "How are you feeling today?"

Gary looked up from scanning the Post-it notes left on his desk and took off his sunglasses. "Sore. I was warned I could end up scarred."

"Mentally or physically?"

"It's no laughing matter."

"I know, but maybe you'll swallow your pride and go to Boots in future."

Gary grimaced. "It won't be for a while, though," he said, easing himself carefully into a different position.

"In the meantime, I hope you've thrown the bloody things away."

"Erm, not yet. I thought you could sell them to Fredo for me and get some of my money back. He'd probably welcome a twenty-four seven sure-thing option, given the demands that waitress seems to put on him."

Alexa rolled her eyes. "Sell them? Is there nothing you won't do for money?" she said.

"Probably not. I'm just like you in that respect," he said. A sly grin spread across his face. "By the way, did you enjoy the pics I sent you?"

"Enjoy?" said Alexa. "That wasn't the word I had in mind when they popped up on my phone as I was about to bite into one of Greggs sausage and bacon rolls. And if you had to send them, one or two would have done. How many were there? I stopped counting after a dozen."

"I was bored, and the nurses weren't paying me any

attention. I thought they might have shown a flicker of interest in my predicament."

"I daresay they've seen it all before. But how about Claudia? What did she have to say?"

Gary pouted. "She was her usual uncaring, unsympathetic, sarcastic self. For all she knew, I was at death's door and all she could say was: 'If you die, I'm going to cut it off and pickle it in formaldehyde as a memento of bygone times.' "

Alexa frowned. "You do realise it's only a matter of time before she questions why you were keeping a deadly spider in your bedroom."

Gary shifted uneasily in his chair and pointed out that the spider in question wasn't the Brazilian wandering type at all but some harmless British specimen. But Alexa was unimpressed.

"That won't wash with Claudia," she said. "The point is you *thought* it was deadly, and she must be aware of that. Did you know she came into the offices the same day you were in the hospital?"

Gary's eyes narrowed. "In here? What did she want?"

"I don't know, but she spent an awfully long time talking to Timea."

"What about?"

Alexa shrugged. "When I walked into reception she was talking about cheetahs. Or something like that. I know she's into animals, but I thought it was a bit odd."

"Odd? This is my wife we're talking about," said Gary. "Nothing is odd where that woman is concerned. And the fact that she called in here probably explains how everyone knows what happened, despite my best efforts to maintain a low profile."

"Ah, I see. Low profile. That would explain the conspicuous attempt to stay inconspicuous by wearing sunglasses indoors," said Alexa. "And while I'm about it, what is that?" she added, pointing at his face.

"It's a beard, what does it look like?"

"That's why I'm asking, because it looks nothing like a beard."

"I think it makes me look quite distinguished," said Gary, stroking the thin, wispy growth on his chin.

"To be honest," said Alexa, "I think it makes you look like a twat. In more ways than one. For God's sake, shave it off."

Gary bridled, both at her disapproval and at a further example of her increasingly aggressive attitude towards him. It was about time she was reminded of who was the senior partner in their relationship. If she wanted to share in his imminent good fortune, she was going to have to work a little harder for the privilege and realise she wasn't the only game in town.

"I've been thinking about Timea," he said, gazing into the middle distance as if absorbed in deep contemplation. "I'm not very happy that she caused this whole unpleasant incident by misidentifying the spider. I'll have to have a chat with her about it, one to one. Let her know she needs to make a big effort to restore my trust in her."

Alexa shook her head. "First of all she didn't misidentify anything – you jumped to conclusions. And secondly, we can't afford you upsetting any more receptionists and costing us another big payout."

There was a sharp intake of breath from Gary. "Are you threatening me?" he asked.

"What?" said Alexa. "If you think I'm threatening you, wait and see what the #MeToo campaigners have to say if they ever find out about you."

"Piffle!" snorted Gary.

"Piffle, is it?" said Alexa. "Well how about Timea's dad? I can just imagine what a man like that might do to you. Although preferably only after you've changed your will, which I'm guessing you still haven't done."

"What do you mean 'a man like that'?" he said, conveniently ignoring the jibe about his will.

Alexa tapped the top sheet of the pad next to her, the one headed 'K Novak Import & Export Consultants Ltd'. "I've found out quite a bit more about Karol Novak that you need to know about. But before I talk about him, I think we ought to discuss our ongoing situation vis-à-vis Bob Flint."

If Gary had started the day in physical discomfort, mention of Flint began to fray his sense of mental well-being as well. "What about him?" he asked.

Alexa turned to the second sheet, the one headed 'Flint Demolitions Ltd'. "He's finally made contact again," she said. "He's renewed his demands for money, only now he wants £10,000."

"What! For failing?"

"No. For starters. And for keeping his silence."

"The man's mad!"

"He's also very dangerous," said Alexa, putting down her pad. "We need to decide if we're going to pay him after all."

"Correction. We need to find out where he is and eliminate the problem. I tried to discover his whereabouts from Catesby yesterday when I was drawn to partner him in the monthly golf competition."

"How did you get on?"

"Not great. To begin with, my stance when I was addressing the ball was a little restricted, for obvious reasons," said Gary, grimacing at the memory, "but the biggest problem was that idiot Catesby. He stood there on the first tee, posing and posturing in his flashy Nike golf shoes and the most expensive clothing in the club shop, before taking an almighty hack at the ball with his top-of-the-range Callaway driver, slicing it into the trees and out of bounds on the right-hand side. So he put a brand-new ball down and tried again. This time he hooked it horribly into the trees and out of bounds on the left-hand side. He then topped his third attempt so it dribbled about thirty yards down the fairway. That's Catesby for you: he looks the part but doesn't have a fucking clue. Mind you, it didn't help that he was trying to play with an eyepatch. He can't hit the ball straight at the best of times, but yesterday he spent more time in the trees than Woody Woodpecker."

Alexa rolled her eyes and sighed. "Fascinating, I'm sure, but all I wanted to know is if he told you where Flint's hiding."

Gary scowled. That was something else that had started to irritate him about Alexa: her lack of empathy. Was that the right word? Whatever. She showed a disturbing lack of interest in the important things in life, like golf and the masons. If she was going to replace Claudia, then she had to buck up her ideas and be prepared to accompany him to all the various dinners and other social events without looking bored witless. To give Claudia her due, she had always gone to these events with him, if only because it gave her a chance to badger the other guests into donating to her animal and children's charities. Not that her attendance was entirely risk-free, as she had been known to claim that impacted earwax had caused temporary deafness if the people she was seated next to were boring her. Or – on one occasion – fart and politely, albeit loudly, enquire if the person next to her was responsible. The poor mayoress hadn't been seen in public for almost a month afterwards.

He would definitely have to talk to Alexa about her attitude at some point. In the meantime, his scowl gave way to a shake of the head. "As I was trying to tell you, the man's useless. He seems to think Flint's in Africa, living under an assumed name. God knows why. I asked him if he'd checked with the telephone companies out there for any new subscribers called Dr Livingstone. He wasn't amused; no sense of humour that bloke. He says his men are combing Africa looking for him."

"Really? Does he realise how big Africa is?"

"Exactly. He's either got more men on his books than Chelsea football club or Newvale Police have got the world's biggest comb."

"Is that all you found out?" said Alexa.

"Yes, I'm afraid so. Except for the fact he was picked up afterwards by this rather gorgeous female who was driving his car. I've no idea who she was, but it wasn't his wife. So maybe it's true she's run off with Flint. Anyway, looking at the woman in the car, I'd say he's come out of it smiling."

"You would," said Alexa, "but if I can just get you to refocus for a moment, Catesby's funny-looking, fingerless detective has been in touch about Flint's company accounts. He's made an appointment to come in and ask me a few more questions about Flint's financial affairs. I think things could get awkward."

"Agreed," said Gary. "We'll have to come up with a strategy to confuse and bamboozle him. Anything else?"

"Just one thing: Karol Novak. I've had a long meeting with him. It seems his business is not doing very well, and his own personal finances are in a real mess too. He's fast running out of money."

"Hmm. Do we sense an opportunity?"

"I think so," said Alexa. "I also found out that when he was a young man he spent some time in the Slovak army."

"And?"

"He trained as a sniper."

THIRTY-TWO

I think I must have supercharged nostrils, Ophelia. Which is the only way to explain my nose for trouble. I've always been able to tell when something doesn't smell right. Then I can get to work on fumigating the problem before it becomes too overpowering. That's why it didn't take me too long to track down the source of the unusual reek coming from Gary last week.

As I suspected, it was the new identikit-blonde receptionist Timea. Having sniffed her out I subjected her to an informal interrogation, as is my wont, but I'm satisfied she's innocent of any wrongdoing – I haven't been seeing a psychiatrist for all these years without learning something about body language. I could bring her back here and subject her to one of my specially designed lie-detector tests, but I don't think it'll be necessary, particularly as the last time I wired up the equipment I blew all the fuses in the house. I only want to check the suspect's biometric readings, not melt their eyeballs. Not initially, anyway. In the meantime, I'm going to keep her under observation, but I suspect she was only guilty of accidental transference. I think that's the term they use in forensic circles.

She admitted she was the one who gave the spider to Gary but only because he asked her to. So what's he up to? Other than no good? If I find out he was deliberately planning to harm me I'll hoist him by something a lot more painful than his own petard.

By the way, guess who I bumped into when I came out of the office: Manisha! You remember her: the girl I worked with at the pharmacy. Or should I say the cross-eyed bitch who stiffed me at the pharmacy. I'd not seen her for years. And when I say I bumped into her, that's not quite true. When she saw me across the street she bolted into TG Jones, but I tracked her down. She was pretending to browse a display of psychological thrillers in the book section. But she wasn't fooling me. It wasn't hard to see she only had one eye on the books, while the other one was wandering all over the shop looking for me. I asked her if she wanted to go to Costa for a coffee – for old times' sake. My treat. She squeaked. I think she was having a panic attack, which was probably triggered by the memory of what happened the last time I gave her a coffee. And why not? Whoever says 'let bygones be bygones' has never met me. It was good to see she was still experiencing feelings of guilt at what she did, though – and fear, obviously, because what good's guilt without fear? I learnt that from my Catholic friends at school. She also looked a lot older and fatter since I last saw her, but I suppose I do, too. Or I did until I started my rejuvenation programme.

Talking of which, when I went to the gym on Monday, I discovered that Flossie has joined, too. She's a strange girl in more ways than one. She kept looking at me in the shower, which was a little disturbing. I thought it was because she was envious of my new-found gym body, but I wasn't entirely sure. And you know me – fight fire with fire – so I began staring back at her. Seeing her without her clothes on, I realised she's very androgynous. Is that what's meant by gender fluid? Or is that something else entirely? I honestly can't keep up with some of the modern terminology; then again, who gives a toss, because I certainly don't. But anyway, Flossie's very muscly, to the point where they stood out like those molehills on our lawn. And the other thing I couldn't help noticing is that she's unashamedly luxuriant down below, which rather surprised me because I thought shaving was à la mode these days. So much so, I had to ask her if she'd got any helpful growing tips, because my bush roses could do with all the help they can get. Not that she minded me asking.

She said: "It's an expression of my individualism, a symbol of my empowerment as a woman and my growth as a person."

I said: "Yes, well, I'm all for feminism and the power of women, but you can stop growing it now before you trip over it."

She then gave me a funny look and asked me: "Are you queer?"

So I looked back and said: "Well, I admit that I'm a bit of an oddball. Does that count?" Enough said about that, I felt.

When we left, her car wouldn't start, so I gave her a lift home. Normally, I don't give lifts to strangers. Not because I'm frightened for my personal safety. Ha! That'll be the day. It's in case they find my secret stash of Haribo that I keep in the glovebox for emergencies. No one is allowed to touch them without my express permission, just in case the thought had crossed your mind.

Anyway, when we got to the ring road, she asked me if I'd be offended if she said something. Put like that, it sounded a bit ominous, so I warned her there was always a chance I might leave her in the ditch with her legs tucked behind her ears. But that didn't put her off: she went straight ahead and told me she was one of my biggest admirers. What the...! I nearly drove into a lamp post! I know I've said nothing really shocks me these days, but that did. I had no idea I had *any* admirers, least of all someone who claimed to be the biggest one of the lot. Makes a change from having persecutors, though. Or is that just my paranoia peeping out from under my skirts? Not that I tend to wear skirts these days. It's a vein thing, rather than a vain thing.

Am I making sense?

She said: "We know all about you and your history."

"You do?" I said. "And who is 'we'?" Because at this point I was thinking, *there's a nice sunny spot at the top of the garden waiting for you and your friends, my dear.*

And she said: "We're a local internet group that likes to chat about true crime. And conspiracy theories about true crime. And you."

Bugger me! And I don't say that lightly.

Flossie told me she's the group's admin and the members are very envious of the fact she knows me. Are they mad? She said the others are dying to meet me. To which I could only point out that death is a distinct possibility if I find out they've been saying nasty things about me behind my back. But Flossie – who goes by the internet name Go with the Flo – assured me they're all fans.

But why?

She said they're intrigued by the number of people I've known who have either died in suspicious circumstances or disappeared. They like to discuss which ones I might have been responsible for and how I did it.

But why?

Flossie said it's because most of them have suffered bullying or abuse of some kind and they admire someone (that would be me!) who has the courage to fight back. Courage? I nearly said to her it helps if you're a sociopath with paranoid delusions and an addictive personality, but I didn't want to ruin the vibe. Besides, I need to find out what Flossie and her internet friends know and weigh up if they're a threat. But on the other hand, there's always a chance I could put my new-found disciples to good use. As you know, I've been looking for a decent hitman.

In the meantime, I've got my diary from 2000 with me, so I might as well tell you about Martin's eventual demise.

Wednesday, 3 May 2000
That's it! I'm done with him! I was in the kitchen peeling the potatoes just now when Martin came in, demanding I make him a sandwich. Demanding! The lazy git knows where the bread and butter's kept, but he expects me – ME! – to wait on him hand and foot after everything I've done to help him. And do you know what he did when I said I was busy? He tried to slap me. He missed, of course, because he was almost too pissed to stand up. But that's not the point. He raised his hand, AND NO ONE DOES THAT TO ME! It's a good job for him he missed, or he'd be lying on the kitchen floor right now with a potato peeler sticking out of his chest. And you know how I feel about sharp objects. The galling part is that I was making home-made bangers and mash for him: his favourite. Well sod that for a game of soldiers: next time he can make do with a packet of Smash and a couple of leftover meatballs. Actually, forget that, because there isn't going to be a next time. Today's mood: incandescent.

Thursday, 4 May 2000
Today I launched my Justice for Geoff campaign, in memory of Martin's former partner Geoffrey Cattermole. At the moment there's only one person working on the campaign: me. But that's OK, cos who better? And there's only one

campaign objective: Martin's demise. It shouldn't take too long, though, because of the amount he's now drinking. That's mainly because Arnold from Barnsley (aka Marcel from Marseilles) has left him. Not that I was in the least bit sympathetic; well, why would I be? You didn't expect anything else from me, did you?

I said to him: "So I suppose he's found someone else to tickle his ivories, has he?"

He cried.

So I said: "It's time to put on your big boy pants and stop climbing into his."

He cried again.

I'm almost ready to take a leaf out of Martin's own playbook. Today's mood: calculating.

Sunday, 14 May 2000

It's late, but Geoff has finally got justice. And me too. To be honest, it took longer than I thought, but Martin always was a selfish, self-centred git. I left him at home while I went to a band concert at the park. Not my cup of tea at all. It was one of those oompah bands: a bunch of bearded dads dressed up in silly felt hats and lederhosen, tooting away on tubas and sousaphones. And in the beer tent were the obligatory fräuleins in their obligatory low-cut white blouses with their obligatory knockers on show, serving obligatory warm beer to all the obligatory neo-Nazis who turned up. As I say, not my thing, but I needed to show my face somewhere. And it was a Sunday afternoon, so where else?

When I got home he was still lying on the carpet where I left him. But, surprise, surprise, I discovered there was still a very weak pulse. So I did what you'd expect in the circumstances: I made myself a Caesar salad and watched *a bit of* Songs of Praise *on the telly before calling for an ambulance. What can I say? Timing is everything. And it wasn't a bad salad, though I say so myself.*

As I tearfully said to the paramedics, he'd obviously gone on a bender while I was out. They could hardly argue with that, judging by all the empty bottles of booze and amyl nitrite surrounding him. I could tell by the way they were reacting they thought he was a no-hoper. So I cried a bit more because that's what people do, although not me. Obviously.

I followed the ambulance to the hospital but took my time because of all the speed cameras on the ring road. And then when I got there I spent half an hour searching A&E after one of the nurses from the resuscitation team told me they'd lost him. Why couldn't she have just told me, "He's dead." I'm a big girl. I can take it.

I'd like to have the following epitaph put on his gravestone: 'He who lives by the sword, dies by the sword'. But doubtless the council will ban it. Spoilsports. They should be grateful – at least I'm not planning to light up the grave with half a dozen solar-powered angels. Today's mood: virtuous.

So that was that. A brief and pointless relationship for all concerned. There was an inquest, but the post-mortem clearly showed it was the cocktail of drink and drugs that killed Martin. The fact that he inhaled all that amyl nitrite *after* he passed out drunk was never going to show up in any forensic pathologist's test. And plenty of his friends testified that he often went on benders. So who was going to argue with that? Arnold turned up and blamed himself for dumping Martin, so I piled in and blamed him as well, telling the coroner the break-up had left Martin depressed. Which it had, so I wasn't exactly lying. And Arnold deserved some retribution, didn't he?

The local paper enjoyed themselves at my expense, pointing out that Martin was my second husband to have died in unfortunate circumstances, in addition to a former boyfriend. And, of course, they had to drag up the business of my mother's disappearance, as if that had anything to do with it. It's probably a good job that Candy is now believed to be in Scotland. I even overheard someone in the Co-op refer to me as The Black Widow. I don't know why, but I quite liked that.

Incidentally, Flossie's just sent me a WhatsApp message asking me if I'd like to join her group. I think I'll do that. I might even call myself The Black Widow.

THIRTY-THREE

Detective Sergeant Kevin Kenneth sighed deeply, knocked and entered the office of his superior, Chief Inspector Julian Catesby, who was squatting on his haunches, holding up a golf putter in one hand and squinting at it with his good eye.

The squint turned to a frown as Catesby stood up and shouted: "Fore!"

"Sir?" said DS Kenneth, quickly taking a step backwards.

"You're standing on my line, Kendra," said Ch Insp Catesby. Satisfied with where DS Kenneth had now repositioned himself, he bent over his club and putted a golf ball across the carpet towards a large glass storage jar, which was lying on its side a mere six feet away. The ball missed its target by at least twelve inches.

DS Kenneth was no golfer, but he fancied he could get closer to the hole than that, even on a crazy golf course with a windmill and a clown's mouth to negotiate.

"Damn patch!" said Catesby angrily.

DS Kenneth peered intently at the floor in search of a water or coffee spillage that might have dampened the carpet. There was nothing he could see, although his boss soon explained the problem.

"This eye is badly affecting my performance," said the chief inspector, pointing to the patch he was still wearing. "I had the misfortune to partner Gary Alcock at the weekend, and his walk was off-putting enough without the handicap of this patch."

"His walk, sir?"

"Yes, his walk, Kendrick. Is there something wrong with your hearing this morning? He was waddling around like a duck with piles. God knows why. He *could* have had piles, I suppose, but I didn't like to ask."

"It's an unfortunate condition," agreed DS Kenneth.

"And it itches like the dickens," said Catesby, who began rubbing vigorously around the edge of the patch at skin that was already inflamed.

"If your eye's still playing up it might be an idea to get it checked by your GP."

"That's what Kate – my sister-in-law – keeps telling me."

"Can't she rub in some cream around the eye to soothe it?" said DS Kenneth.

Ch Insp Catesby shuddered. "God, no. Touching's not allowed. It's the rules."

"The rules?"

"She's a naturalist and they have rules about that sort of thing – a code of behaviour, she said."

DS Kenneth was baffled, even though his face didn't show it. He'd seen most of Sir David Attenborough's TV programmes over the years and he couldn't remember seeing him deliberately *not* touching either man or beast. Hadn't he once play-wrestled with a gorilla? He was beginning to wonder if there was some genetic explanation behind the weirdness that seemed to be affecting Catesby and his family. Or maybe there was something in the water.

"Is she allowed to touch the children?" he asked.

"Just what are you insinuating?" said Catesby. "She only takes her clothes off when the kids are at school or in bed."

"Ah," said DS Kenneth as the penny dropped. "She wouldn't be a member of the Newvale Sun Valley Nudist Club, by any chance."

"Isn't that what I said? You're a bit slow on the uptake today, Keneen. Call yourself a detective?"

DS Kenneth refrained from pointing out there was a world of difference between naturists and naturalists, even if the thought of mixing up the two could be one way of enlivening the BBC's *Springwatch* programme. He tried not to imagine how distracting it must be for Catesby to have his naked sister-in-law wandering around the house when he was trying to cope emotionally with his wife's disappearance. It might help, though, if his boss could come to terms with the reason why she had left him. And there was no time like the present.

"As far as Jennifer is concerned," said DS Kenneth, "it would be helpful to confirm if she is with Flint."

Ch Insp Catesby's eyes narrowed. "What makes you think she's with that man?"

"Well, she's not in the Dordogne. That much is certain."

"She's not?"

"Absolutely not. Try Doncaster instead."

Ch Insp Catesby lifted his putter and waggled it threateningly in his sergeant's direction. "Impossible! That's a foul calumny! Take it back, man!"

DS Kenneth wasn't exactly sure what a foul calumny was, but he got the drift. Resisting the temptation to grab hold of the putter and give it a good waggle under his boss's nose, he explained there had been developments in the case while Catesby had been on leave for a couple of days.

"Our colleagues in Yorkshire were called to investigate a car that had been seemingly abandoned at Doncaster Railway

Station. We've just had it confirmed it was your wife's vehicle, sir. They've checked CCTV footage and found an image – admittedly very grainy, but it could be her – buying two drinks at the Costa Coffee shop in the company of an unidentified male. Although he was wearing a parka with the hood pulled up, we think it could be Flint."

"What makes you think it was Jennifer? Her car could have been stolen."

"She bought an espresso and a chocolate fudge brownie frappé mocha. I seem to recall her telling me once that a chocolate fudge brownie frappé mocha was her favourite drink."

Catesby's shoulders sagged and he laid the putter down on his desk as DS Kenneth added the clincher: "She was also seen giving the cherry off her mini Bakewell tart to her companion. I believe she has a strong aversion to glacé cherries, doesn't she, sir?"

Ch Insp slumped into his chair and nodded. "It could be her," he conceded, admitting that Kate had taken a phone call that morning from her sister to check if the children were OK. "Kate said it sounded as if she was calling from a railway station. She thought she heard a Tannoy announcer in the background say 'Derby Station'."

DS Kenneth sighed. "Why didn't you tell me this earlier?" he said.

"Because I'm telling you now, damn it! I didn't have a chance before you came blundering in here."

The detective sergeant ignored Catesby's blame-shifting bluster and cut to the heart of the matter. "Interesting. If Flint is with her, then it would seem they are travelling by train and heading this way. I wonder why."

THIRTY-FOUR

I can't remember the last time I went to a pub, Ophelia. Usually, I like to stay at home with you when I drink. The company is so much more convivial, don't you think? And you don't seem to mind if I get the hiccups or fall asleep while watching *Miss Marple* on the telly. God that woman is so irritating! No wonder I drink while watching her shows. Calls herself an investigator? She'd need more than a silly hat and a bag of knitting if she came round here, poking her nose in. It's a very big garden and there's always room for one more busybody.

However, Flossie invited me to a face-to-face meeting with some of the forum members this evening, so I thought, *why not?* Better the devil you know and all that. She said they used to meet at her flat, but it's very small and she doesn't get on with her flatmate: apparently the other girl's very messy and Flossie doesn't like mess. Hmm, fancy that – a fellow ataxophobe. And guess what else: when I got to the Golden Lion, Flossie was already in their dingy back room – the one with the tatty old flock wallpaper and the sticky carpet – giving the cast-iron tables and the red leatherette chairs a quick twice-over with a handful of Dettol antibacterial multi-purpose disinfectant wipes. The extra-large ones. Obviously. Because that's the other thing about pubs: you never know whose sweaty arse has been on that seat before yours.

Anyway, I'd only just sat down on my freshly disinfected chair when in walked the first of the forum's members. And you'll never guess who it was: Jasmine Shuttleworth, Timea's predecessor as receptionist. And significantly pregnant too. Well, well. I had no idea she was one of my closet admirers. However, when Flossie told me Jasmine's username was Beatrix Kiddo, she winked at me, so I guessed there was rather more to it than that. I asked Jasmine why she'd chosen the name, and she told me it's because of the film *Kill Bill*. I haven't seen it myself as it's a bit too gory for my tastes, but it seems Beatrix wants to get revenge on Bill for threatening the life of her unborn child. Fascinating, I'm sure, but it still left me none the wiser until I remembered a rumour that Jasmine had been asked to sign a non-disclosure agreement when she left Alcock & Bull.

At which point Jasmine said to me: "I hope you don't mind me saying this, but your husband is a total shit."

"Ah," I said, "tell me something I don't already know."

"What if I tell you I've got a bone to pick with him," she added, rubbing her belly.

"Stick around," I said, finally putting two and two together, "and you'll have plenty to choose from."

Can you believe it? He never found the time, or the wherewithal, to fertilise my eggs but he had no problem giving Jasmine's a good old dousing. What's she got that I haven't? Apart from blonde hair, big boobs and a nineteen-year-old body? Ha! Not that she looks too hot at the moment, not while she's gestating Elmer the Elephant, and everything is sagging and stretching. In any event she deserves to be punished for betraying me, she really does. And yet, I have to take the baby into consideration, don't I? I'm not usually that keen on the idea of redemption, or giving anyone a second chance, but maybe she can earn my forgiveness by proving useful. We'll see.

After Jasmine, the next to arrive was another girl in her late teens called Meera Kumar, who goes by the username Baby Blue. She looked very shifty when she came in, wearing sunglasses, an oversized hoodie and a hunted expression. But that's understandable as she ran away from home after her parents threatened to kill her. It seems they discovered a pregnancy testing kit she'd bought, evidence of her dishonouring the family. Or so they claimed. Not that she looks pregnant, although it was difficult to tell what was going on under that hoodie. Still, someone who's used to defying authority and running around in disguise could also come in very handy.

I was beginning to wonder if the entire forum was made up of impregnated teenies, with raging hormonal issues like mine. But then Hattie Hartopp, aka The Mad Hatter, arrived to even things up a bit, age and fertility-wise. I'm guessing she must be in her late twenties or early thirties, but it's difficult to tell when someone's as mousey as that. I know looks can be deceiving – take me for example – but it's a wonder she didn't scuttle into the room holding a lump of cheese in one hand and preening her whiskers with the other. Because, believe me, that girl has whiskers. I'm surprised Flossie hasn't offered to take her to the salon to wax her face for her. And advised her to get a new hairstyle while she's at it, along with lending her a padded bra. She's never going to get impregnated looking like that. But then who am I to talk?

Anyway, she told me it had been her dream to join the police so she could have the satisfaction of arresting her stepfather. She didn't say why, though I could guess. But the police rejected her. Odd, because I wasn't aware the police rejected anyone these days. Or is that just male recruits? Apparently, she thinks she has an aptitude for police work, based on the fact that she earned an 'Investigating' badge when she was in the Girl Guides. Fifteen years ago. She said the badge helped her to hone her investigation skills and become an expert investigator.

"But they still rejected me because of my A levels," she said.

So I said: "Why, what's wrong with them?"

"I haven't got any," she said.

I commiserated because I'd only just met her and didn't have the heart to tell her it was her own fault and she should have worked harder at school. In any event, she said she's currently studying at Newvale College and thinking of reapplying if she gets her City & Guilds qualification.

So I asked her: "What are you studying?" because I wanted to appear encouraging.

"Millinery," she said.

Millinery. I suppose she *could* be useful if I need a new hat for Gary's funeral.

I looked at Flossie, and she shrugged, before announcing that Derek, the group's token middle-aged male, couldn't make it because it clashed with his Dungeons & Dragons games night. Apparently, Derek, who calls himself The Dungeon Master, is the forum's self-appointed director of strategic operations. He's writing a rulebook and individual character sheets for everyone. What an arse. My guess is one of the others will break the rules and throw him in the canal. Probably before Christmas. And if they don't, I will.

Flossie also apologised on behalf of their psychic investigator, Brenda, who blamed a lack of forewarning for arranging a seance that clashed with this evening's meeting. I kid you not. That'll teach her to look at her diary rather than her tea leaves in future. But although she could only be there in spirit, Brenda The Crystal Gazer sent me a message to say she wants to use her gift to find my mother. Really? What makes her think I'm even looking? And if I was, she'd need more than her 'gift'. Try dowsing rods and a fine sieve, Brenda. But I mustn't be too dismissive. Brenda wants me to give her some object that my mother treasured, which has been imprinted with her sense of self. I suppose I could have given her my mother's well-thumbed contacts book containing all her lovers' details. But after she disappeared I burnt it – both volumes – along with all the Polaroids.

Once everyone had settled down, they began discussing various suspicious deaths that have taken place in the area over the years. And every time a new case was mentioned, they all looked at me. Can you believe it? Talk about giving a dog a bad name. What did they expect me to do? Burst into tears and confess to a string of random murders I didn't commit? Some of the things I do may be a bit mad, but they're definitely not random. Honestly, these people are even crazier than me.

At the end of the meeting, Hattie suggested the group should have a rule like they do at Alcoholics Anonymous. Not that AA would hold their meetings in a pub. That really would be tempting fate.

Meera said: "You mean like we should all become teetotal?"

But Hattie said: "No. I was thinking more along the lines of: 'who you see hear, what you hear here, when you leave here, let it stay here'. I got that from my stepfather. Only don't tell him I told you, for God's sake."

It didn't do anything for me, though, so I said: "If you're going to have a slogan at least make it meaningful. Something like: 'let's do it to them before they do it to us'."

Frowns all round. I think that might have been going a bit too far for them at this stage. But they'll learn; well, they will by the time I've finished grooming them.

I then suggested the group could meet here in future as there's plenty of room and Gary's never around in the evenings to object. Not that I would take any notice of his opinion anyway. Who owns this house: me or that sperm-spraying squatter? Admittedly, the thought of meeting here was a bit triggering for Jasmine, but that was partly the point. The more I can feed her agitation and sense of injustice the better.

After that, I got a bit carried away by the caring, sharing impulse. Which is most unlike me. In fact, by my usual standards it was running amok. Believe it or not, once everyone else had left, I invited Flossie to come and stay here with us. As I said to her, if she leaves her tiny flat and messy flatmate, she can live here and clean the house to her heart's content. And mine. Obviously. There's method in my madness, you know. Not only that, but I'll need someone to help me run the hedgehog hospital and beaver rewilding projects I'm planning. So there's a job on offer too, that's if she fancies a change from waxing women's hairy bits at the salon. She may not, but I could tell she was interested, albeit a touch cautious.

She said: "You do realise I'm a lesbian, don't you?"

I said: "You do realise I'm *not* a lesbian, don't you? But that shouldn't stop us rubbing along together."

"True," she said, "and I'll be on hand if you change your mind. But what about your husband?"

"Don't worry about him," I said, "he's not got round to trying his luck with lesbians yet. He's still plugging away at teenage ingénues."

I told her she can have one of the spare guest rooms for the time being. But once Gary's no longer around – I didn't specify the reason for his imminent departure at this stage – she can move into the main guest room. After it's been deep cleaned of course.

Anyway, she told me the new arrangement will be 'perfect'. And the upshot is she's moving in at the weekend. I can't wait to see Gary's face.

THIRTY-FIVE

Gary and Alexa were in their usual cosy alcove at the rear of Rossellini's first-floor dining area. Out of sight and out of earshot of the other diners. For which they were both grateful, especially Gary.

"There's a noisy rabble in here tonight, isn't there?" he said, glowering at Alexa. He would have preferred to address his complaint to Fredo and glower at him instead, but as there was no sign of the restaurateur, Alexa would have to do.

"It's getting close to Christmas," said Alexa as she picked her way through a tricolore salad with parmesan. "It's always popular at this time of year. In fact, we ought to have booked it for a Christmas get-together for the staff."

"Are you kidding? You can only have a get-together if people actually *want* to get together. Look what happened last year with all those no-shows," said Gary.

"That was only because you were too mean to pay for a proper meal at a nice place like this. What did you expect?"

"Forget it. It would be a waste of money and decent food. Half of those kids wouldn't know the difference between a pork chop and a parson's nose, and the other half are vegans. Unless

185

dinner was served up between two halves of a bread bun with a generous helping of lettuce leaves and a side of chips they wouldn't be interested. Do they even know what a knife and fork are for?"

Alexa sighed. She was beginning to tire of him; there was no getting away from that fact. Instead of turning on the charm with Claudia – at least until his wife changed her will, or he could find grounds to challenge their prenup agreement – he was going out of his way to antagonise her. And his behaviour in general was also rapidly deteriorating. It seemed to her she had hitched her fortunes to a wagon that was in serious danger of derailing itself. And that wouldn't do.

"So tell me," she said, "why are you in such a bad mood? Again."

"I have every reason," said Gary, stabbing at his mushroom and spinach lasagna. "You remember me telling you last week about that emaciated goth girl Claudia's befriended? Well, she moved in at the weekend. Can you believe it? Moved in! I was never consulted. The first I knew of it was when the scrawny vampire turned up on the doorstep before dawn, clutching a couple of battered suitcases and tube of factor 50+ sunscreen. Thank God she didn't bring her pet bat with her."

"And does this scrawny vampire have a name?"

"Flossie," said Gary, almost spitting the word.

"That's unusual."

"You think she's unusual? Try rude. Do you know the first thing she said to me? 'Hi, we haven't been properly introduced yet but I'm a lesbian – just so you know.' "

Alexa raised an eyebrow. "Clearly a girl with priorities," she said, "and they obviously don't include you."

"As if I care," said Gary. "It was bad enough having to share the house with one weirdo, but two! There has to be an ulterior motive. Claudia says she wants this girl around to help run her half-baked projects, but I'm not buying that."

"You're not annoyed because she's ruled herself out of bounds, then?"

"God no!" said Gary. "She gives me the creeps. I thought Claudia's doll was bad enough, but it's getting more like *The Addams Family* every day. The girl came down to breakfast this morning wearing black pyjamas covered in astrological signs and skulls and with these grotesque vampire slippers on her feet."

"I didn't know vampires wore slippers."

"This one does. I'm thinking of sleeping with a clove of garlic around my neck, just to be on the safe side," said Gary as he pushed his plate aside and picked up the menu.

Alexa let him study the desserts in silence for a minute or two before steering the conversation towards an equally prickly subject. "Talking of the girls in your life, Jasmine rang me today."

The menu Gary was holding quivered. "What did she want?" he asked.

"She said she's been thinking about what happened and she's not happy with the way she was treated."

"Well tough titties. She signed an NDA."

"Even so, there may be an issue," said Alexa. "Jasmine has discovered that the solicitor she went to for advice is one of your fellow masons."

Gary put down the menu and gave a dismissive waft of his hand, as if swatting away both Jasmine's complaint and Alexa's concerns. He pointed out that in a small town like Newvale, it was inevitable he would know most, if not all, of his fellow professionals. "Networking's the name of the game," he said.

"Be that as it may, she says she's thinking of ignoring the NDA and revealing all on social media. So what I want to know, Gary, is what she means by 'all'?"

"There is no 'all' to reveal," said Gary with a shrug. "Mountains made out of molehills. It's just the usual 'he said, she said' stuff. You know how precious teenage girls are these days: you've only got to look at them the wrong way and they squeal about 'inappropriate behaviour'." He paused for a moment before adding: "So what does she want?"

"Her pound of flesh, by the sound of it," said Alexa. "I've told her I'll schedule a meeting with her so we can sort something out."

"Yeah, whatever," said Gary with another dismissive wave as he went back to studying the list of desserts.

Alexa had already made up her mind she didn't want a dessert, but what she hadn't decided on was what to make of the Jasmine 'thing'. When she spoke to their former receptionist on the phone, she got the firm impression this wasn't simply a case of Gary being his usual 'handsy' self and making inappropriate suggestions. Jasmine had strongly hinted there was something more to it than that. And without stating what 'it' was, she had sounded genuine. The odd thing, though, was that Gary didn't seem unduly concerned. It was a puzzle, and one that added to Alexa's growing sense of unease.

Gary put down the menu once more. "I think I might have the plum and amaretti *semifreddo*," he said. "Talking of which, where is our host this evening? You don't think he's nipped out for a quickie with his overworked waitress, do you?"

Alexa rolled her eyes. "I think it's far more likely that Fredo's avoiding us in case you start hassling him for some more of his pills."

"No need," said Gary with a wink. "I popped into Boots while the young blonde was on her lunch break. Just so you know, we're good to go once we're done here."

"Really?" said Alexa with a sigh. "Who said romance was dead? But before we abandon ourselves to an evening of unbridled passion, I need to bring you up to speed with Mr Novak."

"Ah yes, our favourite sniper. How did you get on with him?"

"Fine. He appears to be a man with few scruples."

"Ideal then."

"Exactly. He's happy to deal with our Flint problem in exchange for an infusion of funds."

Gary's brow furrowed. "How much?"

"Ten grand."

"What!" said Gary, his brow now shooting up towards the ceiling. "That's as much as Flint wants. We're going to be no better off than if we'd settled with the mad bomber in the first place, and it still leaves Claudia."

"Sssh!" hissed Alexa, looking around to see if any of the other diners were showing an interest. "Keep your voice down! As I recall, it was your decision not to pay Flint. Besides, if it makes you feel better, I've negotiated a two-for-one deal."

Gary grunted. "Even so. Where's the money coming from? It's not as if we can hide that amount in the company's accounts. You know Claudia goes through them with a fine-tooth comb."

"Not if she's dead she won't. But I agree: it makes far more sense to keep this separate from the business. I suppose you'll just have to sell one of your Rolex watches. Or downsize your car. Or tell the golf club you can't afford to be captain next year."

Silence.

Gary glared. He glared at Alexa. He glared at the menu. He glared at the waitress as she approached to take his order. "Go away," he told her, still glaring. "I don't want a dessert after all. I've gone right off the idea."

Alexa smiled apologetically at the waitress. "I'll have an espresso, *please*," she said, accentuating the 'please'. She waited until the waitress had hurried off in the direction of the kitchen before fixing Gary with a glare of her own. "You're so rude!" she said.

Gary gave a truculent shrug. "This whole scheme was supposed to make me richer – us richer – but so far it's threatening to do the opposite."

"You know very well you have to speculate to accumulate."

"I suppose," said Gary morosely. "So what kind of person is this Novak? What am I getting for my money?"

Alexa sat back in her chair as she conjured up a mental image of the would-be assassin. After a moment or two's reflection, she allowed herself a small smile as she told Gary he was about the same age as him, but a bit taller at just over six feet, with short-cropped fair hair. "I would describe him as handsome, in a rugged, manly way; he gave me the impression of being a man of action: a doer, rather than a talker."

Gary might well have sneered at Novak's description regardless, but Alexa's smile made it a certainty. "Sounds like a brainless oik to me. Are we sure he's capable of understanding who he's supposed to be shooting? As much as I detest them, I really wouldn't want any more neighbours needlessly smeared all over the pavement."

"You wouldn't be jealous, would you?" said Alexa, still with the hint of a smile on her lips.

"As if!" protested Gary.

But despite his vehement denial, Alexa knew him, and his fragile male ego, well enough. And even allowing for the subdued lighting in the alcove, she was sure his face had turned a greener shade than the avocado in her salad. Which delighted her. As much as she was growing tired of him, she needed to keep *him* invested in *her* until Claudia was out of the way. After that, well the meeting with Karol Novak had opened her eyes to a new range of future possibilities. She had noticed the way Karol stared at her and knew he wouldn't need much encouragement. Nor, by the look of him – and she had taken a *good* look – would he need the aid of a packet of little blue pills either. And even if all the scheming around the wills failed to bear fruit, she could always sweet-talk Karol into renewing his old smuggling contacts but this time with her as the business brains behind the operation.

Even as her mind started to wander, Gary brought her back to the present. "I suppose the oik will have to do," he said. "We definitely need to sort something out and as soon as possible. I saw Catesby at the club on Sunday, and he told me Flint's still in this country and using the train network to zigzag his way back here. Personally, I can't imagine why he'd want to do that, not with train tickets the price they are these days. Unless he stole someone's walking frame and blagged a Disabled Person's Railcard. I doubt doing something as despicable as that would bother him, seeing as he's already blown a blind man and his wife to Kingdom Come."

Alexa shook her head and, without a trace of irony, said: "As interesting as your imaginative ramblings are, I'll pass on the information about Flint to Novak. Maybe he can keep an eye out for him at the station. Mind you, it could also explain why DS Kenneth postponed his meeting with me yesterday. He said there had been an important development in the case, which was taking up most of his time, and he would have to reschedule our appointment. In the meantime, I'll ask Novak to target Claudia first, providing you can get her will sorted."

"I'll have a go, if I can get her on her own. She did say some of her coven are coming round one evening, but hopefully they'll wait until I'm out."

"Well make it soon. We can't let this situation carry on for much longer."

Gary frowned. "Agreed. But even if she won't change the will, my solicitor says I've got a very good chance of challenging it under the Inheritance Act of 1975. So let's go for it. Are you sure Novak will deal with Claudia?"

"Absolutely. He did seem a little uncertain when I initially mentioned her to him. But once I told him she was using her children's charity work as a front for a child trafficking operation, he became quite enthusiastic."

"Hmm. That's given me an idea. Perhaps we can get him to take out Jasmine as well."

THIRTY-SIX

Detective Sergeant Kevin Kenneth sighed deeply, knocked and entered the office of his superior, Chief Inspector Julian Catesby, who was kneeling on the carpet in front of his desk with his left eye closed and palms pressed together, as if in prayer. His right eye could also have been closed, but it was impossible to tell as it was still covered by a patch.

It was also difficult to detect what Catesby was muttering, although DS Kenneth thought he heard his boss say: "…as we forgive those who trespass against us. And lead us not into temptation…"

DS Kenneth coughed. Politely.

Catesby opened his good eye. "Yes? What is it, Kenington?"

"Sorry to interrupt, sir," said DS Kenneth, hiding his bemusement. "I didn't know you were religious."

"Sometimes I am. Sometimes I'm not. I did once flirt with Buddhism, you know."

"Ah," said DS Kenneth, who wondered if flirting and Buddhism belonged together, at least in the same sentence.

"Kate – my sister-in-law – is a member of the Church of Loving Togetherness."

"Ah," said DS Kenneth again, enlightenment now replacing bemusement. "This would be in addition to her membership of the Newvale Sun Valley Nudist Club, I take it."

"Indeed. She assures me the two are not mutually incompatible. As she explained it to me: 'In our church we shed our sins as we shed our clothes.' "

"Interesting. I can't say I've come across this church before."

"It's very small. At the moment there's only about a dozen members and Kate's the minister. They hold their services in the old scout hut, off St Chads Avenue."

"Cosy."

"Select," corrected Ch Insp Catesby. "Kate has urged me to join. She says that if I become a member, she will no longer be bound by the constraints of the 'no touching' rule. This will enable her to perform the laying-on of hands, thereby manipulating my biofield and facilitating an increased feeling of well-being."

DS Kenneth's eyebrow twitched. "Excuse my ignorance," he said, "but would the laying-on of hands be a two-way thing?"

"Quite possibly. Kate says it all depends on whether our chakras are aligned in harmony. Or something like that."

"I see. So, if you don't mind me asking, where does Mrs Catesby fit into this – if and when she returns?"

Ch Insp Catesby shook his head. "Kate says Jennifer is a lost soul, so I should stop wasting my precious Prana energy on her and start preparing myself for the next stage of my life's journey."

"That sounds like a very philosophical approach to take, sir."

"It does, doesn't it? And I also take comfort in telling myself that Jennifer is going to burn in the fires of hell for all eternity. God willing."

DS Kenneth attempted to scratch his nose with his imaginary finger as he wondered how his boss reconciled this sentiment with the concept of 'loving togetherness'. But instead of pursuing the thought, he said: "Talking of lost souls, for the last two weeks we've been monitoring all the train stations between here and Derby, as best as we can, but there's been no sign of Jennifer or Flint."

"So where are they then?" asked Catesby as he got to his feet and resumed his place behind his desk.

It was a question DS Kenneth had been debating with himself and the rest of his small team of detectives for several days. As yet they had no answers and he could only suggest to the chief that the couple were heavily disguised and paying for their tickets, and overnight accommodation, with cash. "That's unless Flint *does* have an entirely new ID with credit cards to match. Or the pair are camping out in the woods."

Ch Insp Catesby snorted. "Camping? Jennifer? She is a high-maintenance beautician and cosmetologist with her own salon. Stop wasting your time, Kenmore! Living in a tent, at any time of the year, is the last place you are going to find her."

DS Kenneth felt like reminding Catesby that Jennifer's elopement with a rough-and-ready demolition contractor might also have been the last thing expected of a high-maintenance beautician and cosmetologist with her own salon. But it had happened. However, he had discovered over the past few weeks that trying to reason with the man was a waste of breath. Going around him was usually better than trying to go through him, as operational procedure unfortunately dictated.

Yet despite his misgivings over the man's competence, he felt duty bound to report an unusual incident that had occurred ten days earlier. "I'm not sure if this is connected," he said, "but I was in the snug at the Golden Lion last week when I saw Claudia Alcock going into a meeting in the back room with several other women."

"So?"

"Well, my reason for mentioning it is because I thought one or two of them were behaving rather suspiciously. So I asked the landlord what was going on, and he said the room had been booked by a group calling themselves True Crime Lovers Inc. Interesting, don't you think?"

"Never heard of them," said Ch Insp Catesby with a disinterested shrug.

"Nor had I, but we've certainly come across one or two of the individuals before," said DS Kenneth. He paused for a moment, to make sure he'd got Catesby's full attention, before telling him that the room had been booked on the group's behalf by a girl called Flossie McDonald, whom they had arrested the year before. "She was one of the environmental campaigners who glued themselves to the road outside the Newvale Sewage Pumping Station in protest at the water company's release of sewage into the River Newvale," he said. "You might remember her as she works at your wife's salon."

"What? You mean the girl who wears black all the time? Environmental campaigner my arse! She's nothing but an anarchist lawbreaker. I told Jennifer at the time she should have sacked her."

DS Kenneth allowed himself the rare luxury of a frown. "While I don't condone blocking the King's highway," he said, "I rather admire the campaigners for trying to improve the world we live in."

"In that case you've gone right down in my estimation, Kensington. You can bet your pension they're planning something subversive. I overheard Gary Alcock telling someone at the club that his wife's hoping to release a whole army of beavers into the river. Beavers! Can you imagine the damage they'd do to the course? The ninth fairway would be underwater in days."

"Really?" said DS Kenneth. Although the fate of the ninth

fairway didn't bother him – and he couldn't care less where he stood in Catesby's estimation – he *was* intrigued by a possible link between Claudia and Flossie.

Yet while he was intrigued, Ch Insp Catesby was demonstrably agitated by the idea that Newvale could be harbouring a gang of anarchists. "What about the other plotters?" he demanded, thumping his desk with his fist. "Who are they?"

DS Kenneth did his best to ignore the outburst, calmly telling his boss that the only other woman he recognised was Hattie Hartopp, who frequently turned up at crime scenes claiming she was a citizen investigator. "She's the one who keeps pestering our officers to spend a week with them on work experience. Although she's a nuisance, she's essentially harmless," he said. "I often see her with that psychic investigator Brenda Skinner."

"Oh *her*. The Queen of the Tea Leaves. Was she at this meeting, too?"

"No," said DS Kenneth, "but there were a couple there whom I didn't recognise. One of them was a heavily pregnant teenager, so I can't see her offering much of an active terrorist threat. However, the other girl looked a lot shiftier. I couldn't get a good look at her because she was wearing one of those baggy, hooded tops as well as dark glasses. And she scurried in and out of the pub like she was being pursued by the nine o'clock horses."

"The what?"

"It's a local saying, sir."

Ch Insp Catesby shook his head, more in sorrow than anger. "Leaving aside your quaint use of the vernacular, Kenlock, it sounds to me as if they're up to no good. We need to keep a close eye on these people."

"Yes, sir."

"And while you're about it, see if you can find out who these horses belong to."

DS Kenneth silently counted to five before he trusted himself to answer. "In the meantime," he eventually said, "I'm going to interview Claudia again. One or two other things have cropped up that I need to question her about."

THIRTY-SEVEN

Men. What's wrong with them? On second thoughts, don't answer that, Ophelia, or we'll be here all day. For starters, have you noticed that once you reach a certain age they stop noticing you? Which might explain why I was nearly run over the other day. I must have inadvertently put on my cloak of invisibility when I walked down to the corner shop to get some milk. Silly me. Because the next thing I know, that bearded prat from Number 48 came whizzing up behind on his motorised e-scooter and bumped into me, knocking the shopping bag out of my hand. Imagine: a grown man riding a scooter! On the footpath! The clue's in the name, cretin: the path is for feet, not wheels. Get on the road and take your chances along with the cyclists and the badgers. Or, better still, remove the motor and give your silly scooter to a nine-year-old.

He actually had the nerve to stop to complain I was walking down the middle of the path and hadn't given him enough room to get by. I was fuming. Neither the new pills, nor the useless mindfulness advice from the NHS, touched my anger. Mindfulness? Ha! The only thing my mind was full of was a desire for retribution. I picked up my bag and whacked him around the head with it. I'm not sure if a four-pint container of full-fat milk weighs more than semi-skimmed, but he ended up in the Johnsons' privet hedge, squealing like a baby. When he finally got to his feet, he called me a pathetic old biddy and threatened to sort me out. The cheek of it! First I'm invisible and then I'm dismissed as an old biddy! But by then I'd got my 'game face' on and gave as good as I got. Admittedly, I used the F-word and the C-word a bit. Well, quite a lot actually. Which seemed to surprise him as well as the Johnsons, who came out of their house to see what was going on. Nosey sods. I told them to "piss off back inside, if you know what's good for you", which did the trick. To be honest, I would have gone back later and apologised, but the whole street knows they're doggers, so fat chance of that. They're better off indoors, as is everyone else who uses Newvale Common and Woods.

Anyway, I turned back to Scooter Man and waved my Swiss army penknife under his nose. I always carry the knife with me because you never know when you might meet a horse that needs a stone removing from its hoof, or an entitled male who needs reminding the patriarchy has had its day. And he obviously believed me when I said I'd slice him open from his groin to his gizzard, because he ran off home and left his precious e-scooter behind. I threw it over the hedge and into the Johnsons' garden. Not that it'll be of much use for their al fresco activities. Although you never know: I learnt from my mother that you should never underestimate a pervert's inventiveness, especially where battery-powered equipment's concerned.

As for Scooter Man, he whinged to the police, and I had two uniformed officers turn up yesterday while you were having your afternoon nap. The male police officer said to me: "Is it true you threatened Mr Holyoak with a butcher's knife?"

So I showed them my penknife and said: "Best of luck jointing a carcass with that. But then I'm not surprised he exaggerated its size. That's what men do, isn't it?"

After the female police officer stopped smirking, I added: "And by the way, I have a phobia of sharp objects. You can check it out with Dr Rosencrantz, if you like."

The male officer ignored that and said: "It's still an offensive weapon."

So I pointed out that Holyoak ran into me while riding an e-scooter on the pavement, which was also against the law and made *his* weapon equally offensive. But even so, I had to make a statement, and they warned me I might be prosecuted for assault, threatening behaviour and carrying an offensive weapon. Can you believe it? With everything that's happened in my past, they're going to throw the book at me for hitting a whiny twat with a shopping bag. The irony!

Once they had left, I had a follow-up phone call from DS Kenneth, asking if he could pop round later today for a chat. So I said "of course", because I can be very reasonable when asked nicely. In fact, I told him that if he behaves himself, I might treat him to a cup of tea and a Hobnob. And if he tries really hard, I might even stretch to a Twix finger. Which is more than that tiresome county archaeologist is going to get. I had to warn DS Kenneth that Smithson is also coming round. No doubt he's hoping to persuade me to let them dig up the rest of the garden looking for more medieval bodies. But I think you know what my answer to that will be. My rhubarb patch is sacrosanct.

Men. As I said, what's wrong with them? When they're not ignoring us, they're being condescending. Not to mention rude. Take Gary at breakfast this morning. As soon as he saw Flossie wasn't around, he said: "So where's Dracula's ugly daughter this morning?"

Ugly? Has he looked at himself in the mirror recently? That's not a paunch he's growing but a pouch, with a couple of joeys thrown in for good measure, judging by the way it jumps about when he walks.

I said to him: "You do realise this is the twenty-first century, don't you?"

He looked at me in his superior way and said: "What's that got to do with it?"

So I said: "Everything, you arse! Women don't need men's approval or permission anymore."

Not that he agreed. He sneered and shook his head so hard it's a wonder it didn't fall off. Trust me, if he does that again I'll give it a helping hand. Or two.

Anyway, Flossie wasn't around because she's having to work her notice at the salon. She's got appointments booked throughout December, including one with the mayoress on Christmas Eve. She told Flossie she wants to look her best for a festive party she's throwing. I thought, *fair enough*, because what hostess doesn't want to 'wow' her guests? But that was until Flossie said she'd booked in for a full Brazilian. Huh? What kind of party are the civic couple hosting if she has to have the whole of her gubbins waxed? Remind me to RSVP 'no thanks' if I get an invite to their seasonal finger buffet.

By the way, when Flossie was at the salon yesterday, she found out that Jennifer Catesby has definitely run off with the bomber Bob Flint. No one seems to know where they are, but they can't be too far away as the police were asking the staff if Jennifer has contacts in the Derby area. Of course, Flossie might have misheard, and the police were talking about Abu Dhabi. In which case Flossie needs to have her ears waxed, never mind her bikini line.

And talking of puzzles, when I was at the shop yesterday, Francesca told me about another mystery.

She said: "Did you know Gary and Alexa were hobnobbing at the restaurant again on Monday evening?"

I said: "Hobnobbing? In the restaurant? I think you'll find that usually comes later at her flat."

And that's if he's capable of hobnobbing in the aftermath of the Dodgy Blue Pills incident. But to be fair, nothing he gets up to surprises me anymore, so that wasn't the mystery Francesca was referring to. She said that Fredo kept out of their way but overheard them furtively discussing 'shooters' a couple of times. Francesca's worried there might be a new cocktail bar and restaurant opening in town, possibly near the railway station. She wanted to know if I'd heard Gary mention anything about picking up a new client from the hospitality trade. Ha! God knows who – or what – he might have picked up from the hospitality trade recently, but I doubt it's a new client. Although, tell a lie: when I was talking to Timea the other week, she said her dad was transferring his accounts to Alcock & Bull. But I don't think it can be him as he runs an import and export business, rather than a bar or restaurant.

Anyway, that was the front doorbell, so one of my visitors must have arrived. I'll let you know later how I get on with them.

THIRTY-EIGHT

Timea had spent the whole morning waiting for Mrs Pinchess to make some comment about her holiday. Penny had just returned from a week's break in the Peak District but had remained resolutely silent about the experience. And after Mrs Pinchess's ill-tempered reaction when asked about her previous holiday in Wales, Timea had been reluctant to broach the subject again. But by the time Mrs Pinchess returned to the office after lunch, her curiosity finally got the better of her.

"So, how was the holiday?" said Timea, summoning a sunny smile.

"It rained. A lot."

"Again?"

"Again. And it was freezing."

Timea frowned. "You must really like caravanning."

Mrs Pinchess didn't answer immediately. She took off her coat, hung it on one of the pegs in an alcove and then took her place next to Timea at the reception desk, jabbing at her computer's 'on' button as she did so. "Let's get this straight, Timea," she said. "My husband likes caravanning. I don't. He thinks it's good to get close to nature. I don't. I told him nature looks good on the telly, but that's as close as I want to get to it. I've also told him that next year *I'm* going to stay for two weeks at The Grand Hotel in Torquay, where someone else does the cooking, the staff wait on you hand and foot and there's four-star bloody luxury coming out of your ears. But precious little bloody nature. In fact, the closest thing to nature in Torquay are the potted bloody palm trees. *He* can please himself if he comes with me or not."

"Oh," said Timea, who was slightly taken aback by the vehemence of Mrs Pinchess's response. But she quickly recovered to ask: "Why not go somewhere there's guaranteed sunshine, like Spain or Greece?"

"Because it's full of foreigners," said Mrs Pinchess with a shudder. "They're not my cup of tea – present company excepted, of course."

A couple of incoming phone calls stalled any further conversation for a few minutes, before Timea tentatively asked if the holiday had been a complete washout. Mrs Pinchess was about to dismiss the question out of hand but frowned as she recalled an odd incident.

"Now you've mentioned it," she said, "I was walking to the campsite's office one day – last Thursday, I think – when I saw a camper van pull up. A couple got out and the woman looked the spitting image of Jennifer Catesby from The Beauty Spot in town. But I suppose it couldn't have been her because when I waved she took no notice, and they got straight back in the van and drove off. I know I wasn't that close, but I could have sworn it was her. She even walked like her: a bit like a half-starved penguin."

Timea lifted a sculpted eyebrow at the prospect of some decent gossip to brighten an otherwise dull day. "Wasn't there some talk that she might have run off with that car bomber the police are looking for, Bob Flint?" she said.

"You shouldn't listen to tittle-tattle, dear," said Mrs Pinchess, waving an admonishing finger. "It's not the sort of thing we do in this country." But then she succumbed to the temptation to add to the intrigue. "Besides, the man I saw with her didn't look at all like Bob Flint. Mr Flint is quite handsome, in a rugged way. A bit like Charles Bronson."

"The criminal?"

"No, not him. The actor. I imagine he's a bit before your time. He was in a string of films like *The Magnificent Seven*, *The Dirty Dozen* and *Death Wish*."

Timea picked up her phone and began to google images of Charles Bronson. The actor. She held up the screen to show it to Mrs Pinchess. "Him, you mean?" she asked.

"Exactly. Whereas the man I saw at the campsite was fat, bearded, wore dark glasses and had a limp."

Timea thought for a moment. "Perhaps it *was* Bob Flint, but he was acting? Just like Charles Bronson."

"I don't know about that. Overacting, I'd say. If that was the case."

"Hmm. Did you know he's Lithuanian?"

Mrs Pinchess started. "Bob Flint? I never knew that."

"No, Charles Bronson. The actor. That's what Wikipedia says."

"Oh dear. Lithuanian, you say? Now you've put me right off him."

And all the while they had been talking, the radio had been on in the background, tuned to Radio Newvale. The Smooth as Silke Afternoon Show with Sammi Silke was just getting underway with a rendition of 'Rubber Bullets' by 10cc, when the music abruptly stopped. In its place came the voice of the studio's general manager. He was doing his best to achieve a tone of dignified seriousness, but he couldn't hide a slight tremble of excitement.

We're sorry to interrupt the show, but we're just receiving dramatic reports of a shooting in Newvale. We understand armed police and ambulances are at The Avenue after gunfire was heard. We'll bring you another update just as soon as we have more news. And now back to the Smooth as Silke Afternoon Show with Sammi Silke.

Timea and Mrs Pinchess looked at the radio and then at each other, open-mouthed in disbelief.

Timea was the first to react. "Not again," she said.

"Again, by the sound of it," said Mrs Pinchess, standing up. "I need to tell Gary."

"He's not here. Nor's Alexa."

"Where are they?"

"I don't know. They went for a late lunch. Or so they said."

Mrs Pinchess's lips pursed as she picked up her desk phone and dialled Gary's mobile. It went through to voicemail, and she left a message asking him to call her as soon as he could. She then attempted to call Alexa's mobile, but that too was switched off. There was nothing more she could do, except listen to the radio's latest announcement:

We apologise for interrupting the Smooth as Silke Afternoon Show with Sammi Silke once again, but we are now going live to our on-the-spot reporter Kylie McCrystal to bring us more on this afternoon's shooting in Newvale.

Kylie, what's happening?

Thanks, Ben. I'm here in The Avenue where armed police have cordoned off a section of the street. This followed reports of gunshots being fired outside one of the houses. One ambulance has just left the scene with its blue lights flashing, and from where I'm standing, I can see two more are waiting to rush any further casualties to Newvale Royal Infirmary.

Normally, The Avenue is a peaceful, leafy residential street – though not quite so leafy now it's winter, I have to say – but less than three months ago it was the setting for a huge car bomb explosion that killed former missionaries Ernest and Mary Robinson. Police are still hunting for their chief suspect, demolitions expert Bob Flint, who disappeared shortly afterwards. For the moment the police are not linking the two incidents and are refusing to speculate on whether Flint has returned to the area to carry out another attack.

And in yet another twist to this unfolding drama, I have just been told by a resident, who wishes to remain anonymous, about a violent altercation that occurred on this same spot on Monday afternoon. According to Mr Holyoak, he was making his way home when he was stopped and threatened by a homicidal maniac armed with a butcher's knife.

That's all from me for the moment. Back to you, Ben.

Crikey. Thanks, Kylie. More from our on-the-spot reporter Kylie McCrystal as this story develops. In the meantime, it's back to the Smooth as Silke Afternoon Show with Sammi Silke.

Timea and Mrs Pinchess were too preoccupied by the astonishing news to notice the show had resumed with 'The Garden' by Guns 'n' Roses.

"Do you think Mrs Alcock's been the target all along?" said Timea, biting her bottom lip.

Mrs Pinchess shook her head. "I'm not sure about that, Timea. But whatever's happened, I sincerely hope Gary and Alexa haven't been caught up in it."

THIRTY-NINE

Holy mother of crap, Ophelia! I hope you don't mind if I have a couple of stiff G&Ts before bringing you up to speed on what happened earlier.

That's better. Now, where was I?

Ah, yes. So, when I went to answer the door, both DS Kenneth and Mr Smithson, the archaeologist, were standing there. I thought, *uh-oh, double trouble.* And as much as I like *Bargain Hunt*, it was the kind of two-for-one deal I could have done without. I was in two minds to know who to deal with first, which wasn't a surprising neurological state for me. But seeing as Smithson was already wearing his wellies, we went into the back garden to check out my partially excavated pond.

I don't know what he was expecting to find in the hole because nothing's changed since the last time he was trowelling away in there. It's not as if any more dead monks have risen up since then. I'd know if they had. I've been in the garden a lot, and I haven't experienced anything remotely approaching rapture out there. Well, not since my sixteenth birthday when I lured Danny Beckett into Mother's summer house. That was one hot summer's night, I can tell you. Hot *and* sweaty. And very messy. Which was a bit concerning. Still, you don't make a crêpes suzette without breaking a few eggs. I suppose it's a shame what happened to Danny afterwards. But as Édith Piaf used to say, *Non, je ne regrette rien.* Or something Frenchified like that.

Anyway, DS Kenneth decided to come with us. I suspect he was more than happy to have a quick shufti at the garden and make suggestions to Smithson as to where he could dig a few more test pits. Crafty sod. In any event, we were all standing on the edge of the hole when DS Kenneth pointed his stumpy finger at something glinting in the large puddle at the bottom. I half expected to see his fingernail, along with the rest of his missing digit, but when we both bent down to have a closer look, there was a sound like a whip crack, followed by a loud splat. I couldn't believe it! The loud splat turned out to be Smithson. He was lying face up in the puddle with a large hole in the middle of his forehead. Thankfully, there wasn't too much blood and grey matter. Because you know how I feel about that sort of thing.

DS Kenneth got on his knees for a closer look and said: "Good God! He's been shot."

"Well, I didn't think it was a breathing hole," I said. "The puddle's not that deep."

"Get down!" he said and grabbed my arm, pulling me down so we both slithered into the hole next to Smithson, just as there was another loud crack and I felt something whistle over my head. "The shots are coming from the woods beyond your garden," he added, getting his mobile phone out of his pocket, "but we should be OK down here while I call for backup."

OK? That was a matter of opinion. All my life I've fantasised about being in a sandwich between two men. And when it finally happens, guess what? I'm tits deep in a mud bath. And one of them's gone stiff for all the wrong reasons.

As if that wasn't bad enough, I said to DS Kenneth: "What's that smell?"

"It's burning," he said.

"Burning?"

"Yes. It looks like that last bullet burnt your hair."

"What?" I said and put my hand on the top of my head, where the hair felt all crinkly. "Holy mother of crap! The bastard's singed my plume!"

He gave me an odd look and said: "I rather think Smithson would have settled for a bit of singeing."

"Yes, poor man," I said and nodded, as if I'm empathetic. But, quite frankly, I was more concerned about the damage to my crowning glory. Yet looking on the bright side – as I had to do in all that mud – Smithson wouldn't be pestering me to dig any more holes. So, silver linings.

And who knew, when Smithson gazed into the hole hoping to find another body in there, he was foreseeing his own demise? How spooky is that? I've got half a mind to contact the producers of the TV show *The UnXplained* with William Shatner. Maybe Captain Kirk would like to pop along and explain what that was all about. I'm not sure what the other half of my mind's doing at the moment, but it's probably thinking it's a good job DS Kenneth was with me, or some would be blaming me for Smithson's death. Well, half the forum would, no doubt.

More to the point, who was the gunman taking potshots at? Smithson was an archaeologist, for God's sake. He may have been digging into people's pasts but only once they'd been dead for hundreds of years. It's not as if he was a private investigator, like old Gerry Coulson, digging up people's *recent* pasts. I said that to DS Kenneth while we were sitting in six inches of mud, waiting to be given the all-clear by the rest of his mob.

I wasn't happy. I said to him: "How much longer have we got to stay in this hellhole?"

He saw the look on my face and said: "I'm sorry you're having to share space with the unfortunate Mr Smithson."

Ha! As if Smithson's corpse was bothering me. When you've seen one, you've seen them all – providing there's not too much gore. No, it wasn't that. It was all that disgusting gooey water that was seeping through my M&S trousers and into my knickers. That's never a pleasant sensation, regardless of the fluids concerned. And to cap it all, there was a bloody police helicopter whirring about overhead. It was enough to give anyone a migraine, especially me.

DS Kenneth tried to make light of things and said: "It reminds me a bit of that scene with the helicopters in *Apocalypse Now*."

I just grunted. What else could I do when there was a real-life apocalypse happening inside my underpants? Besides, I still wanted to know if he thought Smithson had been the target. Or if he thought it was one of us. Or, more to the point, me. He tried to dodge around the point by asking if I had any enemies.

I said: "Probably quite a few. Starting with the moron who tried to run me down the other day. And not forgetting the police officer who came to interview me. Left to him, I'd have been dragged away in a scold's bridle for disturbing the peace, like they did in medieval times."

He said: "I meant someone who dislikes you enough to want you dead."

Where to start with a question like that? To be fair, the majority of those who might have made the list are no longer with us. So I laughed, slightly, and said: "Well, there's only my husband, who's fonder of my money than he is of me. But that's been the case with all the men I've known."

He looked at me and raised an eyebrow, which was a big emotional response by his usual standards. I didn't know if he thought I was joking about Gary or what. Because I didn't know either. But he took my hand and said: "Not all men are like that."

Interesting. He said it just as we were told it was safe to climb out. And I couldn't help noticing his firm grip as he helped me up, despite the finger shortage. Hmm. Possibilities. Maybe it's about time I unleashed my feminine charms on him. I do have some, you know. Although not when I'm covered in mud. We both were.

So I said to him: "Would you like to take a shower, Kevin?"

He raised his eyebrow again, and I wondered if he thought I was being too familiar. So I added: "Separately. Unless you're a water conservation campaigner like me."

Was there a flicker of interest? You don't think I was imagining it, do you? In any event, he declined and said he had to go back to the station for a debriefing. Silly man, he could have stayed with me, and I would have been happy to oblige. I even offered to give him a rub-down with a stiff brush, in lieu of a shower.

I said: "It'll save your wife the job of cleaning you up."

He said: "Thanks, but I don't have a wife."

Hmm. So I said: "No significant other, then?" Not that I would have been bothered unduly if there had been.

But he said: "Only a mute budgie called Elvis."

A budgie called Elvis who can't sing? *That's Heartbreak Hotel*, right there. It certainly got my sympathy. Poor thing: the budgie, that is, not Kevin.

Anyway, he and the rest of them eventually left without mentioning the Holyoak incident again. No doubt they've got their hands full with Smithson for the time being. Mind you, it took them a while to pull him out of the crater. I half expected them to leave him there and just fill it back in. It might have been for the best. And it would have saved on funeral costs, which are ridiculously high these days. Besides, I'm fed up with people digging holes in the garden, and the pond plan isn't so important now – not since I've switched my focus to the beavers. I'll just have to find somewhere else to stick Gary and Alexa. I know I can be a bit suspicious – well, a lot really – so it wouldn't take much to convince me they're behind both the shooting and the bombing. I talked to Flossie about it when she came home. She was a bit shaken by what happened. Understandably. It's not every day someone's killed in your back garden, even mine.

Flossie said she'll convene a special meeting of the forum to investigate the shooting and any link to the bombing. Not that I think they'll be any more successful than the police. But they could be quite useful if a suspect is identified. There you are, you see – that's me, thinking ahead. As per.

Talking of the forum, I don't think Jasmine's told Gary she's pregnant yet. I told her: "I'll deal with him, if you like."

But she said: "No, it's OK. Leave it to me."

In the meantime, Gary's still not come home and his mobile phone's switched off, so who knows where he's got to?

FORTY

Gary and Alexa were lying propped up on top of her double bed,
watching the evening news on the TV. Both were fully clothed.
It made a change. But not even his recently secured supply of
genuine Viagra pills was sufficient to encourage Gary to engage
in any hanky-panky. Not that Alexa was remotely interested in
such a prospect. Or anything closely resembling it.

"Pregnant," she said, once more, as if repeating the word
made the unexpected development easier to comprehend. "Not
content with cheating on Claudia – *and me* – you had to get
the poor girl pregnant."

"I hardly think she's going to remain poor if we give in to
her demands," said Gary sniffily.

"What do you mean 'we'? You're the one who's going to
have to pay the price for this... this..." Alexa struggled to
find the appropriate words. She tried again. "I hesitate to say
it, but 'cock-up' seems to be a thoroughly appropriate way of
describing it. And I still don't understand why you agreed for
us to meet with Jasmine in a car park. We could have all gone
for lunch somewhere discreet and discussed the situation in
civilised surroundings."

Gary sneered. "As if I want to spend any more money on that girl than is strictly necessary. Especially if she's eating for two. Even claiming the lunch as a tax-deductible expense sticks in the craw. Besides, she was the one who chose the location, not me."

"Yes, but come on, the car park at Newvale Common and Woods? It was all a bit cloak and dagger, wasn't it?"

"It was more discreet than Rossellini's, if that's what you're thinking. I don't entirely trust Fredo's flapping ears. Or his flapping tongue, come to that."

"Flapping?" said Alexa. "What about the couple in the other car that kept flashing its lights at us. What were they up to?"

"Yeah, well, I had no idea the Johnsons frequented the place in daylight hours. They're harmless enough so long as you don't flash them back. Or wind down your windows."

Alexa pulled a face. "Gross," she said. "Who wants to encounter that kind of activity on a nature walk?"

"Depends on your nature," said Gary, grinning at Alexa's discomfort. However, the smile quickly disappeared at the memory of Jasmine's demand: a financial support package for her and the baby, or she would reveal he was the father on social media. And not only that, but she would also provide evidence that Alcock & Bull had helped Bob Flint to hide some of his financial dealings from the taxman, as well as his estranged wife. The only saving grace was that Jasmine had no idea why he and Alexa were so anxious to avoid additional scrutiny of their dealings with Flint. For very obvious reasons.

"Anyway," he said, "you're equally to blame for this 'cock-up', as you call it. If you hadn't sent Jasmine the wrong email attachment, she would never have found out what was going on."

"I am fully aware of that fact, thank you very much. I clicked on the wrong file by mistake. Shit happens. But I didn't expect her to be devious enough to make a copy."

"Perhaps we could threaten to sue her for a breach of confidentiality?"

"Seriously? I think it's a bit late for that," said Alexa as she swung her legs off the bed and stood up. "I'm going to make myself a cup of tea and some cheese on toast. Do you want anything?"

Gary shook his head. "No thanks. I'm not hungry."

Alexa walked through to the kitchen-diner and set about making her snack. She wasn't that hungry either, but the break gave her a chance to think about the meeting with Jasmine and its consequences. She had seriously underestimated Jasmine, dismissing her as merely a pretty-looking airhead who had caught Gary's attention. She never imagined the girl would understand the significance of the file she had been sent in error, let alone keep a copy. Shit had, in fact, happened. Big time. The effect on her congeniality was not dissimilar to standing beneath one of River Vale's raw sewage overflows. Without an umbrella. She had already begun to pivot away from Gary, preparing for a new future, a brighter future, following his eventual demise. But now, Jasmine's intervention was putting those plans at risk. Jasmine wasn't just a threat to Gary but a threat to *her* as well. And that was intolerable.

With the cheese on toast grilled to her satisfaction, she went back into the bedroom, just as the national news programme gave way to the local bulletin. She shook her head at the sight of a reporter, who was chuntering away excitedly to camera. He was floodlit and standing with his back to a line of blue-and-white police tape, with Gary's house just about visible in the background.

"Great," said Alexa, putting down her plate and gesturing at the TV set. "And on top of everything else, they're now confirming that Claudia wasn't the person who was shot."

"Why am I not surprised?" said Gary, reaching over and taking a big bite out of Alexa's slice of toast. "You are developing the unhappy knack of hiring the world's worst assassins. At the rate you're going, Claudia will surpass the eight unsuccessful assassination attempts made on Queen Victoria."

"As if you did any better with your Brazilian bloody wandering spider!"

"That's beside the point," said Gary, doing his best to ignore the painful reminder. "I can't wait to hear Novak's excuse. How could he have mistaken a six-feet-tall, balding beanpole of an archaeologist for a five-feet-nothing, scary dumpling with purple hair? It's beyond me. And that was after I tipped him off that Claudia was expecting Smithson to visit her this lunchtime. As for paying him to kill a council employee, he can forget it. It wouldn't have been so bad if Smithson had been one of their parking enforcement officers."

"I'm sure there was a good reason for what happened. Let's just be careful what we say to him when he gets back in touch. We can't afford to have two aggrieved assassins on the loose. This isn't Dodge City."

Gary glared and took another large bite out of Alexa's cheese on toast before handing back the plate.

"Thanks for that," she said, with a look of disgust at the chewed remains. "But you might as well finish it off yourself now," she added and went back into the kitchen-diner to make some more. For herself. When she came back into the bedroom, Gary was sitting on the edge of the bed and putting his shoes back on.

"I'd better go," he said. "Claudia's left a couple of messages asking me where I've got to."

"What will you tell her?"

"I'll think of something. How about this: we couldn't be reached because we were helping to facilitate clandestine takeover talks involving Newvale Screw and Repetition?"

"The mind boggles," said Alexa.

"At least there's one thing: she won't be hosting that bunch of conspiracy theorists this evening. It's bad enough sharing the house with Dracula's daughter without the rest of town's nutters descending on us as well. I'm thinking of telling Catesby about them and suggesting they were responsible for the bombing and the shooting."

"What kind of conspiracies are they interested in?"

Gary shrugged. "I couldn't tell you. I asked Claudia but she just tapped the side of her nose and said, 'Wouldn't you like to know.' Well, I would, as it happens, but it's supposed to be some big secret, like her diaries, wherever she's hidden them."

"I suppose the fact that no one knows what they're up to is why they're conspiracy theorists."

"Good point," agreed Gary. "Mind you, I've also got to decide what I tell Claudia about Jasmine."

Alexa's eyes narrowed. "Tell her nothing for the moment. When Novak gets in touch about today's shit-show, I'll try and pressure him into taking care of Jasmine as well. Let's call it a compensatory offer."

Gary frowned. "Is that necessary?"

"She knows too much. Besides, blackmailers always come back for more."

"But she's pregnant," said Gary, his frown deepening.

"So?"

"With *my* baby."

"All the more reason," said Alexa, biting into her cheese on toast.

FORTY-ONE

Detective Sergeant Kevin Kenneth sighed deeply, knocked and entered the office of his superior, Chief Inspector Julian Catesby, who was sitting on his heels in front of his desk with a string of beads in his hands. His right eye was still covered, but the black patch had been replaced by a rainbow-patterned one.

"Very colourful, sir," said DS Kenneth, pointing at the replacement patch. "Was that your children's idea?"

Ch Insp Catesby frowned. "No. Why would you say a thing like that? It's a gift from Kate. A spiritual symbol of hope in stormy times."

"Ah. I thought it was a fun reference to that children's TV show *Rainbow*." He had been intending to ask which of the presenters Catesby was supposed to represent: Zippy, George or Bungle. He knew which one his money was on, but he decided diplomacy was the best course of action and stayed silent.

"My kids wouldn't know what you're talking about," said Catesby. "They stopped making *Rainbow* years ago. Do try and keep up with modern life, Kenham."

"I'll do my best," said DS Kenneth, before changing tack. "Is that a rosary you're holding?"

"If that's a roundabout way of asking if I've converted to Catholicism, then the answer's no. I can do without the guilt on top of everything else, thank you very much. For your information, it's called a mala. It's a meditation tool first used in India three thousand years ago for counting breaths. It was another gift from Kate following my initiation."

"Ah."

Catesby stood up and walked round to the other side of the desk. He took a deep breath and sat down in his faux-leather, executive office chair. As he did so, DS Kenneth noticed that on the corner of his desk sat a new photo of his two children; they were scowling. Disapprovingly. Alongside it was a larger photo of Kate; she was smiling. Knowingly. It only showed her head and shoulders, so it was impossible for him to tell if the snap had been taken au naturel at the Newvale Sun Valley Nudist Club or as she presided at one of the Church of Loving Togetherness services. There didn't appear to be any sign of a 'dog collar', but who knew what the custom and practice was at such an offshoot – not to mention offbeat – organisation.

"If it's not a rude question," said DS Kenneth, "how did the laying-on of hands go?"

Ch Insp Catesby smiled. Blissfully. "It was a blessed relief."

"I can just imagine," said DS Kenneth, although he was trying very hard not to. He allowed his boss a few moments of pleasurable reminiscence before bringing him back to the present and something altogether more mundane. "I tried to catch you yesterday, but they said you were at HQ."

"Yes, I was invited to attend the media relaunch of the refreshed Hate Crime and Hate Incident Awareness Policy – Designed for Living in a Multiculturally Diverse and Inclusive Society, together with the associated operational guidance. Unfortunately, the shooting took the gloss off it, but the event went ahead regardless. The chief constable has deemed it our number-one priority. Besides, the caterers had already made the sandwiches."

DS Kenneth went to scratch his nose with his missing finger before abandoning the attempt. "Purely for operational guidance purposes," he said, "can you tell me where other offences such as murder, rape, assault, robbery and burglary now stand in our list of priorities?"

Catesby's nostrils flared. "Do I detect a hint of criticism, Kenhard? Because the chief constable is very clear that we need to be more sensitive in our approach to policing, especially where victims are concerned."

"More sensitivity? Of course, sir. So, bearing that in mind, would now be a good time to discuss Wednesday's shooting?"

"Fire away," said Ch Insp Catesby, demonstrating that the new policy had yet to take root, "but are we sure it was definitely the gunshot that killed him?"

"Well, the rather large hole in the middle of his forehead suggested as much."

"But appearances can be deceptive," said Catesby, who was still fingering his mala. "He could have been a Buddhist. Some of them have a third eye, you know."

"Yes, sir, but this eye was somewhat sightless by the time the paramedics removed Mr Smithson from the scene."

"I see," said the chief inspector, who paused to count a few more breaths while giving the matter some thought. Having duly thought and counted, he turned his attention to the possible culprit and asked if the team was close to making an arrest yet.

"No, sir," said DS Kenneth. "Whoever the sniper was got clean away before we could cordon off the area. At the moment we're focused on establishing who the intended victim was. We don't think it was Mr Smithson because there was a second shot fired *after* he fell into the pit. So, taking into account the previous bomb explosion next door, we believe Claudia Alcock was the target."

"Or you."

"Why me?"

"Why not?" said Catesby, the eyelid of his good eye trembling. "Some people can be intensely irritating without even trying."

DS Kenneth ignored the intended slight and returned to his theory that Claudia was the target. He said he had wondered at one point if Holyoak could have been the sniper, in an act of revenge for the earlier altercation between them.

"Altercation?" said Catesby. "I'd hardly call it an altercation. From what I've been told, that woman committed a heinous hate crime against the poor man. And it's not the first time she's been reported to us for a hate crime, is it? When this is all sorted, we need to throw the book at her, before I have the chief constable shouting abuse down the phone at me. In the meantime, I fancy the perpetrator will turn out to be that philandering murderer Flint."

"I'm not sure about that," said DS Kenneth. He pointed out there had been no reports that Flint had been seen in the area and no evidence that he could shoot, or even owned, a gun. And if it was Flint, why didn't the explosives expert simply climb over the fence separating the woods from the Alcocks' garden and plant another bomb? "Besides, our firearms people tell me that it would have taken a trained marksman to hit the target from that range."

"Well, if it's not Flint, God rot his soul, then there is another possibility we ought to consider. I saw Gary Alcock at the Lodge last night, and he thinks that conspiracy mob – the one led by the ghastly goth girl – are involved. As you know, I think the man's a conniving, oily turd, but he's probably onto something there. And I'm inclined to agree with him that the terrorist cell could be responsible."

Really? DS Kenneth wished he could borrow Catesby's mala so he could count to ten – or at least nine and a half – before responding. When he did, it was to point out that it made no sense for the group to kill Claudia when she was also a member. "Why would they do that?" he asked.

"Because that's what anarchists do: they cause anarchy, killing and maiming indiscriminately. And as for Mrs Alcock, I can't say I'm particularly moved by her plight."

"Even though she's a potential victim?"

"Balderdash! Not only does the woman have a dubious past, but she's still committing hate crimes. A leopard doesn't change its spots."

"Maybe. Though when I called on her the other day, she'd changed her appearance significantly; I almost didn't recognise her. She told me she's been taking part in a programme of self-improvement. And if I'm allowed to say it these days, she looks a lot better for it."

"Good God, Kenhole!" snapped Ch Insp Catesby, gripping his mala beads. "You almost sound as if you approve of her."

"I wouldn't go that far, but there's no denying she scrubs up well. And very intelligent with it."

"And doubtless as mad as a March hare."

"We're all a bit mad, though, aren't we?"

"Speak for yourself, man. And if you take my advice, you'll gird your loins."

DS Kenneth wasn't too sure what Catesby meant by his advice, but he took it as a warning to keep Claudia at arm's length. Or, failing that, well away from any other body part. "I'll bear that in mind when I go round to see her again," he said. "She told me on the phone she's got something she wants to show me. From the hint she dropped, I'm hoping it's proof of a possible link between Alexa Bull and Flint. I've already been to see Ms Bull and thought she was being evasive when I asked her about her firm's business dealings with Flint Demolitions."

"She didn't drop any more hints about Flint, did she?"

"Now that you ask, I also have a suspicion she knows something about Flint and Jennifer's whereabouts."

"Jennifer? Jennifer who?" growled Ch Insp Catesby as he tightened his grip on the mala, and a shower of beads cascaded across his desk and rolled onto the carpet.

FORTY-TWO

I've been looking online to see if there are any courses that teach people how to lie convincingly, Ophelia. But apparently not. There's plenty of other self-improvement stuff, but nothing on how to become a better liar. Shame. Because Gary could certainly do with some help. And I'm not even talking about signing him up for a master's degree in bullshitting, just basic competence. Has he learnt nothing, living with me?

I don't know where he got the idea from to explain his mysterious disappearance. Confidential takeover talks involving Newvale Screw and Repetition? Was that a Freudian joke at mine and Jasmine's expense? I could tell he was lying by the way his Adam's apple was bobbing up and down, like Candy when she ended up in the River Vale. I have to say that girl was remarkably buoyant, considering what was tied around her ankles. And then there was the bottle of gin he brought home to cheer me up, after hearing about the shooting on Radio Newvale. He said it was mentioned on the Drivetime with Dougie Dewis Show. As if I don't know his car radio is permanently tuned to Heat Radio: home of the non-stop bangers. Apparently. That's another Freudian joke, right there.

Even Flossie could tell he was lying. She said to me afterwards: "Did you see the way his vein was throbbing?"

I said: "You want to be grateful you weren't here the night he overdosed on those pills."

She said: "I was referring to the vein in his temple."

"I know," I said, "but you still want to be grateful."

Where was he in my hour of need? Not to mention the hours afterwards. Kevin was here to hold my hand, so where was Gary? Not that I was distressed enough to *need* my hand being held – a couple of Valium and a large G&T would have done the job if I'd needed calming down – but the feeling of flesh pressed against flesh didn't go amiss.

Am I making sense?

Actually, I know where he was because Flossie brought Jasmine round yesterday and she told me all about their meeting. She also mentioned the couple in the other car who kept flashing their lights and gesticulating. She didn't need to describe them – most people round here are familiar with the Johnsons' modus operandi. And you have to give them credit, especially Mr Johnson, because it takes balls to brave those shrivelling winter temperatures in pursuit of your hobby. More to the point, if the Johnsons were doggedly pursuing Gary, Alexa and Jasmine in the car park, they couldn't have been taking potshots at yours truly. Which was a relief because no one wants to be on the receiving end of one of Johnson's potshots at any time of the year. Plus, it narrowed down the list of suspects.

As for Jasmine, I'm not happy that she cheated on me; I think I've made that clear before. But at least she's confessed. And I *can* be compassionate when the mood takes me: remember Birgitte? In a strange way, I'm starting to feel maternal towards her baby, probably because Jasmine reckons it was conceived upstairs in my bed. My bed! Of all places! That's as close as I'm ever going to get to the act of conception. OK, so it took me a while to get over the yukky feeling: all those unknown fluids I'd inadvertently slept in. Thank God I always wear pyjamas. And if I'd known at the time what they'd been up to in there I'd have boiled the sheets, at the very least. Or incinerated them. And when I say incinerated *them*, I mean Gary and Jasmine, as well as the sheets. Obviously.

After our heart-to-heart, I said to Jasmine: "When's the baby due?"

And she said: "Around Easter."

"Oh good," I said, "that'll give me something else to look forward to, along with another showing of *Ben-Hur* on the telly."

They always show that film at Easter, don't they? I can remember when my dad took me to see it at the ABC Empire in town when I was a kid. I was so excited when that lying cheat Messala got trampled to death in the chariot race that I stood up and cheered.

My dad said to me afterwards: "I'm not taking you to the pictures again if you're going to behave like that."

I pulled a face and said: "What? Just because I cheered?"

And he said: "No. It's because you got *so* excited you wet yourself. And me. And the poor woman sitting in front."

I think it was because I was jumping up and down at the same time. Which didn't help. And anyway, who knew that projectile urination was a 'thing'? Well, it is with me.

I told Jasmine that even if Gary is his usual bastard self and disowns her, I'll help. It's one thing punishing Jasmine, but it's not the baby's fault, is it? And guess what: in return, Jasmine told me all about a file that Alexa emailed to her by mistake, which shows she covered up Bob Flint's financial shenanigans. Fancy that. Evidence that Alexa and the mad bomber are in cahoots. I've a good mind to tell Kevin about it. Or at least tease him, so he keeps coming back for more. I'm not daft enough to give him everything he wants on a first date, am I? I've been there before. And come to think about it, I'm not going to tell Rosencrantz that an act of kindness paid off, either. He'll only feel vindicated and increase his fees. And I haven't forgotten my anger at his rejection. Vindication is not at all what he deserves.

FORTY-THREE

Shoes off, Alexa was curled up on the sofa in her apartment. Her legs were tucked beneath her, and her cheeks were suffused with a Prosecco glow, fuelled by the glass of fizz in her hand. Since arriving home from work she had changed out of her business suit and was now wearing a baggy jumper and joggers.

Shoes on, Gary was perched on the edge of the sofa. His legs were tightly crossed, foot jiggling, and his glass sat untouched on the coffee table. He had not changed since leaving work, although he had gone so far as to remove his Armani jacket, which now lay crumpled over the arm of the sofa.

Alexa was demonstrably relaxed. Gary not so much.

He stood up and walked over to the living room window, easing back the curtain to peer cautiously around its edge at the night-time scene beyond. Not that it was especially dark outside the apartment block as the bright new LED street lights provided more than adequate illumination. But although the lights revealed nothing untoward, Gary's eyes continued to sweep up and down the street for a couple more minutes before he resumed his perch.

Alexa sighed and emptied most of her glass in a single swallow. "Any sign of it yet?" she asked.

Gary half turned to look at her. "Sign of what?" he said, the irritation in his voice obvious.

"Halley's bloody Comet or whatever else it is you're hoping to see out there. A meteor shower perhaps. But if you're hoping to catch a glimpse of Santa on his sleigh, you're a week early."

Gary glared as Alexa continued: "That must be the third time you've looked out of that window in the past fifteen minutes. And you hardly touched your takeaway."

"They're out there," he said. "I know it."

"Who is?"

"Someone."

"Someone?"

Gary nodded. "I think someone's following me."

"You need to get a grip."

Not a bad idea, thought Gary, eyeing Alexa's throat with more than passing interest. It wasn't fair. There she was, lounging about like Lady Muck, while he was the one taking all the risks and suffering mental torment as a consequence. Where was the sympathy, let alone the empathy? He was the one who was married to a homicidal maniac with unpredictable mood swings, an unstable psycho who was now threatening to divorce him or worse, with neither outcome being favourable to his lifestyle or longevity. Worse, he was now coming under suspicion following the two botched assassination attempts. On top of which, Alexa was blithely suggesting they should murder Jasmine's unborn child: his child. And to cap it all, someone was following him. Probably. Possibly.

"Have you seen this someone?" said Alexa, looking around for where she had put the bottle.

"No, but I had the strangest feeling on the way over here."

"And not for the first time."

"Excuse me?"

"It's called lust. It's a common occurrence with you."

"I can assure you it wasn't that, you bobble head."

Alexa frowned. Bobble head? She'd never been called one of those before. It sounded vaguely rude, but she let it pass. For the time being. "So, describe this strange feeling then," she said.

"As I said, it's as if I'm being followed by someone. Maybe it's Flint."

"I doubt it. He's been in touch again after reading about the shooting in the *Mirror*, so it doesn't sound as if he's in the area. He wanted to know what's going on, so I told him it had got nothing to do with us. I said there was more to it than the papers have printed and that Claudia was behind it. It's an example of just how dangerous she is."

"Did he buy it?" asked Gary anxiously. "The explanation, I mean, not the *Mirror*. Why would any self-respecting business owner buy *that*?"

Alexa rolled her eyes. "I think so," she said. "Why wouldn't he? I can be very persuasive when I want to be. In fact, I've been trying to think of what we can do to lure him back to Newvale, so Karol can deal with him."

If Gary felt any easier as a result of Alexa's plan, the effect was cancelled out by her use of Novak's first name. It jarred with him. It sounded unduly familiar and failed to reflect the professional relationship that ought to exist between employer and hired hand. Or, in this case, hired gun. But the principle was the same. According to Gary's way of thinking, it was all about maintaining standards. Maybe that was why the assassination attempts kept failing. Maybe Alexa was not being professional enough in her dealings with these people.

"Perhaps I should take over discussions with Novak," he suggested.

Alexa tensed. The muscles in her jaw visibly tightened, the ones controlling her sphincter less noticeably. She sat up. "I don't think so," she said, with forceful determination. "You'll only antagonise him and then we'll have two loose cannons rolling around the deck."

"Well, they're not exactly tied down at the moment, are they?" said Gary. "Who's running this ship? Captain Pugwash?"

For a moment Gary thought Alexa was going to hit him. And for a moment Alexa thought of doing exactly that. "Better Captain Pugwash than Seaman Stains," she said angrily, gesturing at Gary with her now-empty glass. "Just for that you can get me a refill. I think I need it."

Gary thought better of making any further derogatory remark about Alexa's organisational abilities. He stood up, took her proffered glass with a grunt and went into the kitchen-diner in search of the bottle of Prosecco. After refilling her glass, he returned to the living room and handed it back to Alexa, before taking another sneak look out of the window.

"Anything?" said Alexa, a little happier now she had a full glass in her hand.

"No," said Gary as he retook his place on the sofa. He fidgeted in his seat and sighed. "Although there was one other thing, now you come to mention it."

Alexa arched an eyebrow. "Well, spit it out. There's obviously something else that's bothering you, in addition to being stalked by the invisible man."

"I'm not happy about getting Novak to eliminate Jasmine."

"Why?"

"Actually, it's not Jasmine – I couldn't care less what happens to that deceitful, blackmailing strumpet. It's her baby – *my* baby – that's bothering me."

"Oh Jeez! Don't tell me you're developing a conscience. It's a bit late in the day for that, isn't it? So what's the difference between taking care of Claudia, Jasmine and Flint – not to mention the collateral damage to the Robinsons and the archaeologist guy – and her unborn sprog?"

"Isn't that obvious?" said Gary in a high-pitched whine. "Because it's mine!"

"So she says."

"What do you mean by that?"

"Well, if she was quite happy to 'do the dirty' with a married man, who was already having an affair with another woman, then she can't have been too discriminating, can she? If I were you, I'd demand a paternity test before you start getting too lovey-dovey over it. And besides, it wasn't as if you were firing on all cylinders back then, was it?"

Gary's brow furrowed. "Are you questioning the potency of my life-giving essence?"

"Your what?" Alexa laughed. And not in a complimentary way. "It wasn't the potency I was questioning but the mechanics of its delivery. Which left a lot to be desired, as I recall."

Gary fell silent while he pondered Alexa's suggestion. His ego was such it had never occurred to him that Jasmine might have cheated on him. Who did that girl think she was? Didn't they teach morals in school anymore? "Look," he said, having duly pondered, "what if you hold fire on saying anything to Novak about Jasmine until we can sort out a test? Once we know the result, we can take it from there." And then he pondered again. "Please?" he added. It stuck in his craw to plead, but needs must when the devil drives. And Alexa had more than a little of the devil about her.

Alexa smiled inwardly. Outwardly, her expression remained non-committal. "Yeah, whatever," she said. She untucked her legs and swung them off the sofa. "I'm just going to get another refill," she added, as she padded off to the kitchen-diner.

As Gary sat waiting for her return, he tried to convince himself that Alexa would do as he had asked. Or, rather, as he had pleaded. But he had a niggly-naggly feeling she might not. However, it also occurred to him that Alexa was the one who had been in contact with both Flint and Novak throughout. As far as he was aware, there was no solid evidence linking him to either man. Which meant if he had to, he could throw Alexa to the wolves – or at the very least to Catesby and his three-fingered bag-man – and claim plausible deniability. He smiled.

In the kitchen Alexa was also pondering. The email she had received from her sister in Greece had been very concerning. A tax ruling had gone against the family, worsening their financial situation considerably. The growing debt meant there was a pressing need for her to find more money to cover her share of the misfortune. Added to which, there were suggestions that the police were going to reopen investigations into her granddad's death. No wonder she needed a drink.

When she walked back into the living room, she noticed Gary was smiling. It struck her as the smug, self-satisfied smile of a schoolboy who's just bullied a smaller boy into handing over his pocket money. But she didn't mind. She didn't mind at all. It suggested he had accepted her easy lie about Jasmine. He was so obvious. And so easy to manipulate. The thing was, she couldn't allow Jasmine's child to live. Not now, not now there was a risk that Gary might alter his will in its favour rather than hers. That wasn't fair. Who needed the money most? Her or Jasmine's little bastard?

Mind you, there was an alternative strategy.

She snuggled up close to Gary on the sofa and gave his arm a squeeze. "I'm sorry I was so nasty to you about the baby," she said as she gazed up at him, fluttering her eyelids submissively. "Of course we should wait until after a test has been done before we decide on anything. And if it turns out to be yours, then I'm sure I'll get used to the idea."

"Thank you," said Gary, broadening his smile. "I knew I could trust you to do the right thing."

Alexa put her hand on the inside of Gary's knee and allowed her fingers to trace their way teasingly up the inside of his thigh and all the way to his crotch. When they reached their destination, she felt Gary twitch. "You know," she said, squeezing gently, "I've just checked in the bathroom cabinet and there's a couple of your tablets left. If you're feeling up to it, I'll put on your favourite lingerie set for you. What do you say?" She squeezed again, more firmly this time, rendering him temporarily speechless. But Alexa didn't need to wait for verbal confirmation: his body was already telling her what she wanted to know.

She relaxed her grip and stood up. "Give me five minutes to get ready," she said with a mischievous grin and sashayed into the bedroom. She closed the door and began to prepare for the task she had set herself. She went to one of the chests of drawers and took out the outfit she knew always aroused his interest and laid it on the bed. The black fishnet body stocking, complete with integral suspenders, had not been purchased by her. It had been a gift from Gary for *her* birthday. Naturally. Why would he think she might prefer jewellery or perfume? Or even a food blender? From a practical point of view, it was a nightmare to get into, or out of, without the risk of dislocating something. And aesthetically, she thought it made her look like something a Grimsby trawler had just landed on the quayside. But still.

She walked over to her dressing table and took out her ovulation calendar to double-check it. She smiled. If she could also present Gary with a child, would that swing the pendulum back in her favour? Or would she still need to deal with Jasmine anyway, just to be on the safe side?

Tomorrow she would also get back in touch with Flint and try to engineer a truce with him. She needed to pick his brains on how he was able to change his ID in today's all-seeing, all-knowing, all-connected world. She needed a fallback plan. Because every self-respecting planner needs one of those.

FORTY-FOUR

Anyway, Ophelia, I know you've been dying to hear what happened when the group came round for a meeting last night, so let me put you out of your misery, as I think we can probably agree that inflicting misery is something I'm very good at. To begin with, there was a real surprise when Timea Novak turned up. I thought for a moment she'd come to service Gary and had got the wrong day. But Flossie intervened and explained that Timea has just joined the group. I wasn't expecting that, and I'm usually prepared for most things.

Naturally, being me, I was a bit suspicious to begin with and wondered if Gary had sent her to spy on us. But Flossie was happy to vouch for her – more than happy – which made me wonder if there's something going on between them. Who knows? Sometimes it's difficult to tell between a meaningful wink and a piece of grit in the eye. But it's not my place to ask. And I couldn't care less, I honestly couldn't, not now Flossie's doing all the laundry. It might explain, though, why Gary's evidently failed to bend Timea to his will.

In any event, Timea was keen to tell me she was upset by the spider incident and felt guilty I might have come to harm. As you know, she had nothing to feel guilty about, but I wasn't going to tell her that. Not when inspiring feelings of guilt in other people has always been one of my chief pleasures in life. And so rewarding. Clearly, though, the spider thing is playing on her mind, because she's chosen Incy Wincy as her forum name. Each to their own; I'm more than happy with The Black Widow. It suits me, don't you think? To be honest, I've never been remotely wincey. And I've never had the slightest inclination to climb up anyone's spout, thank you very much.

She also told me Mrs Pinchess saw Bomber Bob and Jennifer slumming it in a camper van near Bakewell. What's all that about? What's to see and do in Bakewell in the winter? Apart from the local tarts. And you can see them any time of the year. I thought the pair of them were supposed to be on the run? Sounds more like a Sunday outing if they've chosen a camper van as their getaway vehicle. Still, nine out of ten for originality, if nothing else.

Mind you, I was pretty sure this bit of hot gossip would be of interest to Kevin, so I gave him a call this morning and tempted him with it. I said I'd got something juicy for him, if he'd like to call round. He sounded very interested. Very perky. A woman knows these things, doesn't she? But, as I said before, I won't decide how much to give him until he's round here with his finger poised expectantly on my buzzer. Or what's left of it. The finger, that is, not the buzzer. My buzzer's in perfect working order, thank you very much.

Flossie also introduced three of the forum members I've not met before. First off there was Brenda The Crystal Gazer, who got a black look from me for failing to forecast the assassination attempt.

I said to her: "How come you didn't see the shooting in your crystal ball?"

"I looked," she said, "but the vision was too cloudy."

So I told her: "You should have said sooner. Flossie's a dab hand with a duster and a can of Pledge."

She tried to give me a lecture on divination and what the different coloured clouds mean, but really? In future, I'll stick with Russell Grant. How's that for a forecast? She then asked me if I'm concerned the house may be haunted by Smithson's unhappy spirit 'and those of others' trying to work through their trauma. Those of others? I pretended ignorance. And I wasn't going to tell her this, but it's my head that's demonically possessed, not the house.

Then there was Derek The Dungeon Master, who managed to drag himself away from battling a flock of blood-sucking stirges – nope, your guess is as good as mine – to join us in finding out who shot Smithson and, more importantly, singed my hair, which I can't get replumed until next week, by the way. Bugger! I've thought about doing it myself, but the last time I tried dyeing my own hair I ended up with more orange streaks than a clownfish. It wasn't funny. I had to pretend I'd done it on purpose to raise money for charity. Anyway, I can't say I was that impressed by Derek. He looked more like the Fat Controller in *Thomas the Tank Engine* than someone aspiring to world domination. That's if the Fat Controller's still called that these days. Possibly not. In which case, who's next for the prick of twenty-first-century conscience? Pussy Galore?

And the other one I'd not met before was Colin, aka Mr Kool. I tried not to laugh. If you're in your sixties with a bald head, stooped posture and bad teeth, then calling yourself Mr Kool is a bit of a stretch. I was trying to picture him strutting his stuff on a disco dance floor, when Flossie cut in.

"Mr Kool is the name on his ice-cream van," she explained.

"Ha!" I said, looking at him. "I was about to ask you what you'd done with your medallion."

"It's parked on your driveway," he said, gurning at me.

Huh? I cornered Flossie in the kitchen later and said that Mr Kool seems to be a few sprinkles short of a Fab ice lolly. But she said he has a problem keeping up with conversations.

"It's because his batteries keep going flat," she said.

"Batteries?" I asked.

Flossie shrugged. "In his hearing aids. He insists on buying 'genuine' batteries off e-Bay, which don't last five minutes."

"Well," I said, "there's your problem right there. It's obviously not his hearing aids that are underpowered but what's between them."

Even before we got around to discussing the shooting, the others wanted to express their outrage at me being charged with assaulting Holyoak. Which was OK by me. I like a bit of outrage. They said that if I have to go to court they'll parade outside with placards. And why not? Meera – who's got a permanent scowl, as if she's just spent the last hour trying to get the bloody top off a childproof bottle of Milk of Magnesia (mea culpa) – had a few pithy suggestions for the wording. Her favourite was: 'Holyoak's a lying shit', accompanied by a drawing of a steaming turd and a noose. I wasn't sure if she was suggesting Holyoak should be hanged or the turd. Or both. But although the clarity left a bit to be desired, I admired the sentiment and the underlying passion. As I said to her later, though, sometimes it's best to keep these angry thoughts of injustice to yourself and just let them quietly fester away. That way, you can lull your enemies into a false sense of security. And then, before they know it – wham! – they're swinging from the proverbial gibbet, along with the turd. Albeit, it might have run out of steam by then.

The group also said they'll advertise the protest on social media to drum up support from the sisterhood, as well as the gaggle of virtue-signalling men who tend to turn up to these things. They want to portray me as the victim of male violence, which is fine, because it's absolutely true. But if they're going to use a photo of me, I told them to make sure I don't look *too* much like a victim. It's not a good look. Not at my age. At least let me put on some lippy first. And maybe a hint of blusher. And airbrush the wrinkles. A bit. Basically, I don't want it to end up looking like a Wild West wanted poster for Sitting Cow. Oh, and based on her placard ideas, it's probably best not to let Meera produce a TikTok video.

I'm nothing if not a mentor to these people.

My devotees were equally keen to help track down the shooter. Bless them. We discussed if it was the same person who splattered the Robinsons all over the neighbourhood, i.e. Bomber Bob. But we all thought it was unlikely. According to Timea's intel, he was last seen eloping with Jennifer Catesby in a glorified Transit van along Derby's inner ring road. As romantic gestures go, a trip around the A601 is hardly a visit to Paris in the springtime or likely to rival a sleigh ride through Salzburg's winter snowscape. But love is blind. Or so they say. And I can testify to that, more's the pity.

Derek suggested there could be an evil mastermind behind both attacks, but I wasn't paying full attention, seeing as it was Derek who was droning on and I was trying to open a packet of crisps at the time. So, for a moment, I thought he was referring to me. Don't get me wrong, I quite warmed to the idea of being an evil mastermind, but why would I plan my own assassination? That's not my kind of madness. It really isn't. Fortunately for Derek, I realised he must have been referring to someone else, even if the idea of Newvale nurturing *two* evil masterminds is a bit mind-blowing.

Obviously, Holyoak came under suspicion. And why not? He clearly bears a grudge. The fact he was interviewed by Radio Newvale immediately after the shooting means he was in the vicinity. And I've seen enough true crime documentaries to know that killers often return to the scene of the crime like cheating men who crawl back home after they've been dumped by their hot new girlfriends. Or does that just happen to me? Not that I'm bitter and twisted. Much.

Talking of which, the elephant in the room – other than Jasmine's bump – was my own nearest, but hardly dearest, Gary. We know he couldn't have been the shooter because he was with Jasmine. And anyway, I'm sure the Johnsons would stick up for him if they had to. Well, Mr Johnson would. He's very good at that sort of thing. But is Gary capable of being an evil mastermind? Despite the cheating, the nagging to change my will and the strange business with the spider, I wasn't entirely convinced. And the rest of the jury was still out, too.

"Would he qualify as a Mr Big?" queried Colin, who was now on message following a change of batteries.

"Not from my recollection," said Jasmine scornfully.

"More like Mr Big Mouth," added Flossie, who hasn't got over being called Wednesday, after the girl in *The Addams Family*.

"Agreed," I said. "On both counts."

As for Alexa, she's definitely been up to no good with Bomber Bob. So that made her a candidate as well.

There was then a bit of head-scratching, and Hattie eventually stopped preening her facial hair long enough to suggest putting a tail on each of the main suspects.

"Good idea," I said. "How about pinning a cheetah's tail on Alexa, a rat's tail on Gary and a lying hound's on Holyoak?"

Hattie looked puzzled. "Are you taking this seriously?" she asked.

"Absolutely," I said, doing my best to ignore her twitching whiskers. "You'll just have to excuse the way my mind works." Because, to be fair to me, I'm the only person I know whose mind has a mind of its own.

Am I making sense?

But before she could say anything else, Derek stuck his oar in. "How about I draw up a time-critical rota and action plan to ensure twenty-four seven coverage of the major persons of interest," he said.

"How about you don't," said Meera, who broke off from cleaning out her fingernails with a zombie knife to stare at him.

I wasn't happy. "Put it away. If you're not careful you'll have someone's eye out with that thing," I said, sounding eerily like my mother.

"I know," she said and smirked at Derek.

He deserved it. No question about it. But Meera was also getting nail scrapings in the shag pile carpet, and gunk like that is an absolute horror to get out. Flossie was curling her lip in a most unsavoury manner.

After that little hiatus, things settled down, and we settled on a rota of sorts. Which we achieved without Derek's input. He got the arse and said he was busy all day in his dad's electronics shop. So I said that's all right, he can keep an eye on Holyoak in the evenings instead. It turns out Scooter Man works in a cheese shop in Leicester, which explains the unusually ripe odour he was giving off when we had our little contretemps. I did wonder. But it also means he doesn't get back to Newvale until after 6pm, unless it's his day off, which should be ideal for Derek. Yet he still thought about objecting, until Meera gave him another one of her withering death stares, which saved me the bother. She's got promise, that girl.

Even so, I did wonder if our resident mouse would be more adept at tracking the suspiciously cheesy Holyoak, until Hattie said she doesn't like going out after dark if she can help it.

"Too many strange men about," she said.

"Then why advertise yourself on Tinder?" I said. Not that she's ever had any takers as far as I can tell.

"That's different," she said.

"Ha!" I said. "Men are men, whether they're hiding behind a bush, a fake profile or a false promise. Just ask her," I added, pointing at Jasmine, whose bulge was sprawled over most of the two-seater sofa.

"She's right," said Jasmine.

Praise indeed. But so richly deserved.

So instead of Holyoak, Hattie volunteered to keep watch on Gary during daylight hours, just in case he leaves the office for any nefarious purpose. Which is quite possible. She said she didn't mind because college has broken up for the Christmas holiday, and she hasn't got any other plans. I'm not surprised: she's not got a lot going for her if she can't even get a hook-up on Tinder. Poor girl. On the plus side, even if Gary spots her, I can guarantee he won't give her a second look – providing she doesn't wear that silly Rudolph the Reindeer hat she's made. You have to wonder about some of the things they teach people in college these days. I know it's a millinery course, but there's hats and there's hats.

In contrast to Hattie, Meera had no reservations about going out at night. Mind you, with a zombie knife for company, I wouldn't want to be one of Hattie's strange men. Bush or no bush. Besides, she admitted she'd already followed Gary a couple of times, just to practise her surveillance technique. So we agreed she might as well carry on the good work. As I say, she's a girl with real promise.

As for Alexa, Colin offered to keep watch during the day. He's another one with time on his hands, seeing as there's not much call for Mr Kool's services in the winter. That's OK so long as he parks his van out of sight. We don't want some random child attempting to buy a top-of-the-range double Flake 99 with syrup *and* sprinkles when Colin is about to set off in hot pursuit. Which reminds me, I must ask him how fast his van can actually go. It doesn't look as if it's built for speed, which is a bit of a disadvantage when Alexa drives an Audi TT.

Timea said she'll take over from Colin in the evenings. Which I thought was odd, considering she and Alexa spend all day together at work. But she obviously has her reasons, even though she wasn't telling us what they are. And Hattie was also unsure about the arrangement.

"She might recognise you," she said.

Timea shook her head. "Not with the disguise I'll be wearing."

I didn't like to ask. I just hope she doesn't ask to borrow Hattie's moustache.

We decided Jasmine was too obviously pregnant to waddle around incognito. Especially as any sudden movement is likely to turn the waddle into a widdle, judging from her frequent trips to the loo. God help us all if we're within flooding distance when her waters break.

And as far as Flossie's concerned, she's also too visibly noticeable to take part. Admittedly, she could be hard to spot on a moonless night, providing there's also a power cut, but what are the chances? Besides, she's at work during the day and is busy forward-planning the beaver rewilding project in the evenings.

"And don't forget you also have to fit in the cleaning," I said.

"Perfect," she said and actually smiled. Odd girl. But a godsend.

That only left Brenda, who had spent most of the evening studying her scrapbook of newspaper cuttings about local crimes.

"Whenever I look at his photo I get a strange feeling," she said, pointing at a picture of Ch Insp Catesby.

"Really?" I said, failing to see the attraction. "You haven't been at the mushrooms in my garden, have you?"

She shook her head. "No, but my crystal's vibrating like crazy," she said and pulled out an uninspiring lump of rock from the pocket of her cardi to show me.

It didn't appear as if it was vibrating to me, or even slightly throbbing. But then I've never claimed to have second sight, just an odd way of looking at things. In any event, Brenda asked if she could focus her powers on tuning into Catesby's psychic energy. Put like that, who were we to meddle with things we didn't understand?

Did I say that only left Brenda? That was apart from me, of course.

"In the meantime, I'll concentrate on Det Sgt Kevin Kenneth," I said, "because he's the one who's really giving me the shivers."

FORTY-FIVE

Detective Sergeant Kevin Kenneth sighed deeply, knocked and entered the office of his superior, Chief Inspector Julian Catesby, who was engrossed in arranging a hand-knitted nativity scene on the corner of his desk. It was difficult to detect what Catesby was muttering, although DS Kenneth thought he heard his boss say: "Stand up properly, you little sod!"

Unsure if his boss was referring to him or the woolly object in his hand that might – or might not – have been a sheep, DS Kenneth sought clarification. "Is there a problem, sir?"

"Problem, Kenick?" said Ch Insp Catesby. "There wouldn't be if some of these blessed figures didn't keep falling over."

"Perhaps you should take them back and get a refund."

"You don't think I bought them, do you? Kate knitted them."

"Ah," said DS Kenneth as he stepped forwards to take a closer look. In addition to what were obviously Mary, Joseph and baby Jesus, there were also two sheep and two shepherds, three ornate kings from Orient afar, with gifts, and an angel. There were also a further two animals, whose identity the detective sergeant was having trouble determining. "What's this?" he said, pointing to what appeared to be a pig with long, sticky-up ears.

"Are you blind?" said Catesby. "It's quite clearly a donkey."

"I see. So not to scale then? In which case, I'm guessing this animal isn't some kind of terrier with curvature of the spine?" said DS Kenneth, using his stump to indicate the other mystery creature.

"Of course not. It's a camel! Are you trying to be deliberately offensive?"

"Not at all," said DS Kenneth, trying to recover lost ground. "I'm just surprised Kate had the time to make the set, alongside her ministerial duties at the church and keeping house for you."

"I know, she's an absolute angel," said Ch Insp Catesby, who hurriedly added: "Figuratively speaking."

"Your children must be very grateful to have their aunt looking after them."

Catesby grimaced and looked away, quickly resuming his attempted arrangement of the figures. "Oh Jesus," he groaned as the baby fell out of its crib.

"Here, let me," said DS Kenneth. He wasn't sure if it was the wobbly figures, the chief inspector's eyepatch or a combination of both that was causing Catesby such difficulties. But despite his own lack of dexterity, he righted the crib before putting the baby back in it.

"Thank you, Kenicott," said the chief inspector, grudgingly, as he took his mobile phone out of his pocket and placed it on the desk in front of him.

"No problem. I can't help but notice you're back to wearing the black eyepatch."

Catesby pulled a face. "The chief constable told me the rainbow patch was 'girly'."

DS Kenneth raised an eyebrow. "If you don't mind me

saying so, sir, that was a very misogynistic thing to say. Doesn't it breach his own policy on such matters?"

"The man's a law unto himself. Kate wasn't very happy when I told her. She said I should have lodged a complaint with HR on the grounds of sex and religious discrimination."

"Hmm, the patch is hardly a turban, though, is it?"

"What do you mean by that?"

"Well, the point I'm making is that Sikhism is a recognised religion, practised by up to thirty million people worldwide, while there are nearly two billion Muslims, many of whom also wear a turban. Whereas the Church of Loving Togetherness…" DS Kenneth's voice tailed off.

"Come on, out with it, man!" said Ch Insp Catesby. "You might as well finish what you were going to say."

"Only that there's probably only a dozen of you, as far as I can tell. So you're going to struggle for recognition. Unlike one of the world's major religions." He didn't say it, but DS Kenneth thought that even the followers of Odin or a bunch of voodoo dancers from New Orleans stood more chance of recognition.

Catesby, though, was not cowed or dismayed. With a noticeable gleam in his good eye, he scrutinised his underling, before issuing an invitation to one of their services. "Such ignorance, Keningham. You should come to our Christmas Ritual on Christmas Eve," he said, his tone making it seem more like an order than an invitation.

While DS Kenneth pondered if it really was an instruction, Catesby continued: "When was the last time you nurtured yourself, Kenicuck? I'll bet it's been a while, but fear not: Kate will be there to take you in hand and act as your guide. And before the ritual begins, we'll even spend a few minutes doing some breathing exercises. Alternative nostril pranayama is excellent for settling and preparing the mind to go within."

"You make it sound very… uplifting," said DS Kenneth. He wasn't sure 'uplifting' was the right word, but he was struggling to think of an alternative. "But will everyone be naked?"

Catesby shrugged. "I imagine we'll all be robed, if that puts your mind at rest. The old scout hut can be pretty nippy in the winter. It's got an old oil-fuelled boiler, which is a bit temperamental I'm afraid. And it's also run out of oil, although we've been promised a delivery in time for next Thursday." The chief inspector's shrug turned to a smile of encouragement. "So do come. We'll do our best to give you a warm welcome."

The smile took DS Kenneth by surprise, but it didn't last long. Catesby's sunny disposition quickly clouded over. "I would be very grateful if you *would* come," said the boss, squirming in his seat. "The damnable thing is, Jennifer was in touch with Kate this morning and said she wants to meet her on Christmas Eve to get a few things straight. Kate told her she'll be busy organising the Ritual. But Jennifer was insistent, and we fear she might turn up unannounced at the service, intent on causing a scene."

"I see," said DS Kenneth. That put a different complexion on things. He wasn't remotely interested in Catesby's tortured and tortuous personal relationships, but he was very keen to talk to Jennifer. What's more, based on what Claudia had told him, Flint could very well be close at hand. "I'll be pleased to be there," he added.

"That's good. Very good. Because there is one other little difficulty that might require your assistance."

"Oh?"

"You remember that mad psychic woman who turns up from time to time offering her crime-solving services?"

"Brenda Skinner?"

"That's her. She came to our Vibratory Attunement Ritual. God knows why she came along, but she and Kate took an instant dislike to each other. Kate ended up calling her a disruptive influence and a witch and told her not to come again. But the Skinner woman said we weren't going to get rid of her that easily."

DS Kenneth abandoned an attempt to rub his chin with his missing finger. Given it would be Christmas Eve and police resources were likely to be stretched, he wondered if his attendance at the Christmas Ritual would be sufficient to keep the peace if Brenda Skinner, Jennifer Catesby and Bob Flint all turned up intent on causing a disturbance. Unfortunately, he didn't have access to anything remotely similar to an American-style Swat Squad on standby. The only backup he could hope for was Police Community Support Officer Adam Heggs. Possibly accompanied by his pet spaniel. But even that wasn't a given, if Shirley was still 'on heat'.

He decided that now was the time to tackle the issue that Catesby seemed to be ignoring. "Based on the latest intelligence, there's a distinct possibility that Jennifer won't be on her own," he said.

"Intelligence?" said Ch Insp Catesby. "What intelligence?"

"It's a tip-off from Claudia Alcock."

"That madwoman. And not just any old madwoman but another member of the coven to boot."

"I think the information is credible, though. She said an employee of Alcock & Bull saw Jennifer and Flint in Derbyshire recently."

"In Derbyshire?"

DS Kenneth nodded. "In a camper van."

"Jennifer? In a camper van? Are you out of your mind?"

"I don't think so."

"Really? Because we're talking about a woman who regards four-star hotel accommodation as slumming it."

DS Kenneth didn't voice his suspicion out loud, but he thought it was probably the company she was keeping that made all the difference. Instead, he said: "Maybe desperate times have called for desperate measures. It might explain why they've been able to avoid detection."

"Do we have the registration number?"

"Unfortunately not."

Catesby's brow furrowed. "But if they're headed this way, it won't be too hard to track down a camper van. Not in the winter, surely."

"There's still enough of them about. And traffic is bound to be heavy on Wednesday and Christmas Eve. But we'll do our best to monitor the main roads into Newvale."

The chief inspector opened his mouth to say something, but the alarm on his mobile phone cut him off. And then the something he was going to say turned into something more succinct. "Shit!" he growled as the phone's vibrations sent it skittering across the polished desk, causing havoc amongst the nativity characters. The wise men collapsed like toppling dominoes; both sheep landed on the floor, where one was pinned under the angel, and the baby fell out of his crib. Again. The only ones who survived unscathed were Mary, along with the pig that was supposed to be a donkey.

As his superior battled to turn off the alarm, DS Kenneth sighed and set about restoring law and order to the nativity scene. "There," he said when he had finished arranging the figures, "I think they're back in the right places."

Catesby grunted a thanks, along with an explanation. Of sorts. "I set the alarm to remind me of an important appointment. Rosencrantz is a bit of a stickler for punctuality, so I don't want to be late," he said. "Is there anything else?"

DS Kenneth wasn't surprised to hear his boss was being treated by a psychiatrist. He was familiar with Rosencrantz's name as Claudia had made no secret of being one of the doctor's long-term patients. Which was interesting in itself. But quite how the beliefs of Freud, Jung et al meshed with the beliefs of the Church of Loving Togetherness – or to be more accurate, Kate's beliefs – was equally intriguing.

However, in view of Catesby's obvious desire to bring the meeting to a close, he hurriedly moved on to mention that the bullet used to kill Smithson was probably fired from a .300 Winchester Magnum sniper rifle. "According to our firearms experts, our suspect was more likely to be a professional hitman than an amateur."

"A professional? Even though he missed. Twice. Not exactly the Harry Kane of the sharpshooting world, is he?"

"Even Kane misses occasionally," said DS Kenneth, "but putting that aside for the moment, there is one other thing. We've heard from the authorities in Greece that an important tax case has gone against Alexa Bull's family, leaving them deeply in debt."

"So? What's that got to do with her personally?"

"It remains to be seen," said DS Kenneth with a shrug, "but what's certain to have a more immediate effect is that the police are reopening the investigation into her grandfather's death. As I understand it, new evidence has come to light pointing to her involvement. Alexa Bull is living on borrowed time."

FORTY-SIX

I know you'll find this hard to believe, Ophelia, but I was actually singing at breakfast. Now there's a novelty. Me – singing. There we were – me, Gary and Flossie – all sitting around the table like one happily dysfunctional family, when I burst into song.

"Christmas is coming and the rat is getting fat," I trilled.

Gary looked up with bloodshot eyes and said: "I think you'll find the song refers to a goose."

I stared at him and said: "I beg to differ. I know a rat when I'm looking at one."

"What's that supposed to mean?" he said.

"You know exactly what," I said, "and you're getting fat."

He didn't like that, but it's true. As fast as I'm losing weight, he's piling it on. Is this due to some weird law of physics I've never come across before? Is it possible for one person to transfer fatty tissue to another, as well as bodily fluids? Which reminds me, I keep meaning to ask Brenda where she stands when it comes to excreting ectoplasm. Not too close would be my answer. But then I don't like mess.

As for Gary, he went back to troughing his way through his eggs, bacon, sausage and fried bread. No wonder the

255

weight's piling on. And he looked tired, as if he'd hardly got the strength to lift his knife and fork. It wasn't a pretty sight, which could be why Flossie was sitting as far away as possible. Any further and she would have been squatting on the draining board with only her Bran Flakes for company. How that girl manages to eat such a big bowlful is beyond me. Her bowels must be in a constant state of flux. I'm not surprised she's so thin – any food just gets fast-tracked from one end to the other. Someone once told me that bran would be good for my IBS. Ha! All I can say is I tried it and spent the next three days within touching distance of the toilet. Literally. I wasn't so much wasted by the experience as ghosted. And I was still farting like Tommy the Tuba a week later. These days I stick to plain toast for breakfast.

Incidentally, I've now hit my weight-loss target. So that's something worth celebrating. I'm not a big fan of Christmas – too many ghosts of Christmases past for my mental well-being – but I've decided to treat myself to some new clothes. It's a bit sad, buying my own Christmas present, don't you think? But I can't remember the last time I treated myself, and there's no point asking Gary to do so, because you know how he's treated me recently. So I asked Flossie if she wants to come with me. She said she should be free by lunchtime on Christmas Eve so that's when we'll go and brave the crowds. I don't like crowds very much, but fortunately I'm blessed with very sharp elbows and a mean stare. Hopefully, Flossie will act as a moderating influence on some of my wilder impulses, and I think I'll treat her to a new outfit while we're at it. Preferably not something else in black, but I won't be holding my breath.

Talking of Christmas presents, Kevin came round earlier, and I gave him his. You should have seen his little face light up when I told him about Alexa and Flint. When I say his face lit up, I'm exaggerating a bit, but I could tell he was pleased. Or maybe it was the something else I gave him: compliments of the season.

He'd been sitting there with his coat on for ages, so I eventually said to him: "Are you feeling the cold, Kevin?"

"I am," he agreed.

So I said: "Would you like me to warm you up?"

"What exactly did you have in mind?" he asked, acting very nonchalant, like Paul Newman in the film *Cool Hand Luke*.

"Well," I said, doing my best to sound like a husky-voiced Mae West, "if you take off your coat, I'll show you why Hot Nuts are one of my specialities." I paused for a moment to let that thought register and then added: "I make them with amaretto and Frangelico liqueur, cherry brandy and hot chocolate."

He wavered. "You do realise I'm on duty, don't you?"

I winked and said: "So? I won't tell if you won't."

"Just to be sociable then," he said and held out that funny hand of his for the glass.

I think I'm making progress with him, don't you? Admittedly, he seemed a little dubious when I offered him a mince pie. Maybe he's also got IBS. In any event, I told him: "The time to worry is when I offer you a mushroom risotto."

Aren't I a little tease?

He makes me feel like a giggling schoolgirl. Not that I did much giggling when I *was* a schoolgirl, not with Mother and her gaggle of grunting, groping gigolos in tow.

Did I mention I'm not a big fan of Christmas? That's down to the year that Dad was in hospital over the holiday period after suffering a heart attack. And no, it wasn't brought on by the size of my wish list. If you must know, it was the stress of running his business, and living with my mother. Mainly living with my mother. Fortunately, I was too young to have a heart attack, but that didn't mean I didn't suffer too.

Mother took us to visit Dad early on Christmas Eve because she said she had things to do later in the evening. And as it turned out, that didn't include midnight Mass; try midnight mess, instead. She'd invited a few of her 'friends' to come round for a late-night festive drinks party, so I was ushered upstairs to bed before the BBC had got round to showing Queen's live Christmas concert on *The Old Grey Whistle Test*. How cruel was that? She knew how much I liked Freddie Mercury, despite his funny teeth. She even made a joke about me being in bed by the time Santa arrived. As if I still believed in all that silly nonsense by then.

Anyway, I was woken up at God knows what o'clock by the sound of loud voices and raucous laughter. I lay awake for a while, but when I couldn't get back to sleep, I got up and went to look out of the window to see if it was snowing. And guess what I saw: no, not snow but Santa's sleigh parked in our drive. I couldn't believe it! I was so flummoxed I had to sneak downstairs to see what was going on. Yeah, I know, total naivety. Because it wasn't Santa from the North Pole who'd stopped off at our house but Santa from the Round Table. He and a few of his fellow Tablers had hitched up the sleigh to a Land Rover and had been touring the streets, playing carols and collecting for charity. Then afterwards they'd arrived for Mother's little soirée.

I blundered into the living room and there they all were, having a high old time on Mother's 'special punch' and playing a version of Twister that beggared belief. And to make matters worse, it was my game they were using. And abusing!

I struggled to make sense of what was going on and went to run back to my room but one of the men blocked my way and insisted I tried some of the punch. I don't know where my mother was at this point. I think she was at the bottom of the Twister pile – she'd always prided herself on her flexible attitude – and after the drink I don't remember an awful lot. Except the awful thing I *do* recall is being cajoled and dragged onto Santa's knee so he could give me a surprise Christmas present. I think it was then I became aware that although his wig, false beard and shiny black boots were still in place, he was naked beneath his long red coat.

Everyone thought it was hilarious when he grabbed me by the waist and wiggled me around on his lap. But it's no laughing matter being forced to play Buckaroo while someone's prodding you with a broom handle, I can tell you. They stopped laughing, though, when I wriggled free and snatched the letter opener off the sideboard behind me. "Ho, ho, ho" suddenly turned to "ow, ow ow" as I lashed out. To be fair, it was only a small nick and there wouldn't have been as much blood pumping everywhere if he hadn't had a raging erection. It was like Old Faithful gushing away down there. But he who lives by the sword, dies by the sword, or so the saying goes. Not that he died. Well, not immediately.

He ended up in the same hospital as my dad. Not because of the cut, by the way, but because I also stabbed him in the eye when he got me round the throat and tried to choke me. Not surprisingly, it's a bit triggering when I see an olive on the end of a cocktail stick. Or a pickled onion rolling round on the plate, come to that.

And it's no wonder it put me off sharp objects. And mess. Or that I was messed up before Sarah's joke-gone-bad. Nature or nurture? Try both. And it's not really a surprise that everything to do with relationships, love and sex is all mixed up in my head, is it?

They told the hospital and the police some rubbish cover story about Santa being assaulted by a drunken gang while he was walking home from a party. It was far-fetched, but it was Christmas Eve, and the authorities were overstretched dealing with all the other stuff that was going on. At the same time, Mother warned me if I ever breathed a word of what had happened, Santa would come back to finish what he'd started 'good and proper'. So I said nothing and had to live with that terrible fear. How sadistic was that? I was only nine, for fuck's sake!

Three years later I found out Santa was the man who owned the stationery shop in town. But all's well that ends well, because that was around the same time he died when his shop caught fire. Funnily enough it happened on Christmas Eve. So there is justice in this world. Especially as they never found the arsonist.

And in case you're wondering, I buried my game of Twister in the back garden. You could say it was the start of my special interest in all things horticultural.

By the way, I've never told any of this to anyone else before: not Rosencrantz, nor even my diary. So mum's the word, although an even better one is 'gin'. Because I think I need a really stiff drink before I tell you what else has been going on around here.

FORTY-SEVEN

Gary was slouched, half asleep, on the sofa in his office when Alexa marched straight in without even bothering with the courtesy of a precautionary tap on the door.

"Look at this!" she said testily, waving a sheet of paper in front of him.

Startled out of his mid-morning slumber, Gary shot upright in his seat as if a team of HM Revenue & Customs tax inspectors had just burst into his room, rather than his agitated business partner. "Jesus!" he yelped, clutching his chest in exaggerated fashion. "Don't do that. You nearly gave me a heart attack!"

Alexa scowled at him. "It would serve you right if I had – you're supposed to be working, not daydreaming about our ever more youthful receptionists!" Without giving him a chance to respond, she thrust the sheet under his nose with one hand, while with the other she picked up a copy of *Accountancy Age* magazine, which he had discarded on the seat next to him, and tossed it onto the floor. Having cleared space for herself, she sat down, shaking the paper as she did so. "What do you make of this?" she demanded.

"Hold it still, woman," said Gary. "I can't see it properly."

"You don't need to see it properly. It's quite obvious what it is," she said as she stopped waving it around to point at the montage of individual letters that had been cut and pasted from the pages of a magazine to form a warning message.

But although it may have been obvious to Alexa, Gary was still trying to engage his brain after his rude awakening. "Who's it from?" he asked.

Alexa gritted her teeth. "If I knew that, it wouldn't be a poison fucking pen letter, would it!"

"What I meant," said Gary, furiously trying to backtrack, "is where did it come from? Was it in the morning post? Did a pigeon bring it? Or what?"

"Thanks for the sarcasm, but no, it didn't arrive in the post. Timea brought it into my office separately. It was in an envelope with an 'urgent' label stuck on it. Timea said someone must have pushed it through the door after she emptied the letter box first thing."

Gary snorted derisively. "Who sends poison pen letters these days? I thought people simply bitched about each other on X or Mumsnet," he said. And now that he'd had the chance to read the message, he was equally contemptuous. "In any event, it's hardly very poisonous, is it?" he added and read the letter out loud: "*Stop messing around with married men, or else*. Or else what? Excuse my continuing sarcasm, but is this mystery person going to have you put in the stocks? Or stoned to death alongside the last remaining defender of the British Empire? In any case, who else has any interest in what you and me get up to, other than Claudia? Poison pen letters are hardly her style. Based on her past, she'd simply poison you. And even then, I doubt she'd send you a warning first. If you ask me, someone's trying to wind you up."

Alexa looked at the sheet of paper again. "Maybe," she

said grudgingly. The anger had left her voice, but the note of uncertainty still remained. "It's still a worry, though," she added, glancing involuntarily over her shoulder.

"Ignore it," said Gary, yawning and allowing his eyelids to droop again.

Alexa frowned. "What's up? You're not sickening for something, are you?"

"If you must know I'm absolutely exhausted. I think the technical term is 'shagged out'. Quite literally."

"Are you serious? I thought you wanted to make up for lost time, now you've got your pills."

"Look, I'm not usually one to complain," said Gary, grimacing, "but apart from the night I went to the golf club meeting, we've been going at it hammer and tongs for the past week. Or rather, you have. I don't know what's got into you, but I'm struggling to keep up. There is such a thing as the law of diminishing returns, you know."

Alexa nodded knowingly. "You don't say." She sighed. There was no getting away from the fact that the harvest from their previous evening's laboured encounter had been meagre. So now it was in the lap of the gods, rather than Gary's, as to whether the fruits of his labours would be sufficient to challenge Jasmine's head start in the pregnancy stakes. But just to be on the safe side – or to be more accurate, the unsafe side – Karol had unwittingly made a significant contribution too. Not only had it given her campaign a welcome boost, but it had been delivered in rousing fashion as well. So maybe things weren't too bad.

Then again, maybe the discreet knock on the door and Timea's reappearance suggested they were. Alexa's brief uplift in mood slumped along with her shoulders when she saw Timea holding a similar large brown envelope to the one she had delivered earlier. The receptionist gave a hesitant smile as she handed the envelope to Alexa. It had an 'urgent' sticker on the front.

"It was pushed through the letter box while I was in the kitchenette," said Timea.

"So you didn't see who it was from," said Alexa, more in hope than expectation.

"No, sorry," said Timea, still hovering.

Alexa resisted the temptation to rip the envelope open while Timea was still in the room. "OK, thanks. I'll pop out and have a word with you and Mrs Pinchess in a few minutes," she said, indicating to Timea that her continued presence was not required. Alexa waited until Timea had closed the door behind her before clawing at the envelope's seal with her blood-red nails. She reached inside and pulled out a sheet of paper. It was another poison pen letter. But she already knew it would be. Her eyes narrowed as she read the message to Gary, who had so far maintained an air of languid disinterest. *"I'm watching you,"* she said.

Now that *did* get Gary's interest. He sat up, wide-eyed, his tiredness suddenly banished. "Here, let me see," he said, snatching the sheet from Alexa's grasp and reading it for himself. "What did I tell you last week? I *knew* someone was following me. But all you did was make fun of me."

Alexa snatched the paper back. "It wasn't you they were watching," she said angrily. "It was me!"

"As if," said Gary, reluctant to concede he might not be the centre of attention, even when it was negative. He thought for a few moments before finally conceding: "They could have been watching *both* of us, I suppose."

"Both of us? Do you mean someone's still following you?"

Gary was reluctant to admit he'd been having difficulty keeping his eyes open at all, let alone peeled for suspicious characters who might have been tailing him. "I can't say I've noticed anyone *specifically*," he said, "except for one of those charity collectors. She makes a nuisance of herself whenever I go out. She always seems to be shaking her tin in my direction."

"That's because you never give anything to any good cause. She's probably decided to keep ambushing you until you do."

"In that case she'll still be waiting until long after the famine's over – or whatever it is she's collecting for. Charity begins at home: that's my motto."

"I had noticed. Which is more than I can say for the presence of your charity collector."

"What? You must have seen her," said Gary. He stared into the distance as he tried to recall her appearance in more detail. "She wears a silly hat all the time, looks like Daisy the Cow. The hat, that is, not the woman. Although she's no oil painting either, it has to be said."

Alexa shook her head. "No, sorry. The only thing I've noticed is that old ice-cream van that's been parked on the patch of waste ground at the back. I reckon it's been abandoned, so I'm thinking of ringing the council and asking them to tow it away."

"You don't think it could be Flint, do you?"

"Flint? Driving an ice-cream van?"

Gary wore a puzzled look. "Who mentioned anything about ice cream?"

"You weren't listening to me, were you?"

"I was referring to whoever's been watching me."

Alexa sighed with exasperation. It was too late to go back now, but she began to doubt the wisdom of her campaign to out-Jasmine Jasmine. Gary was such a self-centred narcissist; how could she ever expect him to pull his weight as a husband and father? Maybe she should revert to her original plan and ask Karol to do her a special favour. And then, if she did turn out to be pregnant, she could always tell Karol it was his. Because it could be. It really could. Certainly in terms of quantity, if not quality. And that was open to debate.

But for the moment, there was still Gary's concerns about Flint to deal with. "Look," she said, "I'm absolutely sure it's not Flint who's been watching us. I was in touch with him again last night, after you left, and we've arranged to meet."

Gary blanched. "What? Face to face? Are you mad?"

"Of course not. I've told him we've got his money for him. Except we haven't, obviously. So when he turns up, Novak will be there to take care of him for us."

Alexa had hoped to talk to Flint first about the steps he had taken to change his identity. But things weren't working out that way. And anyway, she could always find out what she needed to know from the Dark Web.

Gary still wore a look of uncertainty. "So when and where is this meeting supposed to take place? Not here I hope."

Alexa smiled. "Flint himself suggested the old scout hut off St Chads Avenue on Christmas Eve. It's a bit dilapidated and only used occasionally by some weird religious sect. But otherwise no one goes near the place. Trust me – it's the perfect location."

Gary did his best to smile back, but he remained unconvinced by Alexa's plan. Or Alexa's intentions, come to that. And the only way he was going to allay his doubts was by sneaking over to the old scout hut himself on Thursday to make sure there wasn't another cock-up.

FORTY-EIGHT

I know I've left it a bit late, Ophelia, but I'm thinking of getting you a playmate for Christmas. It's another Totally Real doll and will keep you company when I'm not around. It'll stop you getting lonely, at least until Jasmine's hatchling comes along. Aren't I thoughtful? And I hope you don't mind, but I want to get a boy this time, just to get a male perspective on our chats. You could say it'll give me a more balanced worldview, especially as balanced opinions aren't really my forte.

I asked the woman from the 'baby farm': "How will I be able to tell if it's male or female?"

"How do you think?" she said.

So presuming it doesn't have designer stubble – which, let's face it, would look very disturbing on a baby – it must come with gender-specific knobbly bits. I was impressed. It's only a tiny amount of extra silicone, but it'll make all the difference, don't you think? You can't fault their attention to detail.

I'm thinking of christening him Freddie in memory of a goldfish I used to have. Sadly for Freddie Mk 1, Mother 'accidentally' flushed him down the sink when she was cleaning his bowl. As this happened right after the Santa debacle, I know she did it deliberately to punish me. An eye for an eye. Or, more accurately, a fish eye for an eye.

When I stopped crying, I thought, *two can play at that game, Mummy dearest.* As you know, I rarely forgive. And I never forget. But even so, it was a couple of years before I got my revenge, when Mother went on a two-week holiday with one of her priapic men friends to the south of France. Dad, as usual, turned a blind eye – he must have kept a ready supply of them in his bedside cabinet – and went along with her story that she was going on a gourmet cookery course. Hardly likely for someone whose idea of haute cuisine was a Scotch egg with crinkly chips. As soon as she left the house, I put a kipper in her naughty knickers drawer and left it marinating for the whole time she was away. The after-effects cramped her style for a while, I can tell you. The kipper's fragrant juices seeped into the wood of the drawer so that, even after a couple of boil washes – as well as a precautionary trip to see her GP – the smell continued to permeate her underwear. Eventually, she had to burn the lot and replace it, along with the chest of drawers.

That's when I learnt it really is true that revenge is a dish best served cold. And not just when it comes to kippers. Delaying gratification gives those feelings of justifiable outrage and injustice a chance to simmer nicely. And giving yourself plenty of time to plan means there's also less chance of being caught afterwards.

I thought this might help you to understand why Gary's still in the land of the living although, having said that, he's definitely looking a little peaky. Could it be he's off-colour because his male ego has been wounded by Flossie's unavailability? Despite saying he finds her repulsive, it seems he can't resist rising to the challenge. I was amazed after breakfast when he shrugged off his lethargy, picked up a tea towel and offered to help her with the washing-up. Gary with a tea towel? That was a first in itself. Ostensibly he was offering to dry the dishes. Ostensibly. But his cover was blown when I heard Flossie tell him: "If you put your hand on my bum again, I'll cut it off."

"Oh yeah?" he leered. "It's a good job I've got another one, then, isn't it?"

"I wasn't talking about your hand," she said, wiggling a soapy bread knife at trouser level.

I was impressed. The girl's learning. She and Meera will make a good team. Unsurprisingly, Gary scooted away with his tail tucked between his legs, while he'd still got one to tuck.

After he'd gone, I asked Flossie if there was anything special she'd like as a Christmas present when we go shopping tomorrow. She needs rewarding, after all.

She smiled coyly and said: "Would you mind if I have my nipples pierced?"

"Why would I mind?" I said. "They're your nipples."

"Perfect," she said and asked me if it was something I would consider doing.

So I had to tell her: "I'm sorry, but you'll have to get it done professionally. I have a thing about sharp objects."

"What I meant," she said, "is if you've ever thought about getting yours pierced."

I shivered. "They'd have to give me a general anaesthetic first. Besides, my boobs are sagging enough already, without hanging lumps of metal off each nipple."

Talking of Meera, she was in fine form when the group met earlier this evening to give their surveillance updates. I'm not quite sure how she did it – well, I am actually: she threatened him – but Meera 'borrowed' Derek's high-powered binoculars from him for her assignment. It was his own fault for boasting that they're Sunagor Mega Zoom Binoculars, which are the most powerful in the world. Apparently. So you have to ask yourself why someone like Derek would need binoculars so powerful they can pick out a pimple on a set of bare buttocks from four hundred yards away. In the dark. Which is a clue in itself. And it didn't take Meera five seconds to guess his dirty little secret and even less time to confiscate the glasses. He wasn't happy, but there's no arguing with a zombie knife and the prospect of a place on the Sex Offenders Register. So since then, Peeping Derek has been sulking. And I hope for his sake he's also been practising his underwater swimming technique, because he's going to need it where he's going after Christmas. We're supposed to be hunting for perverts, not harbouring them.

As for Meera's report, she said Gary spent most evenings at Alexa's flat. Which was not so much breaking news as old news, so far as I was concerned. However, despite that disappointment, she did cause a frisson of excitement when she claimed to have seen UFO activity over Newvale Common. It was on the night she hid in a sand bunker after following Gary to a golf club meeting. What? Aliens in Newvale? I was sceptical. The only reptilian types I've ever seen on the common are a pair of adders, a not-so-slow-worm and someone in an Aussie outback hat who looked a lot like Crocodile Dundee. But Meera reckoned that with the help of Derek's binoculars she could make out a spaceship that had landed on the common about half a mile away.

I said: "A spaceship? Are you sure?"

"Oh yes," she said. "I could see a ring of strange lights."

"A ring of strange lights?" I queried. "On Newvale Common?"

"Absolutely," she said. "They were pulsing on and off."

"Ha!" I said. "Hold the phone call to Mulder and Scully until we check on the whereabouts of the Johnsons and their fan following."

To be fair, all we had to do was ask Derek. He seemed to be pretty clued up on their itinerary – to the surprise of none of us.

As far as Gary's daytime activities were concerned, Hattie reported that most mornings he power walked to Greggs, where he bought a triple chocolate doughnut and a large caramel latte. No wonder the rat is getting fat. Timea suggested the power walk was an attempt to offset all the calories. But Hattie said he was simply trying to avoid the charity collectors he met en route. That sounds about right for such a sponging cheapskate or, to be more accurate, a lying, cheating, sponging cheapskate. I'm surprised he had the energy to power walk in his current state, but then not even the most socially aware *Guardian* reader likes being hassled by those tin-shakers, do they? And Gary has about as much social awareness as a hermit crab.

Colin's report, by contrast, was non-existent. He said the cold weather had played havoc with his prostate. So instead of keeping watch on Alexa, he spent most of his time staring at the wall in the town's public urinal. Or down at the fickle plumbing. Who knows? I wouldn't like to guess, not having a prostate. I've got enough problems without one of those as well, thank you very much.

Colin was very apologetic though. "I'm sorry about the report," he said.

"Can't be helped," I replied, trying to appear empathetic.

He shrugged. "I did my best, but the end result was a bit of a damp squid."

I was going to ask him if he meant 'damp squib', but as I say, not having a prostate, he may have been right the first time.

Besides, Timea chose this moment to drop her bombshell. She said that she had been dutifully watching Alexa's flat every evening from the less-than-salubrious setting of a half-empty builder's skip on the opposite side of the road. There's dedication for you. Because you know what kind of disgusting crap the neighbours dump in those things. Well, that's what I do whenever one of my neighbours has one parked on their drive. It saves getting quizzed by the Shitfinder General who monitors everything you take to the local tip, sorry, the recycling and household waste site. But anyway, back to Timea's bombshell, because on the night Gary went to his golf club meeting, an unexpected visitor turned up. A very unexpected visitor, as far as Timea was concerned. Her dad. And even more disturbingly, he stayed all night. As did Timea, in her skip. Just to make sure. Suffice to say, she wasn't best pleased by this discovery. Nor, I imagine, will Gary be, if and when he finds out. But I daresay Timea's working on how that little subplot plays out.

As it was, she said she had a bad headache and asked if she could be excused from the rest of the meeting. Flossie took pity on her and said she could go for a lie-down in her bed. So after Flossie told us there's a rumour at the salon that Jennifer Catesby will be popping in to see them tomorrow, she showed Timea to her room. I'm not sure if that's all she showed her because the pair of them didn't emerge until I was popping a marshmallow into a mug of hot chocolate around midnight. Still, some people take more consoling than others, don't you think?

Anyway, they missed an entertaining update from Brenda. She said she followed Ch Insp Catesby to the old scout hut near to Dr Rosencrantz's consulting rooms, where it seems he has become involved with a strange religious cult. Brenda said they were holding something called a Vibratory Attunement Ritual, which sounds like it was a not-to-be-missed opportunity for any middle-aged woman who has an up-close-and-personal relationship with her Rampant Rabbit. If only I'd known. But, according to Brenda, it turned out to be a rather different kind of meditation session. They were all wearing different coloured robes in a ritual aimed at 'healing and transmutation by building patterns of harmony through ancient vibratory formulae of colour and sound'. Or so Brenda said. On reflection, I think I'll stick with my trusty rabbit. And I'm not sure if the ritual's harmonics interfered with Brenda's own vibrating crystal, but she took a dislike to the woman who was running the show, even though Catesby seemed in thrall to her. Hmm, I wonder what Jennifer would have to say about that? Mind you, if the rumours are to be believed, she's got her hands full with Flint. In any event, Brenda says she's going along to a Christmas Ritual they're holding there tomorrow. I asked her what it will entail but she said she doesn't have a clue what to expect. Honestly, if there's a worse clairvoyant out there than Brenda, I'd like to meet them. Or maybe I wouldn't.

At that point we were about to wrap up the meeting when Jasmine told us Gary is insisting she takes a paternity test. I can't say I was surprised – that man is capable of anything where money is involved. Even so, Jasmine was understandably upset.

"He's as good as suggesting I slept around," she said.

"But technically you did," I said. "As well as sleeping in my bed, you slept at the Travelodge on the bypass, in the back of Gary's car and at other locations you've so far kept mum about."

She pouted. "That's a bit unfair," she said.

"You may have a point," I conceded, "in that you weren't doing much sleeping in any of these places."

But despite my pickiness – honestly, I can't help myself sometimes – I did reassure her that I'd still help regardless of the outcome of the test. I'm nothing if not big-hearted, when the mood takes me. Have you noticed? However, she then surprised me by saying that Alexa has also been very supportive. Really? You could have knocked me down with a feather, although I'd strongly advise you not to try it. Jasmine said Alexa is even arranging a meeting somewhere tomorrow to find a way of resolving her demands. Why would Alexa do that, I wonder?

It sounds like it's going to be a very eventful Christmas Eve.

FORTY-NINE

Detective Sergeant Kevin Kenneth sighed deeply, pressed the 'call' button on his mobile phone and waited for his superior, Chief Inspector Julian Catesby, to answer. From where he was parked, in the far corner of the old scout hut's potholed car park, DS Kenneth could keep watch on the hut and any comings and goings. So far, the only comings were a dozen people, including both Catesby and Kate, who he assumed must be members of her Church of Loving Togetherness, gathering for their Christmas Ritual.

They looked an eclectic mix, to put it politely. He recognised a woman whose bad poetry featured with depressing regularity, along with her soft-focus photo, in the *Newvale Advertiser*. Someone once told him she was the editor's wife, which explained a lot. However, as the woman also happened to be DS Kenneth's ex-wife, it had led him to develop an irrational dislike for the newspaper, middle-aged 'nepo babies' and poems that didn't rhyme. What was wrong with limericks? Or, at a pinch, the odd ode? Or maybe the joke had always been on him.

Following them into the hut were a couple of ageing hippies who ran a market stall selling New Age paraphernalia.

The man's straggly grey hair hung halfway down his back, making up for its complete absence from the dome of his head, while the woman's equally grey hair was tied in a waist-length ponytail. He'd arrested both of them, several times, for growing and possessing cannabis, although the large plant they were carrying into the hut on this occasion looked suspiciously like a Christmas tree. DS Kenneth hoped for their sakes they intended to decorate it, rather than smoke it, during the ritual. Then again, maybe the congregation would be in need of *something* to smoke if his ex-wife began reciting her incomprehensible blank verse.

Even more unsettling was seeing the owner of the pet shop, where he bought Elvis's bird food, arriving in the company of a unicorn. The fact that the unicorn was bright pink and inflatable only added to the air of surrealism.

His attention was then diverted by a younger couple, carrying a large festive wreath. A few moments later he heard the sound of hammering, and although he couldn't see the front door from where he was sitting, he assumed it was the wreath that was being nailed to it. However, if Catesby didn't answer his phone on this, the third redial, he was inclined to get out of the car and make a safe and well-being check.

He looked at his watch: it was 4pm and the street lights in St Chads Avenue were already attempting to illuminate the gathering darkness. How much of that light would reach the darkest parts of the car park was a moot point; nightfall wasn't going to make it any easier for him to spot any suspicious activity in the vicinity, especially as swirling flurries of sleet were further diminishing visibility. He had inspected the site earlier in the afternoon and had noted that although the hut and its car park had an open frontage to the street, they were extensively surrounded on both sides, and at the rear, by trees and overgrown bushes. If Bob Flint and Jennifer Catesby wanted to observe the hut before making their approach, they could easily hide in all the undergrowth. And the same was true for the mystery gunman if he decided to put in an appearance. And assuming he had a night vision scope for his rifle.

He scanned the car park once more as the driver of the oil tanker, which had arrived a few minutes before, climbed down from his cab and went to inspect the heating oil tank behind the hut. At the same time, Ch Insp Catesby finally answered his phone.

"Do you mind, Keningley?" he rasped irritably. "I'm in the middle of something with Kate."

"It's the oil tanker, sir. It's arrived to make the delivery."

"So? Can't you deal with it?"

"It's not really my responsibility."

"Oh, for pity's sake, man! We're all set to enter an altered state of consciousness that will lead to a greatly reduced external awareness and expanded interior mental and spiritual euphoria. I haven't got time to fiddle about with the driver's nozzle."

"With due respect, sir, I think you should."

There was a pause, during which DS Kenneth could hear a woman's whispering voice, although he couldn't discern what was being said, before Catesby was back on the line. "I'll be out in a couple of minutes," he grumbled, "just as soon as I'm properly dressed."

DS Kenneth's eyebrow twitched. He couldn't help wondering if his ex-wife was also involved in whatever was going on inside the hut, beyond composing a poem about it. Not that he would want to read it anyway.

But of more immediate concern was the appearance of a potential gatecrasher. Fortunately, his call to Catesby was still connected. "Before you hang up, sir," he said, "the psychic, Brenda Skinner, has just turned up in an Uber."

"What the hell's she doing here?"

"From what I can tell, she seems to be using a stick of chalk to mark out a large circle in the car park."

"A circle?"

"Or it could be a pentagram."

Ch Insp Catesby's voice went up an octave. "Arrest that woman, Kenkart, and remove her immediately!"

"On what grounds?"

"I don't care, man, make something up if you have to. There must be some ancient byelaw banning witches you can quote."

"Wouldn't that amount to a hate crime?" queried DS Kenneth. "Only, I thought the chief constable's new policy forbids us from discriminating against minorities."

Catesby's response was so furious it was a wonder his spittle wasn't transmitted over the airwaves along with his voice. "Fuck the chief constable, Kenkee! Do you hear me? Just fuck him!"

"Sir?"

"I'll be out in two minutes to deal with that bloody woman myself!"

The line went dead.

DS Kenneth sighed. He would have preferred to stay in his car and continue his observations, not least because it was considerably warmer inside the vehicle and he still had half a packet of chocolate digestives to finish. But he decided it might be prudent to get out so he could intervene in any confrontation between Catesby and the psychic. However, he paused when he saw a car arrive on the far side of the car park. As he peered through the gloom, a young woman, who seemed to be heavily pregnant, got out of the car. She looked around for a minute or so before taking her phone out of a coat pocket and, leaning against the car door, taking, or receiving, a call. Shortly afterwards, an Audi TT pulled up alongside her and Alexa Bull got out.

Interesting.

Even more interesting was the call from the police control room. The call handler told him that a patrol car had found a camper van bearing a false number plate, which was believed to belong to the missing suspect Bob Flint. It was parked two streets away from the old scout hut.

FIFTY

I'm sorry, Ophelia, but I've been all over the shop today. And not just when I went to River Island with Flossie, although that was a nightmare in itself. The thing is, I mixed up my meds this morning. So I don't know if I've taken too much of one lot and not enough of the other, or vice versa. Or too much of everything, which is far more likely. I wouldn't say I'm 'totally shit-faced', which is how Flossie put it when she insisted on driving. I'd like to think I'm more weird than wired, but then what do I know when I'm in this state?

Unfortunately, it seems to have triggered my compulsive desire to eat Haribo, which has set off my IBS. It reached a pitch, although not in the musical sense, when I bent down to put on my shoes in one of the shop's changing rooms. Well, you've never heard anything like it. I farted so loudly the partition walls shook. I'm telling you, Jericho would have fallen in half the time if I'd been around.

"Excuse me," said Flossie, who was in the cubicle with me, "that wasn't very ladylike."

I shrugged and said: "I'm blaming the tight waistband on these trousers."

"Well take them off," she said, "before you blow the door off its hinges. And me with it."

After that little faux pas, I wanted to buy a leopard-print top with a plunge neckline, along with black leggings. I thought it would bring out the animal in Kevin. It certainly did in me. And there's no doubt it made me look hot. Even the sales girl agreed; she said it accentuated my figure 'within a mature woman aesthetic'. Whatever that means. But Flossie said it made me look like a cougar that's desperate for one last kill before winter sets in. How cruel was that? I pointed out that, as a matter of fact, cougars don't have spots.

She said: "You're forgetting I've just seen your bum."

Cheek. Then, when I went to buy a black leather miniskirt, Flossie said: "I think you need to question if what you're choosing is age appropriate."

I went right off her at that point. She was probably right, but I wasn't going to admit that. Besides, it was time she learnt that one good insult deserves another. So I waited until she was picking out a couple of goth-like black tops and a pair of black lace-up leather-look trousers and said in a loud voice: "I know you've only got a ridiculously small chest, but shouldn't you be buying some bras with a larger cup size?"

She looked at me and said: "What do you mean?"

So I said: "Won't you need bigger cups now you're accessorising your nipples?"

She coloured up and mumbled: "I don't really think that will be necessary."

"I beg to differ," I said. "And as for those trousers, you'll probably need to leave more room for your other piercings."

At that point we decided to go home.

When we got back to the car I apologised, not that I meant it, but I still need her help with the wildlife projects. And the cleaning. Obviously. She was OK about it and said she realised the drugs had messed with my head. I nodded but didn't like to tell her my head had been messed with years ago. But I think she knows that. Even so, I'm not entirely sure we'll be going shopping together again.

Now then, I know we were supposed to be going home for some mulled wine at this point – even if we have to skip the mince pies because of my digestive issues – but you'll just have to be patient. Rome wasn't built in a day. And before you ask, I've no idea how long it took. My brain's not up to it at the moment. Although, if the Romans had had to wait as long as it's taken me to get planning permission for the new summer house, then Gaul wouldn't have been invaded until some time next year. Probably around the Ides of March.

But me and Flossie decided to make a detour when we saw a couple of messages on our WhatsApp group. They said both Gary and Alexa were headed in this direction, so we thought we ought to see what's going on, especially as Jasmine told us she was due to meet Alexa at the old scout hut over there. We thought it was best if we tried to stay incognito, which is why we've parked across the road in Dr Rosencrantz's car park. He won't mind. I doubt he'll want to get into an argument with me after our last little set-to. I think he knows he's on borrowed time after rejecting me.

It's a good job we did make the detour, though, because Derek's picked up a message on his dad's police scanner to say they've found Flint's camper van parked nearby. According to Derek, the police have got the hut under surveillance, although I'm not entirely sure why they think Flint wants to blow it up.

I've thought about popping across the road and asking Kevin, as I can see him sitting in his car over there. He hasn't noticed me because he's too busy watching Brenda, who's on her hands and knees outside the hut. I'm not sure what she's up to, even though I've got Derek's binoculars with me.

I commandeered them from Meera last night as they were wasted on her; she still thinks she witnessed a close encounter with aliens the other evening. Aliens? She was about as close as she ever wants to get to an encounter with the Johnsons. Steer well clear is my advice. I told her if the Johnsons abduct her she won't end up on an intergalactic mother ship, just zip-tied, blindfolded and ball-gagged in the back of their Ford Transit.

Am I making sense?

By the way, in case you're wondering where Flossie's got to, she's hiding in the bushes over there. She decided to sneak closer to Jasmine in case her meeting with Alexa goes tits up because, let's face it, pregnant women have enough trouble with their tits as it is. And besides which, never trust a Greek bearing gifts, especially a cheater like Alexa, whatever her nationality.

Uh-oh, you're going to have to bear with me because it's all starting to happen. Gary's just arrived, and he's marched straight over to where Jasmine and Alexa are talking. I can't hear what he's saying, but he's gesticulating furiously. Mind you, he's always been very good at that, so I'm hoping Flossie has the sense to keep out of range until he's finished.

Whoa! And unless I'm very much mistaken, I've just spotted a moose making its way through the trees. A moose? That can't be right, surely. Since when have moose roamed freely in Newvale? Holy mother of crap, I think my brain's gone into meltdown! How many tablets *did* I take this morning? Unless I've been eating Flossie's CBD gummies instead of my Haribo.

Oh, hang on, that's not a moose: it's Hattie wearing her bloody stupid reindeer hat. Didn't I tell her to wear something else? I hope for her sake the mystery gunman doesn't turn up, or she's going to end up stuffed and mounted over his mantlepiece. Or maybe she's not so daft after all. Who knew wearing a reindeer hat would turn out to be a better strategy than swiping right on Tinder? Having said that, though, it looks like Meera's with her, so that might cool the shooter's ardour. Shame. I was almost beginning to feel pity for the poor girl. Almost but not quite.

And to be honest, I've got my hands full with my own problems at the moment. As if seeing an imaginary moose isn't bad enough, I keep hearing things too, specifically the tune 'Greensleeves'. Which is bizarre because I don't even like folk music. Especially traditional folk music. You don't think I could be suffering from auditory hallucinations as well, do you? I might have to break open my emergency stash of Haribo, as well as the CBD gummies, and sod the IBS.

Ah, cancel that: I've just seen Mr Kool pull up in his ice-cream van, which might explain the music, if not the voices in my head. He's parked the van twenty yards down the road and he's now getting out with Timea. It looks like they're going to join all the others in the bushes. How ridiculous is that? At this rate there aren't going to be enough bushes to hide them all. And they won't want to be huddled together if Colin's prostate starts playing up again. That would put a real dampener on proceedings, make no mistake.

Honestly, it's getting more and more like Fred Karno's Circus over there, it really is. In fact, that could very well be Fred Karno himself, scurrying from the trees towards the oil tank, carrying a large backpack. Then again, he looks suspiciously like Bob Flint to me. Which could be why Kevin's getting out of his car and chasing after him. And why one of those community support officers and his dog are running after Kevin – followed by a pack of other dogs. This is crazy. Can you hear them all barking and howling? Or is that in my head, too?

Holy mother of crap, it's all kicking off!

Rosencrantz has come out of his consulting rooms to see what's going on, and I think that might be Jennifer's husband who's remonstrating with Brenda. But if it's Catesby, why is he wearing an eyepatch and a red robe?

I know this doesn't make sense, Ophelia, but he looks just like the Santa I was telling you about the other day: the one who did all those horrible things. You don't think it could be him, do you? Because he's supposed to be dead! But if he's dead, how come he's standing there, as large as life?

God, I feel really strange, as if my head's about to explode. I've got to go over there and stop him. I can't let him hurt any more kids and get away with it. Not again.

Where did I put that terrible knife I confiscated off Meera?

You stay here. I won't be long.

FIFTY-ONE

Mrs Pinchess looked at her watch and decided it was about time she locked up the office and headed home for the Christmas holiday. She'd been on her own in the building since lunchtime, when Gary, Alexa and the rest of the staff had finished work early, but she had stayed behind to complete a few admin tasks before the week-long break. She didn't mind that, as tidying up the paper clips beat her alternative Christmas Eve task of thrusting a handful of sage and onion stuffing up the arse end of a turkey. And it wasn't as if her husband was intending to lend a hand with the pre-Christmas kitchen chores, as he'd already declared he would be spending the afternoon on some routine caravan maintenance. At least that's what she assumed he meant when he'd told her it was about time he greased the coupling head. Either way, she hadn't been keen on helping him out.

So staying at work for an extra couple of hours had been her preferred option, while Radio Newvale entertained her with their mix of carols and other Christmassy music. She even allowed herself the luxury of listening to one more number as the dulcet tones of the incomparable Nat King Cole sang about roasting his chestnuts on an open fire. *Ah*, she thought, *they don't make them like that anymore,* meaning singers like Nat King Cole, rather than men who were adventurous enough to take such extreme physical risks. Then again... Her thoughts began to wander but were rudely interrupted by the voice of the studio's general manager. He was doing his best, once more, to achieve a tone of dignified seriousness but was failing miserably to hide a quiver of high excitement.

We're sorry to interrupt the show, but we're just receiving dramatic reports of gunfire, followed by a huge explosion, in the St Chads district of town. We understand the emergency services are attending the incident in the vicinity of the old scout hut. Early reports suggest an oil tanker may have exploded, devastating the surrounding area. A fleet of ambulances is ferrying the injured to the nearby Newvale Royal Infirmary, but as yet we don't have any information on the number of fatalities. We'll bring you further updates just as soon as we have more news.

And now back to Kerri and her Cheery Christmas Crackers.

Mrs Pinchess stood looking at the radio set for a couple of minutes after switching it off. "Oh dear," she said with a sigh. "I rather fancy someone's Christmas has been ruined. I hope it's no one I know."

FIFTY-TWO

Detective Sergeant Kevin Kenneth sighed deeply, knocked and entered the office of his superior, Chief Inspector Julian Catesby, who was sitting at his desk, his face hidden by the book he was reading. The detective sergeant deduced his boss's interest in *Jonestown Massacre: Tragic End of a Cult* had almost certainly been aroused by the events that had unfolded at the old scout hut just over a month earlier. But then he was a detective. And he had been tasked with investigating the incident since returning from sick leave.

DS Kenneth coughed politely. Ch Insp Catesby lowered his book, slowly, revealing a reddened face and a green eyepatch covering his right eye.

"I see you've opted for a different coloured patch, sir," said DS Kenneth, as he sat down. "I'm guessing the colour holds some significance for you."

"Well of course it does, Kenlan. You must know what green signifies?"

DS Kenneth mulled over the question. As far as he was concerned, he associated the colour with the artificial lawn his neighbour had laid, the algae growing in his shower tray and cabbage. None of which were desirable. He shrugged, realising these weren't the kind of positive images that the chief inspector was hoping to elicit.

"Come on, man. Try a bit harder," said Catesby.

From seemingly out of nowhere, DS Kenneth recalled that Claudia had green eyes. The recollection was a little disconcerting at this particular moment in time. And it wasn't a piece of information he cared to share with his boss.

Not that Catesby was waiting for his answer anyway. "It's the colour of rebirth," he said. "It's Kate's idea. She suggested we should adopt the colour to signify that the Church of Loving Togetherness is about to be reborn from the fires of adversity."

"Ah, I see. So somewhat like the scene in *Game of Thrones* then, when Daenerys emerges alive from the flames of a funeral pyre with three baby dragons," said DS Kenneth. "Albeit no one emerged from the smoking ruins of the old scout hut in anything other than a body bag. But I understand the symbolism you're striving for."

Catesby fixed him with a malevolent stare. "Sometimes I worry about you, Kenlemann," he said.

The feeling's mutual, thought DS Kenneth.

"The fact that none of the congregation, except Kate and myself, survived the explosion is a major reason why I want to know who was responsible for the atrocity. Have you managed to get a grip on the investigation yet?"

Get a grip? DS Kenneth looked down at his hands, which were resting in his lap. Most of the index finger on his right hand had been missing since his youth. And the bandage on his other hand indicated that the left forefinger was now largely missing as well. How unusual was that? A matching pair of missing forefingers, with the latter having been sacrificed in the line of duty, although in a not-dissimilar way to how he had lost the first. His mind went back to the moment he saw Flint emerging from the bushes, carrying what he assumed to be a bomb. Not knowing whether the device was booby-trapped, DS Kenneth had run over to the tanker driver instead and ordered him to move his vehicle out of range. No sooner had the driver pulled away from the danger zone than the detective inspector had been set upon by a pack of hormonally overexcited dogs. A big bull terrier had only relaxed its grip on DS Kenneth's hand when PCSO Adam Heggs' pet spaniel Shirley – still in season – ran past. Unfortunately, when the ugly brute took off in pursuit, it took most of his finger with it. And although the digit was later recovered, its mangled condition – dripping blood and slobber in equal amounts – rendered it useless as a candidate for reattachment.

Ch Insp Catesby saw him looking at his damaged hand and, in a rare display of empathy, asked him how he was coping with the loss.

"Not too bad," said DS Kenneth with a shrug. "I've not been as inconvenienced as you might think. I suppose I've got used to adapting to this type of injury. But how about you, sir? I see you still bear the marks, too. And if you don't mind me asking, is it just your face or is the whole of your body affected as well?"

"I'm afraid so. Kate's the same and says we should look on the marks as being metaphysical in origin. A bit like stigmata."

"Metaphysical?" said DS Kenneth, attempting to rub his chin with one forefinger and then the other. "I understood the red staining was because Kate dyed your robes just prior to the service and the heat from the fire caused the dye to run. Or am I mistaken?"

"No, that is essentially correct, but it doesn't mean there wasn't a mystical component to what happened."

"Was it painful?"

"Not painful, just infuriating. The fools in A&E assumed we'd suffered major burns injuries and insisted on stripping us both naked. Then once they realised it was just dye, they couldn't wait to get rid of us. It was left to one of the nurses to suggest that when we got home, we should try rubbing each other down with Vaseline or baby oil to remove it."

"And did you?" asked DS Kenneth.

Ch Insp Catesby shook his head ruefully. "I thought it was worth a try, but Kate said we'd suffered enough by then."

"Ah," said DS Kenneth, "but it could have been worse. We were fortunate that the oil tank where Flint planted his bomb was empty and the scout hut absorbed most of the force from the blast."

"Worse? What's worse than the deaths of our entire congregation?" said Catesby, before adding as an afterthought: "Plus the other people who died, of course."

"And let's not forget you and Kate would have been incinerated, too, if you'd been inside the hut," said DS Kenneth. "All in all, it was a regrettable loss of life to add to Flint's other crimes." They were fine words, but was he being entirely sincere? For although the detective sergeant had never considered himself a vindictive man, he couldn't rid himself of the unsettling feeling that the loss of his ex-wife had been no loss at all. Either to himself or the world of literature.

Ch Insp was entertaining similar thoughts of divine retribution. "I can't say I'm displeased to see the back of that mad psychic woman," he said.

"She suffered a grisly fate."

"But so richly deserved. If you dabble in ungodly practices, what do you expect?"

"Yes, but I doubt even a better clairvoyant than Ms Skinner could have foreseen the large metal cross falling off the roof and skewering her so precisely inside that pentagram."

"I've no sympathy," said Catesby. "She summoned the devil and paid the price."

"Perhaps. But I'm not sure the ice-cream salesman deserved his fate. His death was most unfortunate. However, I'm pleased to say that it looks like Ms Shuttleworth's baby is going to survive, despite her very premature birth."

Ch Insp Catesby frowned. "That's all well and good, but is there any word on where Jennifer's got to?"

"I'm afraid not. There's no sign of her."

"Well, she can't have just disappeared in a puff of smoke – unlike Flint seems to have done. What have forensics got to say about him?"

"Not a lot, on account of the fact there was not a lot of him left after the bomb exploded," said DS Kenneth. "We're working on the assumption that the unknown sniper shot him while he was in the act of arming the device, thus triggering the explosion."

"I don't like you making assumptions, Kenleside."

"I know, but all the witnesses agree on hearing two gunshots. One of the bullets hit Claudia, but the other one has not been accounted for. Unless it melted along with Flint."

"How is Claudia, by the way? Dr Rosencrantz told me that what happened may have added to her psychological issues," said Catesby. "An astonishing thought. Can she get any worse?"

"I wouldn't know about that, but when I called round to see her at home yesterday, she struck me as remarkably... enthusiastic."

"You're smiling, man!"

"Yes," said DS Kenneth. "I do believe I am."

FIFTY-THREE

How do you like my hat, Ophelia? No, I thought not. A knitted hedgehog with ear flaps is hardly the height of fashion, is it? And it won't surprise you to know it's one of Hattie's creations. God alone knows where that girl gets her design ideas from. I don't know how hard it is to get a City and Guilds in millinery, but my guess is the bar's set fairly low. When I asked her if I could borrow one of her hats while my hair grows back, I was rather hoping she'd turn up with something a little more stylish. Not that I've got anything against hedgehogs. They're delightful creatures, in their natural habitat. But I think even Chris Packham would agree their habitat doesn't include the top of my head, thank you very much.

She said: "I thought you wanted something to cover up the damage?"

"I do," I said, "but since when has 'cover up' meant 'draw attention to'?"

She was a bit put out, but what are her hurt feelings compared to my suffering? That crazy gunman has got a lot to answer for. Not content with singeing my lavender plume, he returned for a second try, only this time his bullet grazed my scalp and took half my ear with it. So I've ended up with half an ear and half of my head shaved. Ha! After all the time and trouble I went to to get it restyled, my hair that is, not my head; that thought's too weird for words. The point is, if I'd wanted to look like a dog-eared Last of the Mohicans, I would have borrowed one of Flossie's used lady razors and shaved it myself.

So, I'm relying on one of Hattie's hats to cover it up while it regrows, though obviously not the ear: that's well and truly buggered. And the worst of it is that no one can tell me what will happen if I ever need to wear a pair of glasses. I've been searching the internet to see if there's anyone out there who can digitally print me a new ear flap, but so far no luck. And so far nothing from Hattie that I'd even think of wearing outside the house. What I had in mind was something like a sexy French beret that I could wear tilted alluringly to one side. Yes, I know that's a bit of a stretch for you to imagine, but humour me.

So I said to her: "Haven't you got anything chic?"

She looked gormlessly at me and said: "What does chic mean?"

Honestly, this from someone who's hoping to become a fashion designer. So I gave her a useful pointer. "Chic means something that doesn't look like it's been made by a taxidermist on a week-long bender."

She pulled a face and said: "I could lend you the scarecrow's hat I made for Newvale Players' production of *Worzel Gummidge Takes a Holiday*?"

"Just give me the bloody hedgehog," I said.

I suppose I ought to be grateful I'm even here to talk about what happened. I'm told I'd probably be dead if Rosencrantz hadn't rugby tackled me at the very moment the gunman fired. To be honest, what with one thing and another, I don't remember exactly what went on that afternoon. Apparently, I was running across the road, shrieking and waving Meera's knife over my head. The shrieking I can believe, but I think 'running' is a bit of an exaggeration, as I can vaguely recall wearing a pair of leopard-print kitten heels I'd just been mad enough to buy, and no one runs anywhere in kitten heels. Not in the snow, anyway.

Do you think Rosencrantz is now worthy of forgiveness after his earlier rejection? He's told me I need monitoring in case I've been affected 'detrimentally' by the incident, but when he says 'detrimentally' I know he really means 'mentally'. I'm not daft. No, really I'm not. As I told him, at least I've not started making Pedigree Chum sandwiches, like my nan, or been caught breaking into a stranger's home at 3am clutching a plastic water gun and a feather boa, convinced of an alien attack. Well, not yet.

People keep telling me how lucky I am. Are they serious? With all the things that have happened to me. Is that luck? Mind you, at least I didn't end up like Colin. The shock waves from the bomb blast caused his faulty hearing aid batteries to explode, turning his brain to the consistency of one of his double-whipped ice creams. Not nice. And I'm glad I didn't see it. The after-effects of his dodgy prostate were bad enough.

As for Gary, that snake in the grass has somehow managed to impregnate Alexa. How's that for the ultimate betrayal? First Jasmine, now Alexa. Any woman who comes within molesting distance of that man is at risk. Except me. I don't mind admitting it's a bitter pill to swallow, and just a shame Alexa forgot to swallow hers. It's a good job for him he's now moved in with her, although it'll all end in tears, mark my words. Because I'll make sure it does.

I have a gut feeling the pair of them were responsible for what happened at the old scout hut, and you don't want to argue with my guts, believe me. So I've set the forum the task of finding out if Gary and Alexa were in cahoots with Flint, and I'm also hoping they can track down the sniper while they're at it. It's ironic, isn't it, that I've been trying to find a hitman, and he seems to have found me instead.

Talking of the forum, Jasmine's moved in with me and Flossie now that Gary's moved out. It might only be temporary though, just until the poor girl gets back on her feet. Which might take a while after the traumatic business of giving birth in the middle of the car park. That was a shock for everyone but especially Jasmine. I'm told it was a messy affair, so it's probably a good job I was hyperventilating beneath Dr Rosencrantz at the time.

Afterwards, I couldn't help thinking it was a shame it wasn't Kevin who tackled me, rather than Rosencrantz. It would have been worth lying in the slush with my ear hanging off for that. As it is, he called round to see me last night while everyone else was out. How convenient was that? Not to mention cosy. We sat on the sofa with a G&T each and compared wounds. I'm not going to tell you anything more. As far as you're concerned, my lips are sealed. A woman has to have *some* secrets, doesn't she? All I will say is that he was remarkably considerate, and dexterous for a man with two missing fingers.

Who knows? Maybe my luck is starting to change.

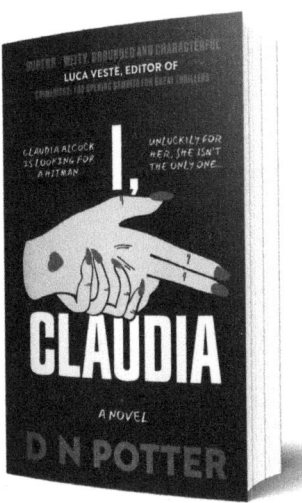

IF YOU HAVE ENJOYED *I, CLAUDIA,* PLEASE
CONSIDER LEAVING A REVIEW ON YOUR
PREFERRED PLATFORM.